The
HUNTED
ASSASSIN

Global Endeavor
PUBLISHING

PAUL B KOHLER

The HUNTED ASSASSIN

The Hunted Assassin is a work of fiction. Names, characters, places, and incidents either are the product of the author's imagination or are used fictitiously. Any resemblance to actual persons, living or dead, events, or locales is entirely coincidental.

Edited by Therin Knite
Cover design by Paul B. Kohler
Interior design and layout by Paul B. Kohler

ISBN-13: 978-1-940740-15-7
ISBN-10: 1-940740-15-0

www.paul-kohler.net

Give feedback on the book at:
info@paul-kohler.net
Twitter: @PaulBKohler
Facebook: facebook.com/Paul.B.Kohler.Author

Printed in the United States of America

First Edition

FOR CHERYL. YOU ARE MY ROCK.

The blackness of space was nearly complete, only faintly interrupted by the glimmer of brilliant stars and satellites shining in the distance. Metal-clad freighters and shuttlecraft of various configurations hovered patiently, waiting for docking authorization from traffic control, no doubt eager to dock in time for the evening's festivities.

The day was special, but the evening held promise to be filled with far more excitement, as the annual celebration of the station's sovereignty, or Founders Day, as the locals called it, was ahead. Light crowds of people ambled about the bazaar, aimless in their journey. Children carelessly splashed away in the large water fountain, central to Taloo Station's grand shopping district.

The reverberating buzz of sitar music echoed out from The Celestial Teahouse as the complexity of Bergamot citrus blended with the scent of exotic Indian spices lingered in the air like a dense fog. An annoying creak echoed throughout the tea shop, reminding Martin once again to lubricate the hinges on the front door.

"Damn," he said from high up on the storeroom ladder. It had been hours since his last customer, and he'd hoped to close early. Most people were either at a local pub or were already in the central promenade. Celebration hour was near and his regular tea drinking customers were notorious for overstaying their welcome. Sometimes hours past closing.

He shrugged his dissatisfaction away and shoved the bin of surplus tea back on the shelf. He gripped the sides of the ladder before slipping his feet off the rung. The station's artificial gravity took over and he slid down three levels to the storeroom floor below.

Popping out onto the sales floor, he found it to be deserted. He was momentarily relieved that he still might be able to duck out early, but before he turned to head back into the storeroom, he sensed something—an instinct embedded in him, a link from his past. As he turned toward the intuition, a hood was draped over his head and a strong grip wrapped around his arms and chest, preventing movement. He felt the brutal strength of his captor and instinctively bent over at the waist, trying to throw him, or her, off balance. But it was futile, as the assailant appeared prepared for the maneuver.

Martin tried to free himself from the hold, but with each movement he made, the grasp became stronger.

Martin jerked his head backward, trying a different approach. The back of his head connected firmly with the assailant's face, but the hold remained. He thrust his head back again, but with much more gusto, and a satisfying crack echoed throughout the store. Martin instantly felt a warm, wet sensation run down his neck. The assailant's blood. The dominating hold lightened slightly, and before the assailant could regain his grip, Martin forced his biceps outward, causing the attacker to back away uncontrollably.

Martin yanked the hood from his head and ran toward the back room. As he passed through the doorway, he felt a fleeting hand grasp the back of his shirt. As the cloth stretched, Martin's momentum slowed, allowing the attacker a stronger purchase on him. Martin's only advantage was that he knew the layout of the storeroom, and hopefully the attacker did not.

He dashed to the left, toward his office, and as he did so, he caught a glint of light reflect off a blade in the assailant's hand. Before he could react, the attacker lunged forward, leading with the six-inch push dagger.

Martin dropped to his knees just as the tip of the blade punctured the skin on his shoulder. The pain was excruciating, but his training had taught him to manage. With Martin's downward momentum, the blade was only able to penetrate an inch or so before it dislodged from the assailant's hand and went flying across the room.

Near the floor now, Martin rolled to his side and landed on his back. The first real sight of his attacker—he was dressed completely in black, including a matching face mask and gloves.

What the hell? Attack of the space ninjas? Martin mused.

The assailant peered at Martin through two slits on his mask, his eyes penetrating and dangerous. He lunged again, but Martin was ready for the assault. He brought his leg up directly into the groin of his attacker. Before the assailant could strike again, Martin shot out with his other foot, blasting the attacker's knee sideways. The assailant screamed in agony as he crumpled to the floor, wrenching at his awkwardly bent leg.

Martin scampered into the office and scanned his desk for some kind of weapon, something that he could use to defend himself. Before he could locate anything, the assailant was back on the attack and was at his heels, wielding the T-knife once again. Martin tried to kick the blade from his hand, but his opponent's reflexes were too quick. With each of Martin's thrusts, the attacker drove the blade forward, causing numerous surgical cuts to Martin's leg, blood instantly cascading to the floor.

Between stabs, the attacker's free hand reached up and gripped Martin's waistband. With incredible strength, he dragged Martin away from his desk. Martin lashed out with both hands in an attempt to grasp something, anything that could impede the attack. As his hands slid across his desk, he latched on to his vintage leather-bound journal—which was of no use—and a silver-tipped mechanical pencil. He threw the journal at his attacker, but he swatted away like a fly. Martin struck the attack's chest with both feet, driving the breath from his lungs. As the attacker gasped for air, Martin lurched forward, fixing the mechanical pencil in the palm of his hand, and drove the sharp silver tip into the killer's eye socket. The penetration was only minimal before it met resistance. But on Martin's second attempt, he broke through the inner eye socket and into the attacker's brain. Hot liquid gushed from the laceration as the assailant's body twitched and convulsed uncontrollably on its way to the floor.

Martin shot back against his desk, panting heavily. It had been several years since he'd needed to use deadly force, and he was shocked at how quickly the ability returned to him.

As he sat on the floor, his breath slowly returning to normal, he contemplated his next move. A noise from the back of the storeroom interrupted his mental process. Someone was trying to jimmy the lock on the door to the service corridor.

Slipping the knife from the dead man's hand, Martin bolted for the rear exit. As he reached the door, the lock clicked. Slowly, the door inched forward as Martin stood just out of sight—the T-knife gripped tightly in his hand. Then, the barrel of a gun slipped through the crack. Martin quickly realized that these were trained assassins, as possessing firearms on-station was a major offense. In the eight years that he'd been on Taloo, he'd not laid eyes on a single weapon of the sort. Even the station police were disallowed to carry a side arm. Something to do with having a stray bullet puncture the skin of an exterior wall.

Martin lunged forward, gripped the barrel of the gun, and ripped it from the assassin's hand. The surprise was instant. He quickly tossed it to the floor behind him then looped his arm around the killer's neck. As he did so, the killer, his body much smaller than the first one, attempted to free himself from Martin's grip. Suddenly, he stopped his protest, as one of his hands disappeared into a trouser pocket. Before Martin could react, the compact killer produced a tactical switchblade in his left hand and began thrusting it backward, narrowly missing the side of Martin's head.

"Enough!" Martin yelled, as his patience ran out. He drove the T-knife into the ribcage of the attacker, and a high-pitched scream blurted from the killer's mouth.

Martin withdrew the knife and released the grip around the killer's neck. As he did so, he latched onto the black face mask, ripping it free. What he saw would have never been cause for alarm or hesitation, but that was years ago. Now, so long removed from his previous life, seeing a female assassin was cause for him to take stock of the situation.

"Who sent you?" Martin demanded.

The killer didn't answer. She widened her stance, awkwardly bouncing from foot to foot. She clearly was favoring her injured side but was still a force to be reckoned with.

"If you leave now, I won't have to hurt you anymore," Martin said.

Again, no reply. Instead, the killer feigned an attack to the left but then thrust to the right, most likely seeing the blood-soaked shirt that Martin wore. Unfortunately for the attacker, Martin was ready for the advance. As the killer's blade got near, Martin swiped his T-knife across her hand, slicing through the glove and lacerating the skin beneath. She lunged again, stabbing quickly at Martin's chest, just barely nicking the skin. Martin once again responded in like force, driving the T-knife into the killer's side. The blade caught on a rib bone, and Martin lost his grip. The killer increased the intensity of her attack now that Martin was unarmed, but the pain she was suffering was taking over. She half-heartedly slashed her knife at Martin's face, but he deftly caught her hand in midair. In a blinding quick movement, he disarmed the killer and drove the knife into the side of her temple. Her body dropped to the floor, lifeless.

Paying no mind to this second dead body in his tea shop, Martin raced to the back door, re-secured the latch, and propped the security bar across the door just to be sure. Then, he rushed back out onto the sales floor to lock the front door as well. He dimmed the lights and activated the obscure glass filter on the storefront.

"What the hell was that all about?" he murmured as he retreated to the back room. Halfway through the sales floor, he stopped and grabbed a few items off of the retail display rack: a pair of sweatpants, size extra-large; a hooded shirt with the saying The Celestial Teahouse Is Out Of This World printed across the front; and a charcoal-colored messenger bag.

Once in the back, he stepped over the first attacker's body and into his office. He quickly changed from his blood-soaked shirt, wincing from the pain with each movement. He noticed the blood had already begun to clot and was thankful that his injury wasn't too severe. He did his best to clear off as much of the blood as he could before slipping on the new clothes.

Suddenly, he heard the back door of the shop rattle again. So, there are more, Martin thought as he calculated his next move. He was confident that whoever was out back would not be able to get through the security measures he now had in place, so he focused his attention on the two attackers' bodies.

Starting with the man, he quickly turned out his pockets to see if there was any sort of ID. There was no wallet or passport. All he found was an energy gun and an assault knife similar to the one currently protruding from the second killer's head. Before he moved to the second body, Martin pulled the mask off the man to see if he recognized the face. Beneath, Martin found a face around his same age. He was clean shaven and was relatively nondescript.

Martin stuffed the knife and gun in his messenger bag before turning toward the female. Just like before, he found no ID or travel permits. He had already disarmed her of all weapons, so there was nothing left to discover on her body.

The rattling at the back door finally ceased, and Martin knew that whoever it was out there, they were probably on their way around to gain entry through the front door. It was time to leave.

Martin dropped the shoulder bag across his chest and made for the front door. As he walked past the sales counter and through the main aisle of the store, he had a sinking feeling that he would never see the place again. After eight years of hiding out there, he was saddened by the sudden loss of this part of his life.

Before regret seeped too far into his mindset, he unlatched the front door and stepped into the bustling foot traffic of the pavilion.

2

Despite the vast differences between living on a space station and living on earth, the environments were not all that different. Besides the obvious—no openable windows or clean, natural air—the surroundings were very similar. There were streets and avenues, for example, but there were no cars, as the streets were more like enlarged sidewalks, complete with curbs and gutters that were most likely in place to remind the people on board where they all came from: earth.

As Martin moved into the street crowd, the undeniable flow of traffic took him toward the center of the pavilion. Without a solid plan in mind, he felt it best just to blend in to his surroundings for the time being. He realized that being in the middle of all these people gave him a great cover, but it also made it difficult to spot more of the assassins. Regardless, this was his best bet at staying alive.

As he merged toward the center of the crowd, he continued to analyze those around him. Most of the people were smiling and being jovial. But Martin noticed some men and women at the perimeter who appeared more rigid. They weren't necessarily just standing around, not enjoying themselves, but they weren't exactly celebrating expectedly. That's when he noticed the next assassin.

Stepping out from a service corridor, a man wearing black pants and a black ribbed sweater stood and scanned the crowd. He'd obviously ditched the black gloves and mask and even rolled his sleeves up in an attempt to blend in with the crowd. The sharply formed bulge at his waistband gave him away though, and it was clear that the assassin was looking for somebody in particular: Martin. Or more precisely, he was looking for the man Martin used to be: Jaxon Rasner.

Martin fished an elastic band from a side pocket and quickly cinched up his shoulder-length hair into a ponytail. He cursed himself for not thinking of grabbing a hat as well, but he did the best with what he had.

Wanting to stay away from the killer, Martin began to drift in the opposite direction until he nearly came face-to-face with yet another man dressed in black.

"Shit," Martin muttered before he discreetly turned his head away and attempted to disguise his height by bending slightly at the knees and shrugging his shoulders over. After he'd moved along several paces past the second assassin, Martin gradually turned his head to see if he was being followed. Thankfully, it appeared that neither of the men had recognized him as they continued to scan the crowd.

Martin realized that, short of a complete disguise, there would be no concealing his appearance and avoiding further assassination attempts. But until he got to his apartment, there wasn't much he could do.

Then, suddenly, Martin noticed that the crowd of people were converging toward the primary station lift. He realized that if he continued with the flow, he would be enclosed in a space with no escape route. Until he was positive that he was clear of any of the pursuing killers, he needed to stay out in the open or in an environment he had more control over. He glanced around the promenade and spotted his target.

Superlative.

As casually as possible, he parted through the crowd to the entrance of the classical 1980s-era dive bar and stepped inside. Surprisingly, there were far more patrons in the establishment than he'd expected, considering the station's big celebration that was about to take place.

Once out of view, he stood for a moment to let his eyes adjust to the darkened environment. Suddenly, he heard his name being called out.

"Hey, Marty! You're here early? Decide to exercise your liver like the rest of us?" Zed, the bartender, asked.

"Crap," Martin said in a low voice. He'd hoped to be able to duck into the bar and not be recognized so quickly. *So much for staying low profile.*

Martin moved up to the bar and smiled at Zed. "Um, yeah. It's been slow over at the shop today, so I figured what the heck."

"Well, buddy. The first one's on the house. We're celebratin' today!" Zed said.

"Hey, thanks. Can you send it down to the end of the bar? I need to take a piss," Martin said as he started toward the back service hall.

"Will do, boss."

As soon as Martin stepped into the hallway, he planted himself against the side wall and peered around the corner toward the front entry. From his vantage point, he could see the light of the pavilion shine in and dance off of the walls of the bar. Nobody came through the door.

Could I have gotten so lucky? he wondered. He stood silently, scrutinizing the entryway for several minutes until the bad news walked in. The killer with the sleeves rolled up boldly stepped in from the pavilion, followed closely by another assailant. They conversed briefly before splitting up and moving deeper into the bar.

Without hesitation, Martin bolted toward the bathroom doors, first popping into the women's room, looking for any sort of access to the service corridors. Having run into a dead end, he stepped out and then into the men's room looking for the same.

"Shit," Martin exclaimed as he stepped back into the hallway. He knew that returning to the bar would be certain suicide, but he couldn't very well just disappear down one of the toilets. He was contemplating his next move when the wall next to the bathrooms suddenly moved to the side, revealing a hidden passageway. As the disguised door opened fully, one of the establishment's barmaids stepped through, carrying a plate of fried bar food, the door closing automatically.

"Hey, sugar. Haven't seen you around for a while," she said as she passed Martin.

Martin smiled and winked at her as she continued her stride out into the bar. As soon as she was out of sight, he pushed on the wall where she had just come from and it gave way again with a click.

Once inside the kitchen, Martin moved past the stainless steel cooktops and prep tables. He was looking for the access point that he knew existed. He was looking for his escape. There, next to a walk-in freezer was a door very much like the one in his tea house. It had the same metal security latch dropped across the face of the door, preventing any unauthorized access.

Martin removed the security bar, and just as he was about to step into the service corridor a beam of greenish-blue energy blasted the wall next to him. He dropped to his knees and turned in the direction of the blast. One of the assassins stood on the far side of the kitchen, waiting for his weapon to recharge. Without hesitation, Martin ducked through the door and slammed it shut.

3

Martin instantly broke out in a sprint, fleeing down the corridor at top speed. The service hallways were generally unoccupied by people but were large enough to accommodate bidirectional delivery-drone traffic. Because of the service nature of the thoroughfare, the walls were lined with sheet metal for protection and the ceiling was highly illuminated. Unfortunately, that spelled for a difficult attempt at seclusion. Martin could run, but there was no place for him to hide.

As he ran past half a dozen closed shop doors, the service-way came to a T. To the right, the corridor continued on for another ten meters before it terminated at a door, most likely leading back out into the pavilion. To the left, the passageway sloped down and away before curving out of sight. Without wasting a single moment, Martin turned left and began the descent into the unknown.

Clink, clink, clink, echoed all around him. It was the familiar sound of metallic bullets hitting the thin sheet metal. Within seconds, the weapons discharge alarm began to blare.

"Jesus, these guys never give up," Martin said as he leaped the final three meters and into a large open warehouse. Scattered about the enormous stockroom stood numerous shipping containers, no doubt filled with supplies for the various shops in the pavilion. Martin darted between two of the containers and hid along the back edge of the warehouse.

As Martin checked himself, he realized that his breath had nearly returned to normal, and his heart rate had stayed at a constant ninety beats per second. He grinned, thankful for the training that he'd endured all those years ago. Training for situations just like this. He also realized that there was only so much running that he could do before the killers caught up with him. He was on a space station, for shit's sake—a proverbial island in the sky. He'd have to face them head on sooner or later.

He removed his shoulder bag and pulled out the energy pistol. A quick study of the default settings and he noticed the intensity was set at its lowest level. He contemplated the reasoning behind it, and concluded that the recharge rate would be quicker that way, and the killers would be more than happy to finish the job with a combat knife once the target was incapacitated from the energy blast.

Martin increased the firing intensity to full power before unlocking the safety. It was a calculated decision; he was confident with his aim and he wanted to ensure that he took the assassin down on the first shot.

With the pistol at the ready, Martin pulled the combat knife from the bag and gave it a quick polish with his shirt sleeve. He then angled the blade around the edge of the container to see the reflection of the service ramp. From his vantage point, he could see anyone approaching.

Within seconds, the first assassin came into view and was side-stepping down the far edge of the wall. He slowed his pace as he took in the surroundings, almost certainly assessing Martin's location.

Martin withdrew the blade and stowed it back in his bag.

Then, he rolled onto the floor and crawled slowly into the space between the containers. With his position low to the ground, the assassin wouldn't see him right away. Martin gripped the pistol with both hands and leveled it straight out in front of him. He pointed it directly at the killer. Still, the killer didn't notice his position.

The killer fully moved into the warehouse, eyes darting all around. Finally, his eyes looked down and saw Martin behind the sight of the pistol.

Martin pulled the trigger.

The discharge was nearly instant, a solid burst of energy, though the pistol had almost no recoil. A splash of greenish-blue light spat from the barrel of the gun, leaving a faint tracer line through the air. But the blast did not have the anticipated effect for Martin. The energy blast struck the assailant directly in the middle of his chest, but it only caused him to stumble back slightly. These killers were well funded, judging by their top of the line gear. To obtain anti-phasor armor was not a cheap requisition.

Martin looked at the recharge meter on the side of the pistol, and it moved painfully slow. At that rate, the killer would be on top of him long before he could even think about getting off another shot.

Martin sprang to his feet as the assassin continued advancing, a menacing grin crossing his face.

One last glance at his pistol's meter, and he realized it was futile. Without thinking, Martin hurled the pistol directly at the assailant, striking him in the middle of the forehead. The force caused him to drop to a knee, probably more out of surprise than injury.

Before the killer could regain his composure, Martin lunged directly at him, his fist striking the killer's left temple with such force that he heard his own knuckle crack.

Again, the assassin was too stunned to retaliate, giving Martin the upper hand. He continued to pummel the killer until he dropped his firearm in protest.

Martin saw his chance and went for the gun. But the moment he stopped throwing haymakers, the assassin tackled Martin from behind. With catlike reflexes, he had Martin in a chokehold—starving him of oxygen. Martin twisted his torso fiercely and swung his legs to the side, causing both him and the killer to lose their footing.

As they fell to the ground, Martin reached for the gun again, but the killer's momentum knocked it away before he could grasp the handle. Feeling his lungs burn, Martin rolled to his left and onto his back just as the assassin came down on top of him. He brought his knee up sharply into the killer's groin, producing a satisfying yelp.

Martin once again went for the gun just as he saw a garrote pass over his head. Within seconds, he felt the metallic wire cinch tight. He thrust his head backward sharply, connecting it with the killer's chin, giving him just enough time to get his hand between the skin on his neck and the wire. The assailant grunted and tightened the garrote once again. The man had enormous strength—far more than Martin was used to. He knew his time was limited. He had to make a move now ... or else.

With all his might, Martin thrust himself backward, driving them out into the open. He continued to drive his feet backward, unaware of their direction, but with each step backward, the garrote loosened a little more. As their momentum increased, Martin thrust his head back once again but missed the killer entirely. The movement, however, was beneficial, as the killer finally lost his footing and they both plummeted to the ground.

The impact happened suddenly, causing the killer to scream into Martin's ear. A split second later, Martin discovered the reason for his pain as a sharp object drove into his own lower back. Then, just as suddenly, the killer's grip on the garrote dwindled and his body went limp.

Martin thrust the wire cord away from his body and cautiously rolled off of the dead assassin. He looked back and noticed that they had landed on a pile of surplus metal fittings, many of them jutting out at sharp angles. One had impaled the killer through the chest and then punctured Martin's back. Thankfully, the killer's torso was thick enough that Martin's own injury was minor.

Martin scampered back to the shipping containers and grabbed the killer's pistol. He retook his position back behind the container and waited for the second assassin. After nearly thirty minutes of silence, Martin concluded that he was safe. The final assassin had either called off the hunt or was searching in a different part of the space station entirely.

M artin repacked his satchel with all the weapons that he'd scavenged from the assassins before doing a final pass through of the warehouse, hoping to pilfer any additional items he might need. Unfortunately, every container was secured with a bio-lock, programmed to unlock at the touch of the owner. And the owner only. In his past, Martin had tried numerous times to trick similar locks into opening, and that was when he was in possession of a random body part of the unfortunately dead owner. The lock was intelligent enough to include a pulse sensor as well as a DNA scanner and fingerprint reader.

Resolved to retrace his steps empty handed, he turned and headed for the ramp. As he got to the edge of the inclined path, Martin found a floor plan plastered on the wall, outlining the entire service pathway system of the space station.

Hurray, he thought, as he pried the plastic shield away from the wall, allowing the map to slip from behind. Analyzing it, he noted the location of his tea shop in relation to his next stop. Then, he found where he was currently at, and determined his path. He was happy to find that the service tunnels led almost the entire way to McKinner's, but the final sector would have to be traversed out in the public thoroughfare.

Martin folded up the map and slipped it into his shoulder bag then bounded up the ramp.

When Martin slipped out of the service door, the surrounding area was much different than that on his side of the station. He so infrequently visited the seedy part of Taloo, he'd almost forgotten how contrasting such a small space station could actually be.

Moving through the grungy neighborhood, he could see the sign of McKinner's ahead, half of the neon light letters burned out long ago. The vicinity was practically empty, most everyone having already joined the celebration at the promenade. That suited Martin perfectly, as it gave him the ability to see any approaching attackers more easily.

As Martin stepped up to McKinner's entry door, he paused briefly, hoping that this forced reunion would pass by amicably. Then, Martin stepped through and into his past.

The inside of the bar was dark and hazy, even though smoking was prohibited on the station. Martin recalled the owner mentioning long ago that he wanted the ambiance of an old biker bar and had installed the smoke machine for effect.

Martin walked further into the bar and discovered that the place was completely deserted. There wasn't a customer in sight, and the only person besides himself that was present was the bartender. The very person he was there to see. Sonja.

He sat down at the bar and looked across the dark mahogany top and into the most brilliant hazel eyes he'd ever seen. "Hi," he said, lowering his gaze slightly.

"Wow, you look like shit," Sonja said, staring at the scrapes and bruises scattered across his face and neck.

"And you haven't changed a bit, my dear."

"First off, I'm not your dear anymore. You lost the right to call me that four years ago when you walked out on me … without even an explanation."

Martin retraced the memories from his past. He'd been living above McKinner's at the time. And having such close proximity to the place, he was quite the regular. That was until he began to recognize various deviations from the norm that caused him discomfort. He'd only been on station for a few years at that point and was still unsure about his new life as Martin Wheeler.

"Yeah, about that—"

To Martin's surprise, Sonja's eyes began to well up. "No. Stop. I don't want your excuses. That's water under the bridge. I'm over it just as much as I think you are," she said.

Martin nodded slowly. "Yeah … that's probably best," he said, wishing that he hadn't waited so long before seeing her again. He did feel terrible for just walking away. And now, here he was, showing up out of the blue, about to ask for something more.

"So. Tell me, Martin, why are you here?"

Martin winced as he adjusted his legs dangling from the barstool. "Do you still have my crate down in storage?"

"That's it? You walk in here after four years and you just want your crate … and then you're on your way again? You sonofabitch."

"No, it's not like that," Martin said, realizing that his words were lies. "I wanted to … come here so many times, but I just couldn't …"

"Yeah, I know," she said sympathetically. "You just couldn't find your balls long enough to give you motivation … I've heard it all. The crate's down where you left it, high up on that shelf that you know I can't reach."

"Sonja, please. Don't be like that. I've had it rough every day since I left, and you don't know how much I regret doing it. But there's more to it than what you realize. And maybe someday, you'll understand everything."

Sonja was about to walk away but stopped. There was something in Martin's words that made her turn back, noticing the blood-soaked shirt for the first time. "My God, Martin, what happened to you? It looks like you haven't shaved in years and your hair is … don't even get me started on the long hair. And it looks like you've just run into the back of a star freighter, and you're bleeding," she said, motioning to his shoulder.

"Long story short, I got jumped," Martin lied.

Sonja's expression changed instantly as she moved to the side of the bar and up to Martin. "And it's not just your shoulder, hon. It looks like they got your back too," she said as she lightly touched the wound.

To Martin, her gentle touch felt more like the stinging spike of needles, and he instinctively pulled away.

"Don't be a baby," Sonja said, lifting the shirt up for a better look. "You can at least let me clean this up."

Martin agreed and followed Sonja into the women's room, where she took over as if she were a triage nurse.

"Let's see just how bad it is," she said as she washed her hands in the sink.

Martin nodded silently and carefully removed the blood-stained shirt before tossing it into the sink. Then, he loosened the drawstrings on his sweatpants and dropped them to the ground.

"Hey, buddy, don't get any ideas," Sonja said, seeing his reflection in the mirror. "I just wanted to tend to your injuries."

"But what about the cuts down here?" Martin said, motioning to his lower leg.

"Jesus, Martin, what did you do to piss these guys off?"

Martin shrugged. He was concerned about disclosing too much information, on the off chance that the assassins followed him here.

Sonja wet a rag under the faucet then turned to him. "Okay, let's see where it hurts. Turn around."

Martin did so and placed his hand on the edge of the

counter for support. Sonja slowly and methodically cleaned all of the dried blood from Martin's skin. She had a motherly touch.

After nearly fifteen minutes of cleaning the wounds, she walked out of the bathroom without a word. Moments later, she returned with a first-aid kit and an arm full of folded-up clothing. As Martin eyed the clothes, Sonja rummaged through the first-aid kit, fishing out the ointment, gauze pads, and surgical tape. Within minutes, she had all of Martin's injuries bandaged up neatly.

"Well, that should do until you get it looked at. Here are some clothes that might fit. Bruno always kept a change of clothes in his locker, and he hasn't been around for a couple of months. He was about your size," Sonja said, surveying Martin's physique.

"Hey, Sonja. Thanks for everything. I mean truly, deeply."

Sonja nodded and smiled. "You get dressed, and I'll go grab the key for the storage room." She walked out, leaving Martin standing in the women's room, wearing more bandages than underwear.

Minutes later, Martin emerged, wearing a pair of brown corduroy trousers and a pullover shirt. "Well? Do I wear it as well as Bruno did?" he asked.

Sonja looked up but didn't acknowledge the comment. She was back behind the bar and slid a key across the bar top. "Remember to turn out the light and lock up when you're done. Stairs are in the back," she said, turning her back to Martin as she mindlessly cleaned a glass that didn't appear to be dirty in the first place.

Wordlessly, Martin picked up the key. He did feel bad about how he'd left things all those years ago, and couldn't help but see a pattern in his behavior. A pattern that he wished he had the power to correct.

He walked through the back and into the stairwell. A quick jaunt down a flight of stairs and he was in another service corridor. It was similar to the one behind his own tea shop but much smaller. It was only used by the handful of businesses in that sector. There were no connections to the other service arteries throughout the station. He felt safe and that was good. He needed privacy, as he was about to open the storage crate. And his past.

Once in Sonja's storage room, he surveyed the layout and found what he was looking for. On the top shelf, along the back wall, sat a wooden crate with the name SABER stenciled in bold letters along its side. Swiftly, Martin yanked at the handle, dropping it down to the ground with a crack.

Along the top of the crate, Martin found the digital padlock that he'd used to secure his belongings eight years earlier. Without thought, Martin entered in the sixteen-digit code from memory. The slowly flashing red light turned green, and an audible click echoed through the compact storage locker.

Martin wasted no time and flipped open the lid. Inside, he found everything exactly as he'd left it. On top were three travel documents. Each one with a different name.

The first one, Jaxon Rasner—his true identity. It was who he always was, and would be again.

The second one, Frederick Deerfield—his last known alias when he worked for the GSA. He tossed it to the side, knowing that using it now would be futile in his escape.

The third passport had the name Graham Campbell, and he felt that a change of identity would be beneficial once he was in Luna City. He set both Jaxon's and Graham's passports aside.

Jaxon had a fourth identity, Martin Wheeler—his current cover—and as soon as he got back to his apartment, he planned on disposing of all traces of the blown identity. *It was blown, right?* he wondered.

Next, he pulled out a large duffel that had the same name, SABER, stitched on the handle. His code name while working for the GSA. Unzipping the duffel revealed the main reason for his trip into the storage locker. Inside, he found a dozen stacks of universal spending credits, totaling more than he'd ever need to live out the rest of his life—in case of an emergency. An emergency such as this.

Beneath the credits, he found an old friend, an MP-96 rapid-fire proton pistol. Next to the weapon lay a box with enough ammunition to fire his way off of the station if necessary.

Along the bottom of the duffel, he found his last bit of good news. It was his custom-made environmental suit, complete with phasor armor. The design had been so advanced when he'd had it made that consumer-grade technology still hadn't caught up with it. *Oh, the joys of being a covert agent.*

Jaxon quickly shed his clothes and put on his environmental suit. The suit was skin tight, allowing it to be worn under regular clothing.

He redressed and then quickly transferred all the contents from the duffel into his new tea house satchel. It was a tight fit, but the touristy satchel drew far less attention than a government-issued duffle emblazoned with his old code name.

Lastly, Jaxon pulled an olive-colored jacket from the bottom of the crate and slipped it on. It was his old Academy jacket, and he was surprised how well it still fit. He contemplated whether or not to take it, but the added feature of a double inside holster sold him.

Stuffing everything back into the crate, he returned it to the top shelf, quickly doused the light, and re-locked the door. A few minutes later, he was returning the key to Sonja at the bar.

"Everything as you left it?" she asked.

Jaxon nodded. "Did you even move it since I put it up there?"

"Nope. Once you told me that it was very important and imperative that it be left undisturbed, I took your word for it. Funny thing about trust, wouldn't you say?" she asked, not really expecting an answer.

"I guess I deserve that."

"At the very least. Tell me, Martin. Was it me? Was it

something else … that caused you to hurt me so bad?"

"No, it wasn't you. It could never be you. It was me and … something that I couldn't control. I still can't control it now, but once I can, I want you to know that I'll explain everything. Until then, I really have to go. I've imposed too much already-"

"So, that's it? I'll probably not see you for another, what? Six years?"

"Hopefully sooner. I have to … leave station for a bit, but I promise I'll try—"

Shocked surprise spread across Sonja's face. "You're leaving? Anything to do with the attack?" she asked, concerned.

"A little. Like I said, Sonja, I want to tell you, but right now I can't."

"All right then. I wish you well, Martin. And before you get too far down your path, you might want to make a stop by the doc's office. That stab wound on your shoulder looks pretty severe."

"Will do, nurse," Jaxon said, winking at her.

Without another word, Jaxon turned and walked out the door.

Jaxon stood in the shadows of a synthetic Beachwood tree and surveyed the landscape ahead of him. The simulated environment lighting was set to synchronize with the time zone of earth below, which happened to be just before 9 PM. Through the dimness of the various streetlights, level seventeen appeared deserted, with most of the inhabitants likely to be at the Founders Day celebration.

The area right near Jaxon's apartment was wide open, giving little to no coverage for a stealthy approach. From years of experience, an ambush scenario should be expected. Time was of the essence, as the multiple weapons discharge alarms blaring across the station would certainly make for a difficult escape.

He adjusted the strap on his shoulder bag and slipped his hand inside his jacket and gripped his pistol firmly.

"Here goes nothing," he muttered as he took a solitary step toward his front door.

The repetitive crack-crack-crack of what must have been an illegal railgun echoed throughout the three-story courtyard.

Jaxon dropped to the ground and rolled beneath a park bench for protection. Slowly, he inched himself forward until he had a clear view of where he thought the shots came from. Second level balcony—he spotted the new assailant. He was kneeling at the edge of the guardrail, a reflective glint bouncing off of his night scope. It was pointed directly at Jaxon. He knew that if there was one, there were probably more. Just how many, he couldn't guess. He also knew that they wouldn't stop coming until he was dead. That's the way he would've done it and that's what worried him the most.

Sliding back beneath the bench, Jaxon removed his satchel and rummaged through the contents. From the bottom of the bag, he withdrew his MP-96 and checked both clips— they were full, with one in the chamber. He flipped on the infrared laser scope and peered through the magenta eyepiece. The off-colored lens allowed him to see the invisible target almost as clear as day. He raised the barrel up and to the left until there was a solitary dot on the chest of the second-floor assailant. Calmly, he exhaled, completely, then squeezed the trigger. A single projectile shot ahead and eliminated the threat, only millimeters off of its mark. Jaxon quickly chambered a new round and began to scan for more assassins. He waited for another discharge alarm, but it never came.

Before Jaxon could locate another target, one of the residents of his quad came out of her apartment, no doubt drawn out by the clamor. It was Mrs. Jarvis, a reporter for the Taloo Tribune. Jaxon wanted to yell out to her, to get back inside, but it was too late. A sniper on an upper-level balcony— just up and to his right—took her out, placing a well-aimed round into the middle of her forehead.

Where the hell were the alarms? he wondered. He wasn't completely disappointed by their absence, giving him a potential edge on escaping the station, and certain death, but they should have been blaring nonstop now. Unless ... they were disabled.

Jaxon rolled out from beneath the bench and into the

clearing. In a swift, fluid motion, he raised the barrel of his gun up to where he thought the second assassin was. The killer was right where he'd expected. Jaxon flipped the pistol into automatic and placed three rounds into the side of his neck, nearly severing his spine with the last penetration. The killer dropped to the ground, lifeless.

Rapid fire shots then began to echo throughout the courtyard from multiple locations, all focused on Jaxon's position. Jaxon scrambled to his feet and bolted for the cover of the balcony above. He landed, his back plastered on the wall directly beneath one of the other shooters. In the distance, just around the corner of the center cluster of units, he saw a shadow move briefly. Jaxon raised his MP-96 once again and fired two shots in that direction. The first shot went wide, but the second entered the killer's right eye socket, blasting blood and brain matter outward.

Jaxon inched forward, about half the distance to the edge of the balcony above, and pointed his weapon up. Then, he took another half step forward and saw the face of the assassin staring back. Before the man above could withdraw, Jaxon squeezed the trigger, obliterating the forehead of the killer.

"One more," Jaxon said as he expertly reloaded his rifle. He knew the final assailant—hoped the final assailant—was to the left and behind a refuse bin. Jaxon took two steps to the right and then reentered the open courtyard, his weapon held steady in front of him. With his stance low to the ground, Jaxon continued walking in that direction. When he reached the middle of the open courtyard, several flashes of light came from the killer's direction as his semi-automatic assault rifle launched several rounds toward him. Jaxon dropped to the ground but not before returning fire, taking out the final assassin with ease.

Jaxon ran to the last fallen body and kicked his weapon out of his hand. He was still breathing but just barely.

"Who sent you?" Jaxon demanded.

There was no response, his eyes quickly losing signs of life.

"How many more are there?" Jaxon asked. "Give me something useful, and I might let you live."

Again, no response. The killer took his last breath, his eyes settling into a sightless gaze.

"Dammit," Jaxon shouted. He holstered his MP-96 and raced toward his apartment. He was still several meters away when he heard the familiar clank and wine of the timeworn elevator come to a halt just to his right. Jaxon sprinted in between the garbage chute and a public recharge station and ducked out of sight.

The doors parted, but nobody got off the lift. Not at first. A cylindrical object flew out of the elevator door and landed near the middle of the courtyard. Moments later it began to spew a green-tinted fog.

Jaxon instantly recognized the smokescreen grenade and cursed beneath his breath. He was close, but wasn't going to get in without a fight. If he could just get inside his flat, he'd have everything he needed to hold off virtually any opposing force that came at him. He leaned out briefly to see his apartment door creak open. He realized at that moment that there would be no gaining access to the place he called home ever again.

He slinked back into his hiding space and quickly drummed up a new plan. The stairwell entrance was just a few meters to his left, and with the right distraction, he thought he could make it. Once inside, he'd expand on his plan of escape.

Without hesitation, Jaxon emptied all five grenades from the launcher at various positions throughout the habitation quad. The last shot he fired directly at the closing doors of the elevator, where the majority of the killers still stood. He could just make out the faint silhouettes through the fog. As each grenade began to detonate in rapid succession, Jaxon bolted from his hiding place and ran toward the park bench to reclaim his satchel. As he scooped it up from the ground, he saw three assailants lying awkwardly on the ground, decimated by the grenade blasts. There were two more fleeting through the fog, toward his apartment door.

Great, Jaxon thought. Out of sight—out of mind. They didn't even see him as he barreled into the exit stairwell.

Jaxon began taking the stairs two steps at a time as he reloaded his MP-96 and extra clip before slipping it back into his holster. As he ascended the stairwell, his mind replayed the events of his last few hours. He could not comprehend how he'd been able to live in secrecy for eight long years, then suddenly, have a whole team of assassins show up at his doorstep. They knew everything about him, where he worked— where he lived. *Have I gotten sloppy?* he wondered.

At level fifteen, Jaxon slowed his pace and inched up to the access door. Silently, he twisted the handle and pulled the door open an inch. Sector 15 was virtually identical to his own habitation level, and it was equally quiet. He re-latched the door and leaned into the center of the stairwell and listened intently. He tried to hear if there were any other footsteps on the stairway in either direction.

Silence.

He decided to go up two more levels, then he could reenter the streets of the station, and hopefully gain access to a lift that would take him to the promenade.

Nearing the limits of his exertion, Jaxon arrived at level thirteen, stepped out, and came face-to-face with one of the most beautiful women that he'd ever seen.

"Hi there, handsome. And you looking for a good time?" the voluptuous auburn-haired woman asked, wasting no time on pleasantries.

Realizing that he'd emerged in the entertainment district, which was known for its adulterous ways, he declined politely.

"Perhaps another time," he said, stepping around her, truly hating life right then.

"You don't know what you're missing," she hollered after

him but refused to give up her position near the stairwell.

Jaxon slowly maneuvered through the crowd of scantily clad women and potential buyers until he caught sight of the elevator. He quickly changed direction and headed straight for it. As he did so, he inadvertently bumped into another prostitute.

"Pardon me," he said as he stepped around her and continued on his path.

"It's all right, I was only *borrowing* this particular spot until you came by," she said, sarcastically.

"Excuse me?" Jaxon asked, not sure he understood her.

"No, no. You appear to be in a hurry, and I don't want to take any more of your time, as it looks like you are in search of a friend," she said, again causing bewilderment to overcome Jaxon.

He stopped in his tracks and turned to face her fully. Jaxon wasn't ashamed to admit that he had frequented the entertainment district a number of times over the years, and each visit meant nothing to him except for the release. Human nature demanded it, and who was he to question that? But, through all those visits, he'd never encountered a creature such as this.

"Sorry, what did you say?" he asked.

"I said that you appeared to be looking for a friend and were in a rush. Are you so sure that your friend isn't right here in front of you?" she asked.

Jaxon contemplated her words. Her approach was definitely worthy of consideration, but his time was limited. Just as he was about to reject her, something flashed in his mind. Something about what she said. *Was he looking for a friend?*

"No? I guess I'm not the friend you're looking for," she said as she began to turn walk away.

Another great tactic on her part. Playing hard to get.

"As a matter of fact, I am looking for a friend," Jaxon said, realizing that she would be the perfect cover for him. The assassins were clearly looking for a single man and not a couple. He would just need her companionship until he got to the space dock.

She froze and turned her purposeful pouty face in his direction. "I don't know." She paused. "How do I know you're not just saying that to get me in the sack?"

"Well, that's a chance you're gonna have to take. I was thinking of taking a trip up to the promenade for an hour or so. Interested?" Jaxon asked.

A look of confusion crossed her face. "So, you really don't want to get me in the sack? You do know what this place is, right?"

"Oh, yes. I know. It's just that, first, I want to take in a little of the festivities, and I would like to have you as my friend and companion for the next hour. After that, I'm game for whatever you have to offer."

She moved intimately closer to Jaxon and slipped her arm through his. "It sounds like a wild time, sugar. But, as you know, I work by the hour and ..."

"Say no more," Jaxon said as he slipped out a few hundred credits from his pocket and held them in front of her. She greedily swiped them from his hand, depositing them into her cleavage.

"Okay. Let's go have that blast that you're so looking forward to," she said as she led him to the elevator.

6

As they waited for the elevator, Jaxon hoped that there wouldn't be any uninvited guests waiting for them when the doors opened. Encountering more assassins just then would have really pissed him off.

Thankfully, when the buzzer sounded, and the doors parted, they were greeted with an empty elevator car. Jaxon led his companion in and pressed the button for the promenade level. The doors closed, and they were whisked up the dozen flights quickly.

"Tell me, sugar. Who do I have the pleasure of spending time with?" the hooker asked.

Jaxon didn't hesitate. "Name's Martin. But my friends call me Marty."

"It's a pleasure, Marty," she said as she slid her arms around his chest. "My name is Starr, just like in the sky. And you know what?"

"What's that, Starr?" Jaxon bit.

"You know what my friends call me? They call me Starr," she said, giggling at her attempt at juvenile humor.

Jaxon chuckled politely as the elevator slowed for their arrival. When they stepped out onto the promenade level, the Founders Day celebration was in full swing. The lights were dimmed, and various strings of colored festival lights were strung throughout the tall rotunda. Rhythmic music filled the air from the live band at center stage. The frivolity-laced dance floor circled the band and was filled with hundreds of station residents, who thrust and gyrated to the music.

At several points along the perimeter, makeshift refreshment bars were put up, ironically near the multiple security booths on the level.

Panic began to set in. Jaxon was fearful that the carnage that had followed him all over the station the last few hours would trigger the station's security officers to pounce on him at first sight.

Wanting to avoid the feared situation, Jaxon led Starr onto the packed dance floor, casually scanning the crowd for suspicious activities. His well-trained eye would certainly pick up on anything out of place. To his delight, he only found inebriated celebrations abounded.

As they neared the center of the dance floor, the rhythm quickly overtook Starr's inhibitions, and she began to dance. Jaxon contemplated dismissing himself from the dance floor due to his rightful possession of two left feet but thought better of it. Being in the middle of the festivities was a perfect cover. Besides, Starr appeared to be having such a good time. He did his best to match her eccentric moves, dismissing the fact that he looked extremely uncoordinated. The image of a dancing squid filled his mind.

Then, he caught something out of the corner of his eye. Odd behavior from several men clustered at the edge of the promenade. As he bobbed and weaved with the music, he coyly studied every detail of the group. At first glance, they appeared to be simply out of place civilians, dressed in khaki trousers and sport coats covering beige button up shirts. Not dressed in the expected black attire as he'd recently experienced. Then, one of them unmistakably touched the skin beneath their ear and appeared to speak to no one in particular.

Shit. They have hypo-comms.

He quickly changed position on the floor, steering Starr in various directions in the promenade, so he could get a better look at the perimeter. Just as he'd suspected, he found three other clusters of casually dressed men, evenly spaced around the rotunda.

Suddenly, Jaxon felt a firm grip on his shoulder, yanking him backward. Instinctively, Jaxon's hand slipped into his jacket and rested on the hilt of his gun. As the momentum pulled him around, he fully expected to come face-to-face with one of the killers, but instead, came eye-to-eye with a very flamboyant man. Jaxon could only stare with bewilderment.

"Hey, man," said the ostentatious fellow. "What are your intentions here with the lady?" He nodded his head in Starr's direction.

Jaxon quickly realized who the man was. Clearly, he was Starr's pimp. Jaxon smiled and slipped his hand into hers. "Hey, we're just here for a good time. Everything's cool."

"Not from where I stand, Bud. The way I see it is that you need to close the transaction, or I need to move the merchandise along, you dig?"

Already expecting the shakedown, Jaxon wanted no additional attention drawn to him, so he quickly peeled an additional 200 credits from his wad and handed them over to the pimp. "I think this should cover Starr for the rest of the night. I'm just here to have a good time, and this should take her off the list, wouldn't you agree?" Jaxon said.

The pimp took the credits and quickly stashed them in his pocket. "I don't know. I think it should be more like 300," he said, taking a step closer to Jaxon.

Jaxon quickly scanned the crowd to see if any unnecessary attention was being drawn, but there wasn't.

"Hey, you're the boss," Jaxon said as he slipped an additional hundred credit note into the pimp's hand.

"Right on, man. I knew you'd see things my way. You two have a good evening, and I hope you tip her well when your transaction is complete," the pimp said before disappearing into the crowd.

Just then, the music set changed from a reggae beat to a modern ballad, and the movement slowed considerably. Starr slipped her arms around Jaxon as they began to wobble from foot to foot in sync with the beat. Jaxon placed his hands on her demure waist and moved her about the floor.

While they danced, Jaxon continued to survey the crowd, looking for an opportunity to escape. To the left of their position, two guards stood on either side of the restricted lift that led to the space dock. As they continued to dance, Jaxon contemplated how he could possibly get around those guards and flee. Ironically, his pleas were answered as a fight broke out a half dozen meters to his right.

Despite the rift between a handful of drunk celebrators, the band played on as security swarmed upon the ruckus, leaving the elevator unattended.

"Hey, you want to get out of here?" Jaxon whispered into Starr's ear.

"You bet," Starr replied, clearly excited at the prospect.

Jaxon took Starr's hand and led her right up to the elevator doors. He quickly punched the call button then pulled Starr close and kissed her passionately. His thinking was that nobody would look twice at two amorous people in a passionate embrace.

As the seconds turned into minutes, Jaxon began to worry that the guards would return before the elevator arrived. Fortunately, his anguish was unfounded, as the doors parted a moment later. Jaxon backed into the elevator, maintaining his lip lock with Starr. As soon as the doors closed, Jaxon ended the kiss and quickly punched the call button for the space dock.

W ow, aren't you full of surprises?" Starr said.

The size of the elevator was twice that of the civilian elevators on the station, and it had walls and ceilings covered in polished aluminum. There were only three buttons on the panel: one labeled P for promenade, one labeled D for space dock, and one button that was ominously unlabeled and required an access key. Through all the years that Jaxon had been on the Taloo Station, he'd been to virtually every corner of its existence, including the space dock. He was surprised that he had not noticed the blank button before.

Jaxon's thoughts were interrupted when Starr pushed him back against the wall of the cab and kissed him firmly. Her hands began to caress his arms and shoulders, before working their way beneath his jacket. Jaxon grasped her hands, stopping her before she found the holstered pistol.

"Don't stop, baby," she pleaded. "I've never done it in an elevator before, especially one that is so off limits." She kissed him again and pulled her hands out of his grasp. She quickly dropped them to his waist and began unfastening his trousers.

"Starr, my dear. I think our time together is about to come to an end," Jaxon said, putting distance between him and the prostitute.

"But, honey, you paid for me for the entire night. I was gonna give you the best time ever," she whimpered.

"At some point in the next few hours, I'm sure I'll regret this, but I really have to go. You should return to the festival and enjoy your free evening. Consider that my treat to you for not having to work tonight."

As the momentum of the elevator slowed, Jaxon watched Starr's expression turn to sadness. He felt sorry for her. Leading such a lifestyle that she'd be disappointed for not being able to turn a trick was unsettling.

"If I go back down there, Robbie, my manager, will just put me back to work. He'll probably wonder what I did wrong to push you away so quickly."

"That's unfortunate. Can't you give him the slip?" Jaxon asked as the doors opened at the space dock. He stepped halfway across the threshold and paused, his body blocking the sensors to keep the doors open for a moment.

Starr's demeanor quickly transformed into fear. "What if I get back down there, and the guards've returned?" she asked, clearly more aware of the situation.

Jaxon contemplated that thought. If he took her with him, there'd be a good chance that she would be hurt or even killed without the proper training. He didn't need to be looking out for another person's life. As these thoughts passed through his mind, he caught a glimpse of movement in his peripheral vision. He squinted and saw two security guards standing still in the distance. Luckily, they hadn't seen him yet, and this new obstacle spurred him into action.

"Okay, new plan," Jaxon said, stepping back into the elevator. "I have two buddies down there that are stranded away from the festivities tonight. How about you go down and give them a good time? I'm positive they'll help you back down to the promenade level, er, after."

Starr's eyes perked up at the prospect. "Are they as handsome as you?" she asked.

"And more so," Jaxon said. He peeled off an additional 200 credits and tucked them into her cleavage, leaving his hand nestled in her warmth for several seconds. "That is for you. It's a little extra so you can give my buddies a night to remember. It's a surprise, so mum's the word on where you came from."

Starr adjusted her outfit and straightened her posture. "Sounds good, baby. Do you want me to give you a signal when the coast is clear?" she asked then winked.

Clever girl, Jaxon thought. Perhaps she'd do okay as a companion on the run. Before he could change his mind, though, she was out the door and walking down the platform.

Jaxon stepped out and stood behind a large support column at the edge of the bay. He leaned around and watched Starr seductively walk toward the guards. As she approached, she added a little bit more wiggle to her step and the guards did not seem to mind one bit. From his position, he couldn't hear their conversation, but their body language clearly indicated that they were pleased. After just a few moments of flirtatious banter, they all stepped into the security shack. As Starr followed them in, she threw Jaxon a thumbs-up then closed the door.

Jaxon gave Starr long enough to get things rolling before he headed out into the docking bay, which just so happened to be on the opposite side of the security shack. He was also concerned with the numerous surveillance cameras throughout the bay and hoped that Starr was good at her job. The guards' diverted attention would certainly be required.

After several minutes, Jaxon took in a deep breath and leaned against the side wall then strafed along the corridor until he was within a few meters of the security shack. He slowed his pace and noticed that on the adjacent wall to the door was a large window, giving a view of the entire docking bay.

"Shit," Jaxon murmured quietly. Yet another obstacle to

overcome.

Jaxon moved close to the window and peered in at the lower corner. He could see the heads of the two men as they sat with their backs turned toward him. Starr was writhing in front of them as she performed a pleasing striptease. Jaxon hesitated momentarily as he watched her seduce the guards. *She certainly enjoys her job,* he thought, as she removed her top and tossed it over the heads of the guards. As it landed next to the window frame, she caught the eye of Jaxon staring at her, and she winked. Jaxon smiled back then casually walked out into the docking bay to begin his survey of ships. He needed a ride off the station.

As he peered across the prows of several ships, he took in the enormity of the bay. It was massive, spanning several hundred meters in every direction. Jaxon guessed that he'd have his choice of more than seventy ships of all shapes and sizes.

He sprinted down the center of the dock, passing by several military-size frigates before he came to a dozen or so luxury yachts. Just what he'd been hoping for.

He stepped past the first two, being of Scottish origin, which he knew featured the obsolete Medcraft engines.

This third ship that he came upon was a Bradbury Max Elite. Its hull was highly polished and appeared to be pure titanium. He'd only seen the ship through publications, but was familiar enough with the specs and was confident that he could manage the helm.

Before boarding, however, he did a quick scan of the rest of the ships with intrigue and knew that there were none faster. He turned back and headed for the ramp of the Bradbury. But, before he took his first step aboard, he heard a voice coming from the other direction.

Jaxon froze and was tempted to pull his gun, but thought otherwise. He turned and saw a third security guard nervously walking in his direction.

"Dammit," Jaxon mumbled. *I don't need this right now.*

"You're not authorized to be here," the guard said as he rested his hand on his night stick.

"Oh, there you are," Jaxon said in a friendly tone. "I've been looking all over for you. Your buddies in the shack back there said you were somewhere in this area."

The guard continued walking toward Jaxon slowly but eased up on his paranoia enough that his hand dropped to his side.

"Ha, foolish me—in such a hurry to join the party, I left all the party favors on my ship," Jaxon said, motioning to the Bradbury behind him.

The guard stopped a few meters away. "I'll need to see your papers before I can let you board. You understand," the guard said.

"Oh, absolutely. I'm glad you guys are on the ball up here," Jaxon said as he reached into his jacket and grazed the butt of his MP-96. By touch, he was able to reduce the power to 30%, assuring that any shot would be nonlethal, but certainly debilitating.

Jaxon took a step forward. "I've got your paperwork right here," he said as he pulled out the pistol and fired it into the chest of the guard.

The look of shock on the guard's face right before Jaxon pulled the trigger was nearly comical.

Jaxon quickly re-holstered before dragging the unconscious body to the far side of the dock. Then, he raced up the Bradbury's ramp. As he rounded the corner toward the cockpit, he slapped a large red button on the wall, retracting the loading ramp, sealing his fate for certain.

8

Jaxon found his way to the cockpit easily enough, and his only hope was that the ship had enough fuel for his escape. Otherwise ... the consequences made his head spin.

As he lowered himself into the pilot's chair, he surveyed the control panel. Most of the digital screens were dark, save for a few monitors displaying essential information about the ship. Batteries were at a hundred percent, life-support: active. Gravity simulator was also in the green. Before releasing the docking clamp and firing up the thrusters, Jaxon continued to survey each of the controls, familiarizing himself with their functions. Despite the eight-year gap between piloting a vessel, the procedures came back to him promptly. He recalled one of his instructors from the Academy telling him that it was like riding a bicycle. *You never forget.* Jaxon smiled as he activated the remaining console lights and controls to full power.

Within seconds, Jaxon began to feel a low vibration rumble up through the floor and into his chair. The ship was waking up. As he adjusted the pitch and yaw settings in preparation to leave the space dock, a broadcasting hail broke the silence.

"This is Taloo Station calling Bradbury 9613, come in," the voice crackled through the ship's speakers.

Jaxon paused for a moment, wondering if he should respond or ignore the hail completely. His initial instincts were to turn the speaker off completely and just make a run for it. But, he felt that, in the end, a little deception might go a long way.

"Yeah, this is Bradbury, um 96—1 ... 3? Over."

"Our readings indicate that you have initiated engine warm-up and are intending to launch. Before you can proceed, you need to file an approved flight plan with control. Power down now and report to station control, over."

Expecting that, Jaxon had a reply at the ready. "Message received. However, if you could please review your records, an approved flight plan *has* been filed, and authorization has been given. Please confirm."

Jaxon knew that the Flight Traffic Controller was doing just that, and he hoped it would buy him at least two or three minutes—plenty of time to finish readying the ship in preparation for launch.

Jaxon continued to monitor his control panel and was happy to see that the ship was already at 75% readiness. In another moment or two, he'd be able to take off. Nervously, Jaxon tapped his foot on the metal deck, waiting.

"Roger that, pilot. Please identify yourself. We have no authorization for your departure. Power down now, or risk suspension of your slip permit."

"Oh no, not that," Jaxon muttered sarcastically. He looked up at the system information board and watched the numbers tick up painfully slowly.

94%. 95%. 96%.

Then, there was a pause. It held at 96% for nearly a minute.

"What the hell?" Jaxon blurted as he tapped the digital readout with his finger. He knew good and well that the crimson numbers couldn't be affected by his motion, but his impatience got the better of him.

"Respond, Bradbury 9613. Identify yourself."

"Dammit," Jaxon yelled. "What's the problem?"

Jaxon stood and peered out the port side window and noticed the dock bay doors begin to flash at the perimeter as their closure mechanism was activated.

Shit! Come on, man.

The digital readout finally advanced to 97%, and then instantly jumped to 100%.

Jaxon's hand at the ready, he released the docking clamp and gripped the control stick then fired the thrusters. The ship began to move forward, slowly. He slid the thruster control forward several clicks, hoping to increase the speed, but the ship continued to move at a crawl. Jaxon realized that there was probably some kind of station-oriented governor controlling maximum thruster speed while inside the station dock.

As the ship crawled forward toward the closing bay doors, the speaker broke the silence once again.

"Pilot. You were ordered to stop. Return the ship to its docking slip and surrender your vehicle. Security is in route."

"Oh, shut up," Jaxon yelled, as he turned down the cabin volume. Next, he dropped to a knee and ducked beneath the control panel, looking for an access panel. Within seconds, he found it and withdrew his combat knife and used the tip of the blade to loosen the attachment screws. Four screws later and the panel dropped to the floor, exposing dozens of multicolored wires and cables. He began to filter through the rat's nest, searching for the yellow wire with the red stripe. He recalled from his cadet training that particular color combination was typically associated with station controls. Finally, located at the back of the compartment, he found it and sliced through it with his blade. The moment that the wire was severed, several warning alarms began to fill the cabin. Jaxon quickly rummaged through the wires once again and found the purple alarm cable and severed it as well.

Silence.

Jaxon returned to the chair and drove the thruster handle forward once again. Instantly, the ship lurched ahead, decreasing the ETA readout from more than four minutes to 53 seconds, 52 seconds, 51 seconds …

"Shit," Jaxon said. It was going to be close, he realized, seeing the quickly closing doors approaching at breakneck speed. He had no idea what the beam of the ship was, but he knew it was most certainly more than the draft, and that he'd be better off adjusting the pitch ninety degrees to minimize the chance of clipping the wingtips. With a steady hand, Jaxon tilted the control stick to the left while pressing his foot on the right pedal. As expected, the ship turned on its edge.

Still concerned that the doors would close before his exit, Jaxon drove the thruster handle all the way forward, breaking even more speed regulations in the station. The intercept timer jumped from forty-three seconds to less than ten.

Nine. Eight. Seven. Six. Five. Four. Three. Two.

The Bradbury 9613 launched into the open space, narrowly missing the closing doors by centimeters. Once clear of all station obstructions, Jaxon engaged the impulse drive and pointed the ship toward lunar base.

Satisfied, Jaxon raised the speaker volume, eager to hear the panicked voice on the other end of the radio.

"… demand you stop at once. I repeat, Martin Wheeler, you are wanted for questioning. Stop at once or suffer the consequences. Security patrol has been notified."

How the hell did they know it was me so soon? Jaxon wondered. Had all of the assassination attempts and carnage been linked to him already? He knew it was only a matter of time, but he'd hoped that it would be several hours before security put two and two together.

Ignoring the pleas from Taloo Station, Jaxon activated navigation control and quickly entered in his final destination. Lunar base. Within a few seconds, the screen read:

Navigational Path Complete. ETA 97 minutes. Engage autopilot?

Without hesitation, Jaxon activated the autopilot, and for the first time in hours, he leaned back in his chair to relax. His repose was short-lived though, as a fiery explosion shook the ship right outside the port window.

"Jesus," Jaxon said, hurling himself from his chair. He activated the ship's radar and noticed security vessels chasing after him. He adjusted the cursor to the ships and brought up their information. They were Evans class frigates, and he knew right away that they'd have no chance of catching up to his superior engine power. The warning shot was just that. They couldn't risk firing upon a valuable ship such as the Bradbury, and he knew that within another six to eight minutes, he'd be out of their firing range anyway. But, just to be safe, Jaxon disengaged the autopilot and took over manual control.

Scanning through the radar screen once again, he saw a diversion tactic that might fit his situation. A few clicks to starboard, he could be heading right to a well-known pleasure cruise belt. If he could put one of the slow-crawling cruisers between him and his chasers, he could virtually eliminate any additional shots fired in his direction.

A few moments later, the first pleasure cruiser came into view. It was an enormous ship, shaped like a jumbo submarine from Earth's navy fleet. But at ten times the size. The attention to detail was complete, as it featured a periscope at the top of the vessel, and twin screws at its rear. Jaxon chuckled as he maneuvered his ship around and past the cruiser until it was situated between him and the chasing vessels.

Jaxon promptly reentered his destination into the navigation computer, and his revised ETA was 113 minutes. Accepting the delay instead of the remote possibility of being captured, he engaged the autopilot once again and leaned back for a short nap.

*Eight years ago — Operation Bohemian Rapture,
above Luna City.*

*Objective: Assassinate Kamil Marsalek and his elite
entourage.*
Timeframe: Immediate.
Threat level: Moderate.
Operatives: Saber, Gillette.
Method: Improvised.

"Robins Nest, to Saber. Do you read?" blasted in my ear. I accessed my environmental suit's controls and lowered the volume.

"I copy. Go ahead?" I said, puzzled by the break in radio silence. I looked across the shaft at Gillette quizzically. He shrugged in wonder as well.

"Checking your status. Mother would like the flock to know that the bird is in flight. I repeat the bird is in flight. Over."

I held two fingers up toward Gillette, then gave the thumbs-up. He nodded and returned the signal, indicating he was on schedule as well.

"This is Saber, over. Could you repeat? Did you say the bird is in flight? Have an ETA?" I asked, maintaining focus on my job at hand. I had already placed three charges along the support rail and had one more to go. Timing was crucial, and if the scenario was to be believable, everything needed to proceed as planned.

"This is Robins Nest, over. ETA: twenty-three minutes. Do you copy?"

Gillette nodded his head as he placed his last explosive charge on the far side of the elevator shaft.

"Copy that. We'll be cutting it close, but should be done in fourteen. Over."

I slid the last detonator into the explosive putty and strung the wire to the relay. I dialed up three minutes and checked my suit display for synchronization. Everything checked out.

I unlatched my safety tether and gently pushed off toward Gillette. As I floated through the airless environment, I pivoted and latched on next to him. Switching off my comms, I motioned for Gillette to do the same. He nodded.

"Timer set," I said, annunciating my words clearly so that Gillette could read my lips.

"Same here. We're actually going through with this?" he asked.

I nodded and unlatched from the safety hook. I slipped the tungsten carbine around the cable at the center of the elevator shaft and pushed off in the direction of Luna City. As I glided down, I turned on my comm's channel and spoke: "This is Saber, over." I waited.

"Ravens Nest here, go ahead."

"Yeah, we're having … can't continue … trouble setting timer … abort, over," I said, purposefully abbreviating my speech as I continued my descent toward the city.

"Saber, repeat. Your transmission is breaking up," said Capt. Evans from his orbiting transport ship on the far side of the moon.

Evans received static in return.

"Director? It's Evans," he said into his secondary microphone. "It appears we have a problem."

"Go ahead. What's going on?" the director asked.

"I was in communication with Gillette and Saber up until about a minute ago when we lost their signal. The last clear transmission indicated they were on schedule, and—"

"Then, what's the problem?"

"Their last communication was scrambled and fragmented, and Jaxon's last word was abort. I'm not sure if it was a question or a comment," Evans said. "What should we do?"

The director gave no response and Evans re-keyed the microphone. "Director? Did you copy that last—"

"I did," the director said from behind Evans. "Precisely, what did the message say?"

Evans replayed the last transmission from Jaxon. "That was nearly three minutes ago," he said.

"Well, unless we can raise them again ... we proceed as planned. Like they said, they're on schedule and will have time to clear out before—"

"Robins Nest, this is Saber! Severe malfunction! Detonators not responding. I repeat, not responding. Timer won't set, and—" The broadcast broke into static.

"Saber, this is Robins Nest. Do you copy?" Evans asked.

Static continued to blare over the speakers as Evans and the director stood by.

Evans brought up the external video feed of the space elevator and directed it to the wall display. Moments after the display focused on the cylindrical shaft jutting up into space from the moon's surface, an enormous explosion severed the shaft at its midway point.

"Oh, my God," Evans gasped.

All they could do was watch in horror. The top portion of the shaft tilted to the side as debris from the explosion shot out in all directions.

"Director, I—" Evans said, not finding the words to express the shock of what they just witnessed.

"Yes, I know. But right now, we need to be someplace else. There can be no trace of our presence in this sector."

"Director, can't we—"

"That's an order, Perry. Get us out of here, now," the director said before walking out of the communication center.

Mission conclusion: failed.

Comments: Operatives lost in unexpected explosion during implementation phase. Bodies unrecoverable due to zero atmosphere.

10

Vibrations rose up through the hull and nearly shook Jaxon from the pilot's chair. As he snapped to attention, he wiped the sleep from his eyes, pushing away the memories from his past.

Having already disabled the proximity sensors and alarms on the ship, he was unaware of the attack. Now, it was too late.

He brought up the ship's sensors and noticed several approaching ships, coming from both the moon base and the space station. He checked his ETA to moon base: sixteen minutes. At the speed of the advancing ships, he knew that he'd never make it. He cursed at himself repeatedly for his extravagant exit from Taloo Station.

After assessing all of his options, it became apparent what his next move would be.

"It's time to play possum once again," he said aloud.

Jaxon activated the defense shields and reconfirmed the autopilot's program. With everything still good for a moon base destination, he stepped away from the control panel to headed for the belly of the ship.

Having passed through only the main corridor of the ship when he first boarded, Jaxon was unsure if the Bradbury was properly equipped.

In nearly every ship manufactured in the past ten years, at least one escape vessel was included. But only as an added option. He found it odd that even with the advancement of space travel in the last quarter century, escape pods weren't mandatory.

As Jaxon rushed along, he hoped that the buyer of this particular vessel picked up at least the minimalist form of escape.

As he reached the back of the ship, he found a ship's ladder leading down. Quickly descending into the darkness, Jaxon found himself standing in the cargo hold. It was too dark to see much, but he could just make out a faint glow on the side wall. The control panel. A quick tap on the touch screen and the ship's systems were at his fingertips. A few more taps and the overhead lights brought him from the darkness.

Being able to see clearly now, Jaxon moved ahead, dismissing the various crates and cargo bins lashed to the side walls. At the forward end of the long cargo bay, he found what he was looking for, and silently thanked whoever it was that was looking out for him. It was an escape pod.

Wasting no time, Jaxon analyzed the locking mechanism and access panel then initiated activation protocols. Within moments, the pod's lights flickered to life.

Ignoring the continued warning shots exploding just outside the hull, Jaxon gripped the grab bar at the top of the entrance portal and kicked his legs into the chamber.

"Sonofabitch," he mumbled. The pod was no bigger than a vintage telephone booth back on earth.

How in the hell did they expect the whole crew to escape in a pod sized for a single person? he wondered.

As he rested on the launch couch, he looked over the minimalistic control panel, familiarizing himself with its use. There wasn't much he could control, though. Other than setting a destination and clicking ENGAGE, it was virtually useless.

Because of its compact size, the speed was limited to the stored energy power at the base of the vessel. It was some kind of energy drive that was no doubt limited in its distance capabilities as well. Seeing as he was less than twenty minutes away from the moon, he disregarded the concern and activated the remaining exiting procedures on the panel. The display indicated that escape would be possible in ninety seconds.

Jaxon crawled back out into the Bradbury and retraced his steps back up to the bridge. Once back in front of the main control panel, he disengaged the engines and felt the momentum slow instantly. Next, he accessed a submenu for exterior door closures and scanned through the list of portals until he found what he was looking for. He initiated full exterior door lock up and hit execute. As he watched the display, the exterior view of the ship filled the screen. To his satisfaction, each of the thruster and impulse outlets were closing as ordered. His happiness quickly turned to worry as he saw the escape pod door close as well.

"Shit."

Jaxon dropped to his knees and ducked beneath the control panel once again. He withdrew a bundle of wires, sorting through them until he found the right one. Jaxon quickly severed the wire with a firm yank. Leaning back up to see the display, he was happy to see the escape pod door reopen.

Standing back up, he grabbed his satchel before entering the final command into the control panel. He transferred full engine control to the cargo bay before racing back through the ship.

Once back in the cargo bay, Jaxon opened his satchel and removed all of his collected weapons and ammunition. He tossed them on the floor, annoyed that he'd be arriving on the moon unarmed. He knew though that, ever since the terrorist attack on the space elevator all those years ago, security was at a heightened state. Even eight years later. He knew that he would never make it into Luna City carrying so much as harsh language. He un-holstered the last two weapons from his person and tossed them to the ground as well.

Finally, Jaxon brought up the ship's engine controls and re-engaged the impulse engines. He'd already disengaged the safety measures in place that prevented it from firing with the rear hatch closed, and he knew that he'd have less than a minute before the system overloaded and a hull breach would destroy the ship.

He ran forward and quickly dropped back into the escape pod, closing the door and activating hailing frequencies at the same time.

"Mayday—Mayday. This is Martin Wheeler on Bradbury 9613. I have an engine failure warning, and I can't deactivate it. Mayday—Mayday. Send ..." Jaxon flipped off the comms and jettisoned the escape pod.

As the pod launched away from the Bradbury, Jaxon deactivated all forms of power, except life support. He hoped that it would appear as just part of the ship's debris after the explosion. The explosion that was about to light up space as far as the eye could see.

Ten seconds later, it happened. The damage began at the rear of the ship, right where the impulse drive doors blocked the output. The carbon fiber reinforced metal shrouds began to glow from the intense heat, then they disintegrated. The damage was already done, though, and the engines overheated, blowing off the rear quarter of the ship. As debris began to jettison away from the ship, the forward two-thirds of the ship imploded due to the sudden pressure change. The force blew even more debris out into space.

Jaxon was thankful that none of the debris from the exploding ship flew directly at his escape pod. It was a calculated risk, but it was one that he was willing to take. One that he had to take, or risk being captured. Or worse: being killed.

All he had to do now, was wait. With any luck—luck that he might have already used up on his escape—the chasing security ships would survey the area and determine the ship destroyed: no survivors.

As those wishful thoughts ran through his mind, he suddenly realized that the escape pod might have some kind of homing device installed that would certainly foil his plan. As fast as he could, Jaxon tapped away at the control panel, searching for some form of rooted directory that mentioned anything about system automation. After several minutes of cycling through every category on the display, he concluded that if the escape pod was equipped with a homing beacon, it was not wired into the computer system. He had to rely on luck.

"Damn," Jaxon cursed.

Patience was not one of Jaxon's strong points. He continually fought the urge to enter his destination of Luna City into the control panel and hit execute.

To pass the time, he opened all radio frequencies and keenly listened for any chatter between the pursuing security ships. All he heard was silence.

Seconds turned to minutes, and Jaxon could only wait. He disengaged his safety harness and floated toward the single view portal in the vessel, hoping to catch a glimpse of any approaching ships, but the constant drift and rotation of the escape pod made it nearly impossible for him to determine which direction they would be coming from.

Frustrated at his helpless situation, he refastened his harness and thought of something, anything to take his mind off his current dilemma. Before long, more flashes from his past took his mind from the present.

Nine years ago — Berkley, California, Earth.

"I can't believe this," Lily gasped. "Why are you even telling me this?"

Jaxon stared at her for a moment longer before shifting his eyes to the seven-year-old girl playing across the room. "Isn't it obvious? It's because of her." Jaxon nodded in the child's direction.

"If you think I'm going to tell her now, just because ..." Lily began.

"No," Jaxon insisted, returning his gaze toward his old flame. "Not at all. I just ... I don't know. I just thought that if you knew ahead of time, it wouldn't come as such a shock. I'll leave it up to you whether to tell her who I really am ... er, was."

Jaxon's attention returned to the girl. She was busy pouring make-believe tea for her party guests—two inanimate dolls propped up on small plastic chairs. Jaxon had lied: he did want Celeste to know who he was so he could hold her, as her father, just once. He wanted her to know exactly how much he loved her and how important she was to him. It was because of her and Lily that Jaxon had even come up with the absurd idea in the first place.

The silence in the room was uncomfortable as they both continued to look on as Celeste continued her tea party. Finally, Lily broke the silence.

"Do you know how much of an asshole you are right now?" she asked, her cheeks turning red from the anger building up. "You are nonexistent in our lives for the past five years, with no word or mention of where you are or what you are doing, then, you just show up here, unannounced? And then you drop that news that you're going to kill yourself like it's just a regular event ... like brushing your teeth?"

"It's not like that, Lily. You know why I couldn't contact you. It's this goddamn job," Jaxon said.

"Still, a postcard would've been nice," she said. "At the very least. You know, even just saying that you're alive and have a nice day."

"I know you're upset, but there are reasons why I'm doing this now."

"So you can run away ... from all the world's trouble on your shoulders ... to stick your head in the sand?" she asked.

"Partly. I don't know ..." Jaxon paused, contemplating how much he should tell her. "I don't want to put you and Celeste in any danger. The less you know, the better your life will be. Besides, I'm not really going to kill myself."

"Oh, sorry. I had no idea that you were going to be deceitful about killing yourself. That makes everything so much better," Lily said, her words dripping with sarcasm.

"Trust me, Lily. This is the best scenario. You know they'll never let me just quit, and I'm tired of being their in-house mercenary. I always thought that joining the GSA meant so much more."

"Have you even tried to talk to Perry about leaving? I was able to get out, or did you forget about that?" she asked.

Jaxon did remember her leaving the GSA shortly after the Academy. The situation was quite different. She was pregnant with his child, and she had not gone covert yet. Of course, the company let her out.

"I talked with him. Well, not in a straight up, 'Hey man, I want to quit' approach, but we've talked around the subject a few times."

"You see? That's why you're never going to amount to much in life. You're too much of a coward to confront what's important to you. That's why Celeste will never know who her father was." Lily wiped a fleeting tear from her cheek. "So. When is this masquerade going to happen? Does anyone else know?"

"Gillette knows. We've got a couple opportunities to pull it off in the coming weeks, but nothing is for certain yet."

"And Gillette's okay with this? Of all people, I thought he'd be the one to talk some sense into you," Lily said.

"It was his idea. He's … going with me. He's just as tired of being the company's assassin."

Lily winced at hearing Jaxon's true profession. In all the years that she'd known him, he never actually told her what he did, but she knew how nefarious his profession could be. Actually, she was quite relieved all those years ago when she had gotten pregnant. Just a few years in the Academy was long enough for her to realize how dishonest the Global Security Agency really was.

"I'm sure there is going to be a big investigation after the event, and you have to promise me that no matter what happens, you have to protect Celeste. You cannot let on that you knew about any of this. For your safety and hers."

"You actually think they'd come after us?" Lily asked.

Jaxon shrugged. "Hell, I don't know. I can only trust a handful of people in the company, and it just depends whose desk the news crosses first."

"Then why tell me at all?" she asked.

"Like I said. Because of Celeste."

Concern spread across Lily's face as she looked at their daughter. She envied her carefree outlook on life.

Lily placed her hand on Jaxon's arm, soothingly. "You have my word. I don't agree with your decision, but I understand why you're doing this. After you're … gone, I will tell Celeste all about you."

Warmth and relief filled Jaxon. Thankful for his worry to be put to rest, he placed his hand atop Lily's. "Thank you."

Suddenly, warning alarms blared inside the compact pod, pulling Jaxon back to the present. He blinked away the hazy fog and focused on the control screen in front of him. It was a navigational sensor alarm indicating that he'd continued to tumble, randomly, through space and was nearing the point of no return unless he took immediate action.

12

Jaxon muted the alarm then accessed the external sensors. Despite being frustrated at the lack of detail on the miniature display, he zoomed out as far as he could. Rotating the directional vector array in various aspects, he searched for any approaching ships.

None were visible.

Glancing at the clock, he saw that he'd been dozing for nearly an hour. He knew that the likelihood of any lingering ships in the vicinity was still possible, but slim at best. Chances were they'd all returned to moon base or Taloo Station, respectively.

Marginally confident that any navigational maneuvering he'd do now would go undetected, Jaxon promptly entered Luna City as his destination and hit execute.

Beep, beep, beep.

Jaxon pressed execute again but received the same warning alarm. Looking deeper, he found that the warning was telling him that he'd entered a destination further away than he had enough fuel for.

"Shit," Jaxon mumbled.

He flipped the display back to close range sensors and pivoted the display to the surface of the moon. As he scanned for a secondary port, suitable to receive the escape pod, additional warnings began to blare.

"Give me just a minute, dammit," he yelled.

The new series of warnings told Jaxon that immediate action was necessary to avoid an unrecoverable decline to the surface of the moon.

Tapping his fingers much more quickly, he found his best option to land was not terribly far from his current position. It appeared to be some sort of surface mining facility that had a small clearing which he hoped was suitable for a dust off and landing.

He checked and double checked the coordinates before entering them into the computer. As soon as he hit execute, he began to feel a pit of uneasiness build up. He hoped that whoever it was that occupied the facility was of the non-confrontational variety because he was really tired of all the killing.

Seconds after the computer accepted the destination, the slow tumble of the escape pod ceased as miniature thrusters leveled out its trajectory. Then, the rear engines fired, jettisoning him toward the mining farm.

As the escape pod bounded toward the moon's surface, Jaxon became increasingly concerned with his approach speed. Having years of piloting experience under his belt, he knew that unless he reduced the thrust of the engine, he'd be coming in far too fast to make a clean landing. He cycled through several screens on his display but found no manual override. He flipped back to the main radar screen, and the surface of the moon continued to increase in size exponentially. ETA flashed ninety seconds, in crimson numerals.

Jaxon gave up on searching for an override and grabbed his satchel. He pulled out his mask and helmet shield and quickly slipped them on. He knew that a rough landing was imminent, and there was no telling how the escape pod would perform.

With the last of his environmental suit connected and secured, he braced for impact. The digital readout on the display counted down as the surface of the moon neared. He did one last check of his safety harness before gripping the side walls for support.

Eight, seven, six, five ...

Suddenly, the rear thrusters cut out and the bow thrusters kicked in. The escape pod pivoted around ninety degrees, before gently setting down on the moon's surface.

The landing took Jaxon by complete surprise, as it was one of the smoothest automated landings that he'd experienced in all his years in space. He smiled as he powered down the computers. Lastly, he released the locking mechanism on the escape hatch and unfastened his safety harness.

"Honey, I'm home," Jaxon mused as he climbed up and out of the escape pod.

13

J axon stood on the surface of the moon, taking in the vast expanse of nothingness. As he walked around the escape pod, his eyes remained fixed on the horizon until the image of Earth dissected the sky beyond. Despite having frequented the moon many times throughout his career, seeing the spectacle was awe-inspiring. He wondered if there would ever be a day when he'd be able to return to the planet, or if he was destined to live a life on the run. The last several hours certainly did not bode well for him.

After several minutes of analyzing his immediate surroundings, Jaxon rolled up his coat sleeve, revealing a flexible vid display stitched into his environmental suits arm. A couple taps on the screen with his gloved hand and the condition of his environmental suit filled the display.

Oxygen level: ninety-six percent.

Time to depletion: three hours, forty-seven minutes.

Power level: eighty-four percent.

Time to recharge: seven hours, two minutes.

Happy that his suit had maintained its reserve levels so

well while sitting in a crate for such a long period, Jaxon cleared the display and brought up a proximity guide to sort out his current location.

As the map slowly generated, Jaxon continued to scan the horizon, hoping to glimpse some kind of structure or habitat that he could head for. After several minutes of squinting across the moon's surface, a notification alarm dinged in his ear.

The map displayed the escape pod's location—on the edge of Rehlo Crater, just a few dozen clicks from Mare Cognitum. According to the readout, that particular parcel of the moon's surface had been leased out for private strip mining. Jaxon quickly tapped the more info button, but no further information could be displayed.

Returning to the map display, an amber-colored arrow blinked slowly at his current location. He increased the magnification level and found a substantially sized structure just outside of the crater's edge. It was just under three kilometers toward the southern pole, and it wouldn't take him all that long to get there.

Jaxon stretched, took a series of deep breaths, and began to walk in the direction of the structure, noting how strange it felt to be walking in such low gravity again. As his pace increased, he concluded that the distance might pass much quicker than anticipated due to the lightness of his footsteps. Each step expending much less physical energy than what he was used to.

With a moderate walking pace established, Jaxon's mind switched to survival mode. He analyzed his life on Taloo Station and wondered where he might have gone wrong. He'd made it eight years there before being discovered. At least as far as he knew, that was. Then, nearly a dozen assassins were sent to take him out.

His first question: who sent the killers? Was it someone that he'd wronged somehow in his past life? Could it possibly be the company coming for him after discovering that he was alive all along?

Second question: where could he go now? Jaxon's mind chewed on that thought for some time.

The answer to the second question was very much related to the first. If he knew who it was that was after him, he'd much better be able to determine the length he'd have to travel for self-preservation. There was no use heading for another inner-ring space station if the facial recognition present at nearly every entry portal would certainly give him away. Same thing for entering Luna City. That's assuming that it was the company that was after him.

Jaxon sighed deeply. It became apparent that his only alternative might be to head to the outer ring, where crime and corruption were the daily norm. The company would be less likely to pursue him there. That's also assuming that he could even survive long enough to get there. The question still remained: Who was after him, and how far would they go to kill him?

Having hiked the first kilometer without any contact, in the far distance Jaxon could make out what appeared to be some kind of surface vehicle. A moon buggy. And it was heading directly toward him.

"Looks like it's about game time," Jaxon mumbled.

Jaxon continued on his current heading as he watched the buggy grow in size as it closed the distance. Within minutes, the transport was nearly upon him. Seated behind the clear bowl-shaped windshield was an older man with a gray beard, much longer than Jaxon had seen in years. He wondered just how somebody with that much facial hair could even wear an environmental suit.

As the buggy stopped, the old-timer waved at Jaxon then motioned him in. Cautiously, Jaxon nodded and moved to the side of the vehicle where a hatch was beginning to swing out.

Once the door was open, Jaxon climbed in and cycled through the pressure chamber before moving further into the vehicle. Making his way forward, he verified the environment was safe to breathe before removing his helmet and face shield. As he finished stowing them in his satchel, the old-timer opened the door to the cockpit.

"Well, what we got here?" the old man asked. "Looks like yer having a bit of car trouble, eh?"

Jaxon was a little baffled by the codger's slang and ancient earth accent. "Oh, you mean the escape pod?" Jaxon asked. "Yeah, I had a thruster problem on my ship and had to bail before I went down with the vessel."

"Yep. I reckon that's what that flash was a while ago. Ain't that thing got any better distance?" he asked as he stroked his beard, probably out of habit.

"You'd think, but here I am. Sorry about landing on your property," Jaxon said as he nodded in the direction in which he came.

"Ain't no thing. I reckon yer probably gonna be looking for a ride to the nearest call station?" the old man asked, surveying Jaxon with a peculiar look.

"If it isn't too much trouble," Jaxon said. "I'd be willing to pay you for your time and effort. I'm …" Jaxon paused to determine what name he should be using. "I'm Jaxon," he finished, deciding that Martin Wheeler might have taken his last breath in this sector.

"Names DeWitt. Yeah, I can give you a ride. I was fixin' to head that way anyway, so you can keep yer money." DeWitt turned and stepped back into the cockpit. Jaxon followed and took the copilot seat.

"About how far of a ride is it to Luna City?" Jaxon asked.

"Luna City? Are you out of your mind? It's at least three hours away. No sir, I'm headin' to Carver Outpost. Yea, should be able to secure transport through the tunnels on into Luna City, if that's yer destination," DeWitt said as he adjusted a few controls on his dashboard before engaging the drive.

"Okay, then. How long until we get to Carver?" Jaxon asked, conceding that landing where he did was probably a blessing as he wouldn't have to explain his arrival at the docks of Luna City.

"Thirty minutes. Max," DeWitt said as he pointed his moon buggy toward their destination and engaged the autopilot.

Jaxon caught DeWitt giving him a sideways look again, his curiosity certainly piqued by his sudden appearance.

"Tell me, DeWitt, what is it you mine out here?" Jaxon asked, hoping to divert the attention away from himself.

"Oar, mostly. There's some heavy mineral deposits all over the surface, and the moon is littered with meteorites," DeWitt said, turning directly toward Jaxon.

"Isn't that the truth?" Jaxon said. "But hasn't the surface been picked clean? I know nine or ten years ago, the reports indicated that most of the meteorite salvage had been exhausted."

DeWitt nodded. "Yep. Sounds 'bout right. I got this parcel pretty cheap around about that time. You're not really from around here, are ya?" DeWitt asked as he sized up Jaxon's attire.

"Oh no, not at all. I spent a good deal of time here a decade or so ago but not so much since," Jaxon said as he adjusted his posture, attempting to betray a sense of confidence. It had been years since he'd had to use the technique, but he was confident that he hadn't lost his touch.

"Listen, I got to ask you a question, Jaxon, was it?" DeWitt began. "Where in tarnation did you get that environmental suit? If you ask me, you look like some kind of futuristic techno-nerd. Because that suit looks out of this world. I've been up on this rock looking down on earth for coming up on six years now and boy, let me tell you. That is one, fancy, suit yer wearin' there. That must've set you back a pretty penny."

Oh, shit, Jaxon thought. He instantly regretted not stocking his go bag with used riggings as opposed to the top of the line company-issued gear. What could he tell the old guy without sounding too farfetched?

"What, this old thing? I, uh, picked this up off of a freighter about a year ago. I think the merchant said something about it belonging to some government guy that got blasted out into space. Sometimes I feel it's a size or two too small for me, know what I mean?" Jaxon hoped that his improvisational skills were up to snuff.

DeWitt nodded, contemplating Jaxon's marginally believable story. "Sometimes it's all about being in the right place at the right time. Like I said earlier, I got this here plot of land for a song because the miners felt they had cleared as much useful salvage from the surface that they could. Shortly after closing escrow, a buddy of mine down on earth heard about this new gizmo that's able to strip mine the surface much more thoroughly. The device set me back the rest of my savings, but ever since, I've been laughing all the way to the bank by what I've been able to haul in," DeWitt said, returning his attention to the controls.

Jaxon nodded and listened for the next fifteen minutes as DeWitt continued to regale him about his mining adventures on the moon. It also gave him time to reflect a bit about the choices he'd made. Although the environment up on Taloo Station was a virtual Shangri-La compared to the moon's surface, at least here on the moon you had something. Something that you could call your own, and the ability to get away from it all. Up on Taloo, all you could do was escape as far as the confines of the station would allow. And none of it was yours. It was all a leased life, and Jaxon wondered where his own lease on life would end up.

Before long, Jaxon could see Carver Outpost grow along the horizon. He couldn't help but wonder if he could've done more to alter his appearance before ditching the Bradbury. He made a mental note that when he set up his next go bag that he would include a bottle of hair dye and some clippers to change up his physicality. It's the least he could do on short notice.

As they pulled into Carver, Jaxon compared the facility to something like an old Western town set on the edge of the plains. Desolation spread as far as the eye could see and there were only four or five structures clustered together like an oasis in the sand. DeWitt maneuvered his moon buggy through an automatically controlled gate and parked next to the entrance to the station.

DeWitt turned to Jaxon and said, "Well, this is it. Hope I didn't bore you too much along the way."

"Not at all. You sure I can't give you something?" Jaxon asked, pulling a fistful of credits from his pocket.

"Nope. I've got all I need. I've got a little business inside, but I hope you have yourself a nice day."

As the all clear sign turned green, DeWitt opened both hatch doors, and they walked out into the outpost. DeWitt was off on his own path without another word. Jaxon cautiously surveyed the facility, paying extra attention to the potential presence of more assassins. Slowly, he made his way through the streets of the open market, circling back to the station's entrance doors.

Satisfied that the place appeared to be occupied by no more than the locals, he relaxed a bit and was off to take care of some things.

The first line of business was to trade in his environmental suit. He found a secondhand merchant store and walked right up to the counter.

"Excuse me, but I'm looking for a new environmental suit."

The man behind the counter turned and looked Jaxon up and down. His eyes widened slightly, but he quickly dismissed his surprise. "Sorry, fella. We don't sell new here. We only have used."

"I'm sorry," Jaxon said, "I don't necessarily mean new. Just new to me. I have grown tired of this one, and I'm looking for ... something different. You take trade-ins?"

Jaxon had the salesman's full attention as they bartered out a deal for an older model environmental suit that fit his needs. Ten minutes later, Jaxon walked out with a fistful of credits that the shop owner paid him extra because his suit was so nice. Walking through the streets suddenly felt so much different, and so much more awkward. The top-of-the-line suit that he'd just traded in felt like a second skin and this POS, that he almost certainly overpaid for, must have weighed ten times what he was used to. He swallowed his pride and accepted his new sense of blending in as he sought out the transport hub to Luna City.

Several minutes later, Jaxon came upon a stairway that led down to the subway. Unfortunately, the entrance was cordoned off, and a sign was plastered across:

CLOSED FOR REPAIR.

"Excuse me," Jaxon asked an attendant off to the side of the entrance. "How long will these repairs take?"

"Well, that's a big unknown right now. There's been a cave in a few hundred meters down the track. It's those damn rebels. They think they own the moon, but they don't want to pay for anything. So, they vandalize the hell out of everything, and it really makes life hell."

"Are we talking hours or days?" Jaxon asked.

"Honestly, mister. Probably more like weeks. It's been this way for the last ten days."

"Sonofabitch," Jaxon mumbled. "Any other form of transportation to Luna City?"

"Well, a surface shuttle just left about an hour ago. I think the next one's scheduled for the day after tomorrow. We'll occasionally get a low-flying orbiter through here, but there's no saying when those are coming around because they're all private contractors."

Jaxon thanked the attended for his time and rushed back to where he last saw DeWitt. He just hoped that he hadn't left yet.

As Jaxon blasted through the entrance doors, he saw that the stall where DeWitt had parked was now empty. His heart sank a little as he felt the doom of being stuck in that shit hole for an extended period of time.

He quickly ran around the yard and found DeWitt's moon buggy parked next to a fuel-cell with several hoses connected to it. He was refueling.

Moments later, Jaxon stepped up to the front of DeWitt's buggy and put his thumb out, portraying a hitchhiker's stance. DeWitt motioned him in.

"Thanks again for your time, DeWitt, but I need another favor."

"Shoot," DeWitt said.

"Looks like the tube to Luna City is closed for repair for the foreseeable future. The moon shuttle just left about an hour ago, and another isn't due until a few days from now. I really need to get to Luna City, and I'd love to make it worth your while," Jaxon said as he pulled out the fistfull of surplus credits from the sale of his environmental suit.

"Well now, how much are we talking?" DeWitt asked, eyeing the handful of credits.

Jaxon promptly organized the credits then counted them back to DeWitt. "Looks like sixty-three credits," Jaxon said, shoving it toward DeWitt.

DeWitt reluctantly picked through the pile, siphoning out a mere thirty credits. "That's far too much for me to take just to give you a ride. Besides, I should be paying you for the company."

"So we have a deal?" Jaxon asked.

"Yep. As soon as we're fueled up, we'll hit the road."

Within thirty minutes, DeWitt had paid for his refill and was steering his moon buggy toward Luna City. Despite DeWitt's comment about companionship on the road, after the first few minutes a conversation, DeWitt turned on the audio system and blared classic country music throughout the cockpit.

It wasn't long after the second verse of the opening song that Jaxon drifted off to sleep.

"Four, three, two, brace for impact," I said as I reached for the rung closest to me. I lashed my safety cable onto a secure hook just as the explosion went off far above our heads. The explosion was silent, but I could feel its intensity through the massive vibrations on my handhold. I looked at Gillette and was not at all surprised at the cavalier expression plastered across his face. It was like just another day at the office for him.

As the vibrations began to subside, I knew that unless we moved quickly, the authorities would be swarming our location. Our timing had to be precise, and we were a mere three or four meters away from the designated access hatch laid out in our planned escape.

"Time's a wastin', buddy," I said to Gillette as I floated past him and grabbed ahold of the lever securing the hatch. Surprisingly, the latch did not budge. I applied more pressure and tried again. Same result.

"Step aside, young lad," Gillette said as he wedged himself between me and the hatch. He gripped the handle, and in what appeared to be an effortless motion, lowered the lever and pushed in.

"Yeah, whatever. I loosened it for you," I said as I followed him in and resealed the door.

Once inside the maintenance passage, we began to feel the pull from below, as the effects of the artificial gravity grew. The further into the passageway we got, the closer to Earth's gravity we felt.

When we reached the one-hundred-meter mark from the main junction corridor, Gillette and I were at a full speed run, hoping to make it inside the station before maintenance locked down the facility. If we were caught outside of Luna City's environment when that happened, our fate would be sealed. And that would be a death that neither of us wanted to experience.

A few minutes later, we slowed our pace and walked through the unlocked door and cycled through the rarely used pressure chamber. As we emerged out the other side, we quickly changed out of our environmental suits and donned outfits that we had placed in the vacant corridor weeks before.

"Okay, Jaxon. Stick to the plan," Gillette said as we worked our way out into the streets of Luna City. "We both have new identities, and we just disappear. No more contact."

I nodded, patting the lanyard around my neck with the name Martin Wheeler. "Got it. Do you know where you're going to end up?" I asked.

"Nothing against you, Jaxon, but I think it best that neither of us knows where we're going. If one of us gets nabbed after this, there's no use in both of us being tried for treason," he said, patting me on the back. "Listen, it's been great knowing you. I hope you have a great life. Now get out of here!"

Not being very fond of long goodbyes, I faked a sucker punch in his belly and walked past him, and into the crowd. I never looked back.

My first stop in Luna City was a barber to get a buzz cut and to lose my goatee. Next, I stopped at a tattoo parlor and got LOVE and HATE tattooed across my knuckles. After that, I found a small hostel and paid cash for the week. I only stayed a day. After that, I drifted away.

Jaxon felt a tug on his shirt sleeve, and he turned to see what was the matter. He opened his eyes to the blurry image of DeWitt, the gray-haired codger, who was staring back at him.

"Boy, I tell ya. Yer the worst traveling companion ever. Don't you know that the navigator's job is to keep the driver awake?" DeWitt asked as he pivoted his seat back to the control panel, shaking his head in disbelief.

Jaxon peered out the front viewscreen and saw that the desolate moon surface had transformed into low-formed habitats and portal entrances in every direction. In the far distance, Jaxon spotted the remains of the once fully functional space elevator. He cringed at the actions of his past.

"Sorry about that, DeWitt. It's been a long day," Jaxon said as he straightened himself up in the copilot's chair. "I see that we've made it to Luna City."

"Yep. Pulled in just a few minutes ago. The trip was pretty much uneventful, as expected. I don't much get to these parts of the moon, so it's always nice to see the hustle and bustle of how the other side lives," DeWitt said, steering the moon buggy into the subsurface transportation dock.

As DeWitt maneuvered through the underground facility, Jaxon organized himself. With his satchel packed, and sure that he had everything he brought with him, he looked over at DeWitt.

"Hey, I really do appreciate the ride, DeWitt. Here's an extra twenty credits for your time," Jaxon said, slipping the credits into his hand.

"Well, you needn't do that, but much appreciated just the same. As freely as you throw your credits around, you must be loaded. What did you say you do again?" DeWitt asked as he stuffed the credits with into his pocket.

"I didn't. I'm kind of in between jobs right now," Jaxon said as he stood and headed for the exit door.

"Fair enough," DeWitt said, following Jaxon. "By the way, are you planning to have your escape pod picked up anytime soon? Don't get me wrong, there's no rush and all, but I'm just curious."

Jaxon stepped to the ground, then turned to face DeWitt. "Well, the ship was a complete loss, and I have no immediate plans on buying another, so ... why don't you salvage anything off it that you can?" Jaxon said.

DeWitt's eyes brightened up, and a grin crossed his face. "Thank you kindly, sir. I've been meaning to do a few upgrades around the habitat, and what I can get from some of those parts should come in handy. You take care now, Jaxon."

Jaxon bowed his head, turned and silently walked away. As he made his way into the heart of Luna City, he was surprised just how familiar the whole place seemed. It had been nearly a decade since he'd set foot in the first colonized station on the moon and it had held up fairly well.

Jaxon's first priority was to get some rest. Even though he'd dozed on and off during the trip from Carver Outpost, he still felt exhausted. And he knew that exhaustion led to mistakes. Right now, a mistake in pinpointing potential killers in the crowd before they identified him could mean certain death.

As he moved through the city streets, he noted several rooms for rent and various hotels intermixed with the multitude of shops and restaurants. But he knew that it was best to find someplace a little off the beaten path. Also, he couldn't help notice the strange looks that he was getting as he moved through the crowded streets, and it only took him a block or two before he realized that he was still wearing the bulky, outdated environmental suit.

"Shit," he mumbled. He had to get out of sight and change into something more appropriate before he drew the wrong attention to himself.

After a few more blocks, he found what he was looking for. It was an access corridor that led to the service thoroughfares that circulated beneath the city streets themselves. He ducked into the dimly lit alleyway, and once he was out of sight, he shed the environmental suit quickly. He attempted to stuff it into his satchel, but there was absolutely no room to fit the bulky suit. Jaxon cursed repeatedly under his breath for making the knee-jerk reaction of selling his custom-tailored suit back at Carver.

Frustrated, Jaxon rolled up the environmental suit and stashed it behind a refuse bin with the intention of coming back for it before leaving for the outer ring.

Emerging back into the pedestrian flow, he felt better about blending in, wearing his civilian clothes. As he walked along, hunger pangs rumbled throughout his core. Just then, he realized that it had been quite some time since he'd eaten anything. He instantly changed his priority: get something to eat.

Jaxon looked up and down the street, reading the various food signs, looking for something that sounded appealing, when his eyes fixated on a familiar sign. The Calypso Cantina was down a few blocks on the right. He remembered that the place had just opened up about the time of his and Gillette's

Houdini act. It was as good a place as any.

As he moved toward his destination, Jaxon couldn't help but notice something that stood out. Probably one out of every ten pedestrians on the streets was dressed in clothing similar to what the assassins wore on Taloo Station. *Was it a coincidence or was there something more to it?* he wondered.

Casually, Jaxon pulled the hood up over his head and hunched his shoulders, attempting to disappear into obscurity. The closer he got to the cantina, the more out of place characters he found. When he was about a block away, he came upon a group of four individuals standing at the center of an intersection, each one peering off in different directions. They were clearly looking for something or someone, and Jaxon hoped that it wasn't him. Instinctively, Jaxon slid up his sleeve to access his suit's display but suddenly realized that that was no longer an option. It was sewn into his old environmental suit back at Carver.

New plan, Jaxon thought. He needed to locate a communication device and see if there were any news reports about the incident on Taloo. He could easily step into any one of the tech stores and buy what he needed, but most of those were monitored by video surveillance. He didn't want to be caught on camera just yet. His second option was to resurrect yet another skill from his past. Personal larceny. He needed to *lift* one from some unsuspecting civilian.

Just then, Jaxon noticed a crowded tourist shop, and he quickly stepped in. The shop carried all sorts of souvenir items, from moon rocks to T-shirts with Luna City plastered across the front. The shop was narrow and long, and from Jaxon's quick survey, it appeared there were no cameras in the facility.

Purposefully, Jaxon began to stumble and collide into a number of people in the shop, apologizing for his clumsiness. As he made his way toward the back of the store, he picked up a few items along the way, namely a new canvas jacket and a large duffel bag suitable fit his environmental suit. After paying for the items, he continued his bump and stumble maneuver back toward the front of the store and out onto the street.

Blended back into the crowd, he donned his new jacket and quickly stashed the half a dozen personal communication tablets that he'd pickpocketed from the store's customers. Jaxon grinned at his own astonishment that he hadn't missed a beat in his last eight years.

With his new duster on, he strolled past the four men at the center of the intersection without a second thought. Within moments, he was walking into the cantina and asking for a table in a dark corner.

An attractive waitress sat him in booth practically in the kitchen, but it was just what he'd asked for. He thanked her and ordered an Astro beer and asked for some time to decide on his food order.

As soon as the waitress had disappeared, Jaxon pulled the first of several comm devices from his pocket. He held the transparent device along its edges and tapped the activate button. It was password-protected, just as he'd feared. He tossed it to the table and pulled another from his pocket. He cycled through several of the stolen devices, each one arriving at the same conclusion. His fifth attempt was different, though. It was unlocked and fully charged. Jaxon drifted his fingers across the flat screen, deactivating several standard tracking features on the device until he was confident that his device usage couldn't be followed.

Moments later, the waitress delivered his beer and took his order for street tacos. As she walked away, Jaxon began searching for some form of transportation from the moon to the outer ring. With each new search, Jaxon felt the pit of his stomach tighten. He knew it was a dangerous proposition heading to the outer ring, but he saw no other option. Taloo Station was clearly no longer safe for him, and having only been on the moon's surface for a few hours, he felt nearly as unsafe as he did on station. No, he needed to flee further out. He had to disappear once again.

After several minutes of introspection about his future, the waitress returned with his food. The street tacos of the day were fish, and Jaxon was only mildly curious as to what the main ingredient really was. His starvation convinced him that that it was nothing to worry about.

As soon as the waitress returned to the kitchen, Jaxon started his next series of searches on habitation. He needed a place to stay for a day or two until he could arrange for transport. Based on his searches, there were no commercial passageways to the outer ring. He knew then that he'd have to locate private transportation on his own.

As he continued searching for a place to flop, the more uneasy he became. His mind continued to bring up the images of the numerous assassins that he'd encountered on Taloo Station as well as the streets here in Luna City. He knew that every eye on the street would be on the lookout for someone just like himself. That meant that staying in a public facility was out of the question. Feeling like he was at the end of his rope, he had one last-ditch effort for a place to stay. He mentally crossed his fingers as he typed in the name: Cliff Hartley. After several seconds of an ever-turning hourglass on the display, the screen froze up.

"Come on, come on. I know you're here," Jaxon said as he shook the device, hoping that the owner hadn't reported the device stolen already. Finally, after nearly a minute, the screen went blank before displaying the name and address of Gillette, under his disguised persona. Just as Jaxon had anticipated, Gillette stayed in Luna City and disappeared into the outskirts. According to the address, he was living in Sector 39, which was about a fifty-minute shuttle ride through the bellies of the city.

Ecstatic at finally coming around to seeing someone from his past reality, Jaxon proceeded to eat his imitation fish tacos and drink his beer. His excitement was so much that he'd consumed his entire meal inside of seven minutes and paid his check before walking out the door.

16

Staying clear of the main thoroughfares, Jaxon found a subway access on the edge of Sector 1. Before entering, he circled the block twice then doubled back a block before approaching the subway entrance in earnest. He wanted to ensure that he wasn't being followed.

As he descended the three flights of stairs to the subway platform, he was pleased with himself for being able to resurrect aspects of his tradecraft after so many years of inactivity. At the same time, though, he was disappointed with his complacency on Taloo Station. He'd become lazy, and that had taken over his daily, monotonous life on Taloo Station. He realized that he might not even be in this situation if he'd been just a little more cautious and careful with his daily activities.

Stepping out onto the platform, Jaxon found a relatively small crowd waiting for the next train—maybe a dozen other passengers—most of whom were self-absorbed in their own lives. Most importantly, none of which were dressed as the assassins were that he'd encountered up until now.

The wait was minimal, and without great fanfare, the train

arrived and departed like clockwork. Jaxon took a seat in the rear car of the train so that he could face forward the entire trip to Sector 39. It was a wise precaution, but the action was quite unnecessary in the end, as the thirty-minute ride passed by uneventful.

Having traveled through most of Luna City in his past life, Jaxon was familiar with virtually every sector of the station. That was only true for the commercialized areas, though. The residential sectors, 11 through 45, were virtual unknowns to him. But if you'd seen one, you'd seen them all, and Sector 39 looked quite similar to every other one that he'd seen.

Pulling his stolen communication tablet out, Jaxon brought up the sector map. It showed his current location on the platform at center screen. From there, there were a multitude of residential units in clusters of eight, fanning out from his location. He punched in his destination, and the map highlighted the most efficient route through the clusters. After a few minutes of reviewing the map, he waited for the immediate vicinity to clear of any wandering eyes before heading out.

If Jaxon had taken a direct route to Gillette's flat, he would've been knocking on his door inside of four minutes. But Jaxon's knowledge of diversion tactics dictated that he take a distant path and circle back through the far end of the sector.

After rounding Gillette's cluster twice to verify that he wasn't being followed, he arrived at unit 273, the number displayed in some futuristic font that made Jaxon chuckle.

Knock, knock, knock.

Jaxon stepped away from the door and nervously waited for his old friend to hopefully welcome him back into his life. After several uncomfortable minutes, Jaxon was about to knock again when the door sprang open, momentarily startling him.

The man that answered the door stared at him. He looked familiar but not at the same time. He'd certainly aged since the last time he'd seen him. And if it was possible, Gillette's hair had grown out longer than his own. Also, he had a beard that could challenge DeWitt's in a length contest.

"Well, if it isn't my old friend Saber," Gillette said with an enthusiastic grin. "How the hell are you, man?"

Gillette thrust his hand forward and took Jaxon's in his own. One quick pump of their hands and Gillette yanked Jaxon forward into a great bear hug.

"You know, it's strange. I was just thinking of you the other day," Gillette said. "I trust you weren't followed?" he asked nervously, trying to look past his surprise guest.

Jaxon winked as he stepped past Gillette into his apartment. "Absolutely. I walked through Sector 39 for nearly fifteen minutes just to be sure."

Gillette leaned out into the corridor to verify that they were alone. Satisfied, he stepped back in and shut the door and latched seven different locks. "Well, I wouldn't expect anything less than your absolute precision," Gillette said. "What brings you to these parts of the ... wait a minute, how did you find me?"

"Long story, my friend. I am in a bit of trouble, and I need some help."

Gillette took a seat at the large island separating his kitchen from the living area. "That sounds ominous. What kind of trouble are we talking?"

"Not sure. I'd been living on Taloo Station, and quite peacefully I might add, until about eight hours ago."

"And you decided a trip to the moon was in your best interest?" Gillette asked in his typical humorous fashion.

Jaxon ignored his friend's sarcasm. "That's when at least three separate assault teams were sent to take me out."

Gillette's whimsical grin vanished instantly. "You certain?"

"Yeah, unfortunately. The first attack came right as I was closing up my tea shop, and I was able to take out both of the assassins quietly. After that, another pair chased me down, and I was able to neutralize them with a little more effort. Finally, a much larger team ambushed me at my apartment. I was able to take most of them out before fleeing the station."

"Jesus! And they were all there for you? Are you certain?" Gillette asked again.

"Positive, buddy. We've been in this game for far too long to be mistaken. Whoever hired these mercenaries paid well. They were well-equipped and highly trained. If they'd been sent for anyone else, it would've been over quickly. I just thank the stars that I had the training to persevere."

Gillette stood and paced around his compact apartment. A look of doom spread across his face. "Jesus, you led them here!"

"Relax, man. Like I said, I was cautious."

"I'm not sure how much I can help. Besides, it looks like you're doing pretty fine on your own, escaping Taloo, getting through Luna City, and to my front door with hardly a scratch on you—"

"Trust me, pal. I have the injuries to show for it," Jaxon said as he adjusted his jacket. "What I need is help getting off of the moon."

"But you just got here. Can't you just hole up in a vacant apartment until the shit storm passes? It worked for me."

"Well, I'm not too certain that will be anytime soon. As I made my way through the city, I noticed several suspicious goons on the lookout. Not sure if it was for me or someone else."

"Sonofabitch. This is real."

"No shit, buddy. So? Can you help an old friend out?"

Gillette circled back into the kitchen and pulled an aluminum bottle from the refreshment center. "Beer?" he asked.

Jaxon nodded and accepted the cold beverage.

Gillette grabbed another beer and took a seat at the island. "Listen, Jaxon. What you've gone through sounds like complete hell. And trust me, I'm sympathetic. But—"

"But you're not willing to risk your ideal situation to help me," Jaxon said, finishing Gillette's statement.

"Yeah. Something like that. Where do you want to go? Not back to earth, I hope."

Jaxon took a long pull from his beer and wiped his lips. "No, I was thinking of one of the stations in the outer ring."

"Jesus, Jaxon. Did you hit your head during the attacks? That'd be suicide for you. There's some bad guys up there, and I'm sure they'd love to have you as a guest."

"Well, I'm not sure what else to do right now. You're right about not going back down to earth, and any of the stations in the inner ring are out of the question as well."

"How so?" Gillette asked.

"Surveillance. The inner ring has really tightened up ship since I settled down there, after ..."

Gillette nodded.

"I was hoping that I could start fresh here on the moon, but from what I just saw in the city, I think I need to get away from everything, at least for the time being."

"Well, I wish you the best, but I don't think I can help. You're more than welcome to crash here for the night, but I think it best that you move along first thing tomorrow."

Jaxon felt fainthearted as his old friend declined to help. He really couldn't blame him for the reluctance, but it still weakened him.

"Thanks, Gillette. I'll be out of your hair before the earth rises."

Gillette finished off his beer and pulled two more from the dispenser, handing one to Jaxon. "Listen, I was just about to cook up some grub. Are you hungry?"

Jaxon chuckled. "I did just have some fake fish in the city, but I could always eat something ... real."

Over the next hour, Gillette and Jaxon reminisced about their time at the GSA. They laughed when remembering the good times, and were sorrowful for the bad. At the end of the evening, Gillette produced a fold-up cot from the storage closet and tossed Jaxon a blanket.

"Hey, man, no hard feelings, right?" Gillette asked. "I'd love to help you out, but I just—"

"Don't give it a second thought, Gillette. I knew it was a long shot even coming here. I just appreciate your ear for the night and the warm meal. I'll figure something out tomorrow, I'm certain. Right now, I'm fighting to keep my eyes open."

"I can imagine. Well, sleep tight, buddy. I'll have a good breakfast for you tomorrow before you take off."

Gillette walked out of the guest room and closed the door. Jaxon collapsed onto the cot and was out in minutes.

The smell of freshly brewed coffee and cooked bacon wafted through the morning air, stirring Jaxon from his fitful sleep. Slowly, his eyes flickered to life, and he rolled onto his back. He stretched his sore muscles, feeling—more than hearing—his joints creak in protest. He swung his feet to the floor as he sat up.

Standing upright, he stretched again and inhaled deeply. The sublime aromas were still present, satisfying Jaxon's fear that they weren't just part of a dream. It had been so long since he'd actually had pork bellies that it nearly made him salivate just thinking about it.

Having slept in his clothes, Jaxon wasted no time stepping out into Gillette's apartment. The vid screen displayed a scenic view from earth: the sun rising above a grassy horizon.

"Oh, wow. I'd say that it looks like you got a good night's rest, but to tell the truth, you look worse now than you did last night," Gillette said as he poured Jaxon a cup of coffee.

"Yeah, thanks for that. As you can imagine, I tossed and turned all night, reliving the events from yesterday." Jaxon sat at the island, practically worshiping the steaming cup of coffee.

"Hopefully, this will perk you up. Plus, I got bacon!"

"Real bacon? How'd you get that up here?" Jaxon asked as he drooled over the plate of crispy strips of heaven.

"It's the real thing. I'm able to get a pound every now and then from a connection I have in the city. This one's been sitting in my freezer for the last two months, so I figured it'd be a great way to kick off the day."

Jaxon didn't hesitate stuffing a piece into his mouth. The salty goodness that can only come from the flavor of bacon melted on his tongue. He closed his eyes as he chewed, savoring every morsel.

"Jesus, Jaxon. Do you two need to get a room?" Gillette asked as he slid a plate of toast across the island.

"My God. That bite was almost pure nirvana," Jaxon said as he slid two more pieces onto his plate before grabbing a slice of toast.

"Well, you better eat well. We're going to get you up to the outer ring today, and I think you're gonna need all the nourishment you can get," Gillette said.

"What's that? I thought you were on the cautionary side of my predicament," Jaxon said. He stopped eating, pushing his ravenous appetite to the side for a moment.

"Yeah, well, that was last night. Went to bed thinking how much of an ass I sounded like, not willing to help a buddy out. I'm sure if the tables were turned, you'd be the first one to help me—if I was in your position. So, I was up early and reached out to some friends. Looks like you're in luck today."

Jaxon's eyes widened in surprise, dumbfounded by his buddy's change of heart. "I … I'm speechless. I don't know what to say. I, I owe you, buddy."

"Don't thank me quite yet, Jaxon. First off, it's going to cost you. Three hundred credits, all in advance."

"Done. I still have my rainy day stash—I've barely even touched it."

"Then, there's the shuttle. It leaves at 10 AM, and it's ten minutes after nine right now."

Jaxon looked at the digital clock on the wall: It read 9:11 AM. "And you don't think you could've led off with that as opposed to wasting time with eating breakfast? Shouldn't we be getting there and—"

"Relax, Jaxon. We're good. I trust this guy as much as you trust me. Finish your breakfast and we'll be on our way."

"But isn't the city a good forty minutes away at this time of day?" Jaxon asked

"Don't fret, my man. Because this isn't a publicly authorized departure, you will not be leaving from Luna City station. There's an old surface access just on the far side of Sector 45. Once you get to the surface, there will be a ship waiting."

Jaxon relaxed and picked up another piece of bacon. "All right. No use letting this fine swine meal go to waste, then."

18

Twenty minutes later, they walked out of the apartment. As Gillette spent several minutes securing the myriad of locks on his apartment door, Jaxon scanned the immediate vicinity, looking for any sign of the assailants.

"All locked up," Gillette said. "Are we clear?" He and Gillette had complemented each other so well for so many years, and he felt a resurgence of strength with his old partner. *Just like old times,* Jaxon mused.

"Nobody in sight," Jaxon said, nodding his head over his shoulder. "Not sure what we'll encounter on the tube, though."

"We're not taking the tube. At least not on the way there. Once you're off, I'm almost certain things will cool off for the rest of us innocent inhabitants of the moon," Gillette said, his comments full of mockery.

"Oh, nice. Way to make a hunted assassin feel good about himself," Jaxon scoffed. "If we're not taking the tube, how are we going to pass through six sectors and not be late?"

"Long before the subway tubes were built, access to all sectors was by underground thoroughfares. Even though everything is already sub-terrestrial, the depressed, or lowered platforms, stretched from sector to sector. They were large enough to handle full-sized vehicles and were actually used for the initial build-out as each new sector came online."

"And you think using an enclosed pedestrian tunnel is better than taking the speed of the train?" Jaxon asked, confused by his friend's logic.

"For starters, they're not as confined as you might think. I use them almost exclusively when I'm heading out to 45. It's actually much faster than taking the train. Especially at this hour. We're at the end of rush hour, and taking the tube just six short stops could take more than an hour. Besides, I want to arrive at the town center on our terms, and not be thrust right into the middle of an unknown situation, unprepared."

"You're the boss," Jaxon said, standing to the side. "Lead the way."

Gillette did so, leading Jaxon through the maze of residential corridors until they came to a wide open stairway. A little puzzled, Jaxon wasn't sure how he'd missed it when he first arrived in Sector 39 the day before. He'd circled around most of the sector before arriving at Gillette's doorstep.

"What do you know about Sector 45?" Gillette asked, descending several flights of stairs.

"Not much more than what you've already told me. The last time I was in Luna City was with you, and we never made it out past Sector 11, if I recall."

"Not only is the surface access there, Sector 45 is really just a smaller-scaled city center. It was established so that those living in these distant sectors didn't have to travel into Luna City for everyday living essentials."

Jaxon followed Gillette into the surprisingly well-lit underpass. The ceiling was nearly four meters high, and the channel was almost twice as wide. Despite the welcoming conditions, the thoroughfare was practically deserted.

The journey through the underworld passed in relative silence. Gillette led the way and kept an earnest pace, while

Jaxon continued to dwell on what, or who, they might encounter in the end. Visions of Taloo Station continued to dominate his mind.

As they approached Sector 45, their pace slowed. "For the most part, Sector 45 has only ever been partially occupied. Its remote location makes it far less desirable for those that work in the city. By tube, it's more than a ninety-minute ride, taking all the stops along the way into consideration," Gillette explained.

"Sounds like a great location for someone to lay low," Jaxon said, contemplating his decision to get to the outer ring.

"You'd think, but those that do live out here are usually government officials and security personnel. Most of them use the surface access and then fly in short-range air shuttles to get to the city center in a fraction of the time."

"What prevents civilians from doing the same?" Jaxon asked.

"Cost, mostly. The short-range flyers are typically priced out of the normal person's budget. Plus, there's the cost of dock space, both here as well as in Luna City. It really is just for the elite, who can afford it, or the city workers, who get it for free," Gillette said.

"Then I hope this is a brief visit to Sector 45," Jaxon said, fighting back his uneasiness over the situation.

"I think we'll be fine. It's after the morning rush hour now, and Diego has a reputation for being thorough," Gillette said.

"For being a character conducting illicit behaviors," Jaxon added, smiling to Gillette.

Gillette winked as he led Jaxon out of the underpass and up the stairs.

As they reached the landing, Jaxon gauged that they were on the edge of the commercial district by the bleak surroundings. Gillette continued to lead them toward the town center. It was just as Gillette had described: a miniature version of Luna City. There were bars and restaurants, intermixed with several boutique shops. As it was still relatively early, there were very few people milling about the town.

As they continued their trek, Jaxon spotted two men that seemed out of place. They stood at an intersection at the edge of the city square and happened to be wearing gear that was strikingly similar to those back on Taloo.

"Gillette," Jaxon said, nudging him with his elbow.

"Yeah, I see them. Let's get off Main Street. We can get to where we're going another way," Gillette said before crossing the street and heading away from the potential foes.

Jaxon followed, diligently evaluating the populous. Besides the two back in the square, he was feeling more comfortable the further they walked. Regardless, Jaxon continued his heightened awareness.

When they neared the next intersection, Gillette stood next to the side wall and peered around the corner. The side street was empty and gave direct access to the surface stairway.

"Okay, it's just a few blocks up on the left. I think if we cross here and work our way up, we'll be just about home free."

Jaxon nodded silently, wishing that he had his MP-96 that he'd left on the Bradbury.

Gillette crossed the street and continued down the block. About halfway down, Jaxon spotted one of the space ninjas a few blocks ahead. Gillette was too far ahead of him to point the man out, and he didn't want to call out to him because it would probably alert the assassin at the same time. He had no choice but to continue following along with Gillette's rapid pace.

As they reached the end of the first block, Gillette finally slowed, and by the time Jaxon caught up, it was too late. The assassin caught sight of them and whispered something into his sleeve, almost certainly calling for backup.

Without hesitation, Gillette turned down the crossing street, veering away from their destination that was now just in sight.

Jaxon hoped Gillette knew a different path but was relieved that they were out of the assassin's sight for the time being.

As they neared the end of the next block, Jaxon assumed that it would lead to yet another cross street, but it didn't. It dead ended at a rock wall, course drill markings on its surface, indicating the extent of the coring rig used to dig out the city streets.

"Wrong turn, buddy," Jaxon said as he crouched near a side wall.

"Yeah, I see that. I thought this would double back toward the surface stairway. We've got to go back and then up the next street," Gillette said as he slid along the side wall.

Jaxon cursed under his breath at the clear misjudgment on Gillette's part. If he'd thought any less of Gillette, he might have considered that his buddy led him right into a trap. In the end, he heeded that Gillette's furtive abilities were just out of shape, and it was an honest mistake.

He fell into stride behind Gillette, and as they reached the edge of the street again, their perilous situation became clear. There were now two assassins on each of the three intersecting streets, and they were all heading in their direction.

"Shit, man. What did you get us into?" Jaxon asked.

"You don't think I did this on purpose?" Gillette demanded.

"I don't know, did you? Your sudden change of heart to help me out should've been my first clue," Jaxon snapped. He stepped around Gillette, trying to get a better handle on their situation. He needed a way out.

"Listen up, Jaxon. Think what you want, but I'm right in the middle of this with you. This is just an unfortunate circumstance that we need to get through. Are you with me?"

Jaxon didn't have any other options. He was unarmed in an unknown environment. "What do you have in mind?"

Well, it's you that they're after, so I'm going to try to get past them and cause some kind of diversion. You just need to hang low until you see the sign."

"That's your plan? Save your ass while you leave me here, cornered?"

"If you have anything better, I'm all ears," Gillette said, holding steady.

Jaxon thought through their situation. Neither of them had a weapon, and they were cornered in the alley. There was no other option. "Okay. Go on, then. What's the sign going to be?"

Gillette smiled. "You'll know it when you see it." He stood up and walked out into the intersection. Confidently, he glanced up and down the adjacent street then nodded his head. As he nearly reached the other side of the street, shots were fired from an unknown direction. The first shot went wide, glancing off of the metal ducting at the side. The second shot hit Gillette, dropping him to the ground.

"Gillette!" Jaxon called out.

Gillette rolled along the ground until he was behind a stack of shipping crates. He leaned up against the wall and motioned for Jaxon to get down.

Jaxon was thankful to see that Gillette's injuries weren't life-threatening. He did as instructed, lowering himself as close to the ground as possible. Then, Gillette reached into his daypack pulled out a cylindrical device that Jaxon recognized instantly. It was a concussion grenade, and he wondered why Gillette didn't tell him about having weapons earlier.

Wasting no time, Gillette removed the cap from the grenade and pressed the trigger button. He held it for several seconds before launching it into the air, toward the approaching assassins.

The grenade dropped to the ground and detonated, easily deafening anyone in its vicinity. Jaxon was prepared and had tucked his head between his biceps. As the reverberations subsided, Jaxon peered through the drifting smoke toward Gillette. Once the vapor began to clear, Gillette peered back, having just uncovered himself from debris.

"Run! Run, now," Gillette yelled as he crawled along the building's edge.

Jaxon wasted no time and sprinted toward the surface

access point. As he reached the corner of the next street, he heard several shots being fired behind him. He turned and saw Gillette convulse with each bullet. His body dropped to the ground, face down and lifeless.

Until that point, the death toll had consisted of only the killers after him. Now, it was Gillette's blood that had fallen, and all he could think about was avenging his death. But he knew it would be suicide. He still had no weapons and he was still in an unfamiliar area. All he could do was run.

He turned up the street and saw the entrance to the surface stairway less than a block away. He dug deep and increased his speed toward the door.

As he reached for the door handle, he hoped that there would be no unforeseen obstacles on the other side. He gripped the handle and wrenched it open, blindly springing himself into the stairway. It was dark, but it was thankfully vacant.

Maintaining his momentum, he shot up the first flight of stairs. As he turned at the first landing and began to ascend the second flight, the door behind him opened and closed.

They're right on my heels.

Not wanting to slow his pace to see if his suspicions were correct, he barreled up the second flight of stairs at twice the speed. As he climbed, he glanced up the center of the stairwell and could see that he had at least a dozen flights of stairs before he got to the top.

That's when he realized he had yet another problem: how to don his environmental suit while running up the stairs. He carried it in the backpack slung over his shoulder and had figured all along that he'd have time to put it on long before actually arriving at the moon's surface. His only hope was that he had more stamina than those following him and that he could somehow have time when he reached the top to adequately protect himself from the moon's lack of atmosphere.

As he turned the next landing, he unslung his pack, pulling the suit out in the same swift motion. He gripped it and slung it over his shoulder before dropping the duffel on the stairway. He decided that after banking the next landing, he'd pause long enough to slip his feet into the legs and continue climbing as he finished slipping his arms into the sleeves.

When he reached the fifth landing, he stopped and quickly dropped his right foot into the first pant leg. As he raised his left foot, something dropped from above, catching his attention.

It struck the landing and bounced down the stairwell before it detonated. The explosion of the grenade nearly knocked him to the floor.

The closeness of the explosion stopped Jaxon in his tracks. He knew that there were killers coming up from below, but who dropped the grenade from above? Hopefully, the grenade took out at least a few of his followers down below.

Suddenly a second grenade dropped and landed right next to his feet. Before he could grab it and toss it away, it detonated, the flash causing near blindness. The blast launched Jaxon several meters into the air, and he fell hard against the steel stair treads. Jaxon was still conscious and was surprised that he was still alive after such a close detonation.

It must have been a flash grenade, he thought, as he had few injuries. He tried to stand but quickly fell back from the dizziness.

He tried again but had the same result, falling down the stairway even further.

As he lay there, only marginally aware of his condition, the edges of his vision continued to blur. Within seconds, he was almost to the darkness in front of him when he saw several pairs of combat boots approach. Then he blacked out completely.

Eighteen years ago — Live training, mission number one, Ixtapa, Mexico.

Objective: assassinate Ignacio Guzman (El Tonto).
Timeframe: Immediate.
Threat level: Severe.
Operatives: Saber.
Method: Sniper Rifle.

The gentle roar of the ocean crashing against the sandy beach rolled in from my right. The salty air thick with humidity caused beads of sweat to constantly roll off my skin. Any perspiration that remained quickly evaporated, leaving a sticky residue in its place.

Concerned about a potential malfunction, I cycled through my rifle's chamber. Or was it out of nervous habit? I lifted the bolt up and back, ejecting the .50 caliber bullet from its chamber. I caught it in midair and examined the condition of the casing before reinserting it. I drove the bolt forward and slapped it back down, confident that for the fiftieth time, everything would go as planned.

I readied the rifle to my shoulder and peered through the scope. At the center of the crosshairs, the world moved at an exaggerated rate as I swung the rifle, slowly, from left to right.

There wasn't a soul in sight in the luxurious courtyard, but it was early. Having gone through nearly four years as a cadet, and an additional year and a half of specialized training, I was ready. Eager, but ready. I just hoped that I wouldn't fuck it up.

I continued to study the patio and the surrounding veranda, alternating between my scope and a pair of binoculars that had inferior optics, but gave me a bigger picture of the situation. In between endlessly scanning the area, I continued ejecting the cartridge from my rifle. I was nervous.

Then, just as I'd taken a moment away from my obsessing, I leaned back in my chair and noticed the door burst open into the courtyard across the way. A quick glance through binoculars and I knew it was time. One by one, people started coming through the open doorway. The first half dozen men through were armed guards, most likely there to protect El Tonto. Then, a handful of women and children scampered out into the courtyard. Finally, El Tonto walked out and into the brutal sunlight.

After many weeks of intense training, I was finally at the precipice of death. I had visualized the man's face in my crosshairs thousands of times, and here I was, at the moment of his departure. Strangely, I froze. I suddenly saw a real person in place of what I'd only envisioned as his likeness, an image of himself. The person in front of me was now a living, breathing individual. I began to panic.

A crackle in my ear brought my wandering attention back to the present.

"Eagle's Roost, to Saber, do you read?"

I touched the skin beneath my ear and pressed down, activating the implanted hypo-comm device. "I hear you, Eagle's Roost. Loud and clear, over."

"Roger that. Are we ready to dance? Over."

"That's affirmative, Eagle's Roost," I said. "The ballerina is on the dance floor."

"Understood. Do you anticipate any difficulties? Over," Eagle's Roost asked.

Ignoring my concern of the humidity or my own psyche, I said, "There's a slight breeze, but it's nothing that the digital sight compensator can't handle. Over."

"Copy that. You now have full authorization to proceed. The time is finally here, Saber. You've had a great training run, and you'll be a prized asset. I'm going radio silent now, but I will be monitoring the comm line."

I took a deep breath and raised my rifle to my shoulder. He was right. I did have a great training run, and I knew it. I felt like a natural and nobody was going to take that away. I had anticipated this moment for so long, I only feared the sadness that would come after it was done.

Forcing the thoughts out of my mind, I sighted through the scope. It was a nice one, far nicer than my personal rifle back home. This model had digital readouts, showing distance and wind speed, and it was even equipped with optional low-light compensators. It truly was the Cadillac of sniper rifles.

"Distance to target: 200 meters. Windage: 2 kilometers from the south."

I lowered the rifle and verified the auto-adjustments on the scope before shouldering it once again. I panned through the crowd until I found my target. El Tonto. He was standing in the middle of several men, full of arrogance and gusto, speaking excitedly to the crowd. Those that surrounded him cheered and joined in the celebration. It was his birthday, and if you were present, you were part of his personal entourage, or you were family. Both of which were very important in their culture.

I thumbed the safety latch to off and slid my finger around the trigger. It was time. I monitored my breathing, taking in a slow, deep breath before exhaling fully. When my breath was completely exhausted, I refocused my scope on the target and firmly squeezed the trigger.

A teen boy ran across the patio from just outside of my scope's view. At the precise moment I squeezed the trigger, the child crossed through and into the crosshairs. It was too late. The report of the rifle echoed throughout the city, startling birds into the air. Instinctively, the multitude of people in the courtyard cowered at the sound. I knew timing was everything, and I needed to be on my way before the echo of the gunfire subsided, but I had to see. Did I hit the kid or did I take my target out?

I shouldered my rifle once again and peered through the scope at the calamity across the city square. It was chaos. People were running franticly, screaming in fear. The armed guards took defensive points around the wide open courtyard. They were scanning the surrounding buildings, looking for the killer. The assassin. They were looking for me. I focused my rifle on the last position that El Tonto stood and found no one there. I lowered my scope slightly and found two bodies lying on the floor, both of them covered in blood. I scrutinized the scene, and it was horrific. El Tonto was down, and the left side of his chest was obliterated. The wound was deep, wide, and covered in blood. Mission accomplished. I panned my rifle to the second body and cringed. It was a boy, probably around sixteen, and the side of his face was covered in blood. His condition: unknown.

"My God, what have I done?" I mumbled.

"You have to move, now, Saber," crackled into my ear.

So much for radio silence, I thought.

Stunned, I cursed at myself for being so careless. How could I have overlooked the potential of injuring another person, let alone a child? I tried to keep my hands from shaking, but it was difficult. Then the crackle came once again.

"Saber, do you read? You have to move now. El Tonto's guards are already on the move. You've got sixty seconds to get out of there."

Forcing away my remorse, I lurched into action. With a

practiced hand, I dismantled my sniper rifle and slipped each of the parts into a compact briefcase, just like I'd done hundreds of times through training. I closed the window and shuttered the drapes in the small hotel room. I rushed to the far side of the room and slipped the briefcase into an exposed cavity in the wall. Once in place, I slid the bureau in front of it before doing one last pass through the room, being sure not to leave anything out of place.

Calm and collected, I stepped out into the corridor and made for the exit stairwell. I knew that as soon as I reached street level, El Tonto's goons would be all over the place, most likely being assisted by the local police.

As I descended the stairway, I pulled out a wig of slick brown hair and donned it over my tightly cropped sandy blond hair. Then, from my inside pocket, I slipped out a dark brown mustache adhered to a piece of cellophane. I paused momentarily, long enough to apply the critical piece of my disguise.

Finally, on the move again, I slipped off my jacket and discarded it in the stairwell. My undershirt was of white linen, with sweat stains in the armpits. I now looked like a Mexican worker that had been slaving away in the sun for many hours. When I reached the first-floor landing, I picked up a broom and dust pan that I'd previously placed in the inside corner, completing my disguise. I stepped out onto the street.

20

A stinging pain overcame Jaxon as he rolled to his side. He was waking up. He tried to reach up and soothe the back of his head, but his hands didn't cooperate. They were bound at his sides.

He opened his eyes and blinked several times, trying to remove the blurriness from his vision. After several moments of uneasiness, his surroundings started to come into focus. It was clear to him that he was in some sort of cargo facility by the multiple lashing points around the perimeter. At the far end of the bay, the wall was slanted up and away and had signs of substantial use. A retractable loading ramp. He was on a military supply ship.

To his right, there was a ship's ladder leading up to a platform with a single man-sized door. Leading into the rest of the ship, he assumed.

Jaxon tried to stand, but the restraints at his side were lashed to the bindings at his seat. He looked down and found that he was not only bound at the wrists and waist, but his ankles were shackled as well.

"What the hell?" Jaxon murmured, trying to get a grasp of his situation.

As if on cue, the door on the landing above grinded open, and a man in black military fatigues stepped out. He gripped the sides of the ship's ladder and slid down to his level then headed right for Jaxon.

"What's going on here?" Jaxon asked, attempting to raise his hands.

The man in black walked by Jaxon, ignoring his question. He continued past and sat a few seats away.

"Hey, are you deaf? Why am I in handcuffs? Who are you?" Jaxon asked again.

A faint smile crept across the stranger's face. He fastened his seatbelt and pulled a magazine from beneath his seat and began reading.

Jaxon rolled his neck to the side, attempting to release the pressure building up on his spine. The pain was excruciating, and it felt like he'd been run over by a truck. He thought back to his last moments of consciousness, but most of it was a blur.

He was with Gillette on the moon base, and they were attempting to … to do what? *What were they trying to do?* Jaxon wondered, running through multiple scenarios in his mind.

Wait a second, he thought. *Why was I even on the moon?*

Slowly, Jaxon worked backward through what had happened, and few seconds later, everything came flooding back. The ambush at his apartment, the assassination attempts in the service tunnels as well as at his tea shop. Everything rushed into his mind like a freight train.

"Okay, if you don't want to tell me who you are, can you tell me why you want me dead?" Jaxon asked, trying a different approach.

The man shrugged as he flipped through the pages of his magazine.

"Come on, man. You've got to give me something," Jaxon pleaded.

"Ain't got to do shit," said the man in black without looking up.

"Okay, fine. Can you at least unhook me from this chair? I'd like to stand and stretch my legs," Jaxon asked, already calculating potential escape routes. *But escape to where?* he wondered.

Surprisingly, the man in black stood and unlocked the steel cable that had been run through the shackles at his feet and waist. "Don't do anything stupid," he said.

Jaxon stood and promptly sat right back down due to dizziness.

"How long have I been out?" Jaxon asked.

"Not long," the man said.

Jaxon stood again, and waited for him to expound, but it became clear that he was a man of few words. He'd already sat back down and resumed flipping through his magazine.

As soon as Jaxon's equilibrium was balanced, he began to shuffle his shackled feet up and down the cargo bay, trying to formulate his plan further. Experience told him that the difference in the artificial gravity and the momentum he felt in the ship's superstructure meant that he was, in fact, flying through space. Besides living on earth for most of his life, Jaxon had spent a significant amount of time on the moon, or on various space stations. Each environment had its own distinct level of gravity that he'd learned to recognize. The gravity beneath his feet right now was unmistakable and doom quickly set in as he realized that he was out of luck for any attempt to escape. Unless he could get out of his shackles, he was at the mercy of his captors.

But who were his captors? Where were they taking him? His only guess was to the outer ring, which oddly enough was his initial destination.

After a bit of time pacing back and forth, the man in black called.

"You better sit back down, boss. We'll be landing soon, and we'd hate to see you get ... knocked around," he said with a wry smile.

Reluctantly, Jaxon agreed. Depending on where they would be stopping, the landing could be rough. He retook his seat and the man in black leaned over and refastened his seatbelt.

"Got to stay buckled up, you know? It could be bumpy," he said.

Shortly after, Jaxon felt the momentum of the ship change and the pit in his stomach rose. They were dropping. Oddly enough, the gravity beneath him changed as well. It was much stronger, and he knew instantly where they were heading. They were returning to earth.

21

The floor plates beneath Jaxon's feet began to vibrate. Jaxon gathered that the landing thrusters had just been engaged and the moment of his reintroduction to the Earth's surface was imminent. The reunion after eight peaceful years living in hiding.

As the ship continued to pitch and roll, adjusting for the landing platform, Jaxon thought more about a potential escape. Flying through space created certain difficulties for breaking away, but once he was in a breathable atmosphere, the playing field was level.

He looked down at his shackled ankles and judged his stride to be about 12 inches. The bindings at his waist allowed his arms to freely move about the same distance in each direction, but not enough to effectively aid in any heroic maneuvers. He had to get out of the shackles first. At least he was free of the lashing cable, being held securely by a simple seatbelt now. Perhaps if his timing was right, he could pop his release button and spring onto his captor and immobilize him long enough to search for a key to his restraints.

Jaxon looked at the man in black, trying to gauge his alertness, when he suddenly returned Jaxon's gaze. It was almost as if he knew precisely what Jaxon was thinking.

"Don't try it, buddy," he said, dropping the magazine into an empty chair. The man in black sat upright and crossed his arms, glaring straight at Jaxon.

Well, the cat's out of the bag on that plan, Jaxon thought.

Moments later, a loud concussion reverberated throughout the cargo bay as the landing gear touched down. The vibrations beneath his feet subsided almost instantly. That's when Jaxon felt a faint movement, almost as if he was on the water. *Have we actually landed on a sea platform?*

Jaxon was aware that several private organizations had been using the floating landing pads since earlier in the century, but they were only utilized for non-habitable missions. Jaxon wondered what else might have changed since he last set foot on earth.

As this new situation began to set in, Jaxon returned his thoughts to his escape plan. He knew how to swim, and despite being off earth for such a long period of time, he still remained in good physical shape. He was confident that he could swim with ease, despite being shackled as he was. Granted, he'd have to swim like a fish, utilizing his abdominal muscles and leg kicks for propulsion. He just wondered whether it would be a better alternative than staying captive to who knows who.

With a rough escape plan in place, Jaxon decided that his best chance for success was to get near the edge of the landing platform. If he could then catch his captors off guard, he could simply jump out into the water. The likelihood of one of them following was pretty slim. Or so he thought.

The man in black unfastened his seatbelt, stood, then adjusted his posture. A common maneuver when returning to the gravity of earth after a long space flight. "Up," he said, staring directly at Jaxon.

Jaxon attempted to stand, but his own seatbelt was still fastened. "A little help?" Jaxon smiled.

The man leaned down and unfastened Jaxon's seatbelt before gripping him firmly by the shoulders, lifting him upright.

"Thanks."

The man in black guided Jaxon forward, toward the cargo bay door. As they neared the door, Jaxon felt the grip strengthen around his arm and slowly pull him backward. With his other hand, the man triggered the door release, and the pressure seal whispered softly. The pressure equalized with the environment outside and the door slowly grinded open. Once it was clear, Jaxon saw a ramp already touching the landing platform below. The man shoved Jaxon forward, causing him to nearly trip down the ramp.

The salty air infiltrated Jaxon's nostrils instantly. "Ah, earth."

As Jaxon was guided down the cargo ramp, he glanced back to see the type of ship they were flying on, hoping to determine its origin. No visible insignia appeared anywhere on the hull. There wasn't even a vessel number stenciled on the hull, which he thought was mandatory for galactic travel.

Once on the landing platform, the man guided Jaxon toward the edge of the platform, practically inviting him to carry out his plan. Jaxon watched the water carefully the closer they got to the edge, judging the swells of the sea. In the distance, Jaxon saw the horizon, where the sea met the sky. There was no land in site in any direction. They were at least a few miles from the coast and that worried him. His ability to swim was not in question, but the presence of sea life was. The ocean was full of predatory mammals, and Jaxon knew he would be nothing more than an appetizer for any one of them.

When they reached the edge of the platform, Jaxon quickly decided to deviate from his plan when he noticed a stairway leading down. About halfway down the steps, Jaxon was met with two more men coming up. They had equally menacing looks on their faces.

"Hi there," Jaxon said, trying to be disarming in his

approach. "How're you doing today?"

They both ignored Jaxon as they squeezed by, continuing up to the platform.

Confusion began to set in. Jaxon had thought they'd have more guards around. And the first two people he encountered, besides the man in black, walked by him without concern. *Who are these people?* Jaxon wondered.

As they reached the bottom of the stairway, the man in black steered Jaxon in through a portal, then down a long corridor that ran the length of the landing platform. About midway down the hallway, they came to an unmarked door. The man in black straightened then knocked.

Motion could be heard from the other side of the door seconds before it swung open, instantly revealing the identity of his captors.

Perry Evans stood before him.

"Well, if it isn't Jaxon Rasner," Evans said, thrusting his hand out to greet Jaxon.

"In the flesh," Jaxon tried to accept his hand, but because of the shackles, it was nearly impossible.

"My God, man. Dispense with those bindings, now," Evans said sternly. The man in black quickly obeyed, removing the restraints from around Jaxon's waist before kneeling down and removing the shackles from his ankles.

"Now, where were we?" Evans asked. "Oh yes, it's good to see you, old friend," he said, pumping Jaxon's hand at the same time.

22

"You son of a bitch," Jaxon snapped as he ripped his hand back from Evans. Evans' face turned from happiness to surprised shock.

"I ... I don't understand. I thought you would be at least a little bit glad to see me, considering—"

"What? After you tried to have me killed? Can't you tell when somebody's trying to remain unseen?" Jaxon asked, his anger building.

"You've got it all wrong, Jaxon. It was me, us, the company—we saved you. If it weren't for Miles here, you would have certainly been killed in Sector 45. He and his team had been tracking you ever since the fiasco on Taloo Station."

"Then if it wasn't you, who was it?" Jaxon asked, confused. "And you knew about me being on Taloo Station?"

Evans smiled. "Absolutely. I've known about you and your little tea shop for quite some time. I recognized the signs of burnout in your eyes years ago and knew precisely what your next move would be. I talked with the director at the time and convinced them that it was okay to let you out ... for the time being. As for who it is that's trying to kill you, my guess is as good as yours. Perhaps it's somebody from your past, and they are seeking revenge."

Jaxon began to pace in circles, trying to reassemble the past 48 hours of his life. The fact that the company knew that he was alive the whole time further baffled his mind.

"And what about Gillette? Did you know about him as well?" Jaxon asked, stopping his gait.

Evans lowered his gaze. "It appears that Gillette wasn't as fortunate as you. Yes, we knew that he was alive and well in Luna City, but he wasn't our target ..."

"But you said that I wasn't on your hit list. What do you mean *your target*?" Jaxon demanded.

Evans held his hands up to assuage Jaxon. "Slow down, Saber. It's not what you think. Yes, you were targeted, but for employment reasons only. You have to trust me when I tell you that our relationship is much deeper than a working relationship. I've been your handler, and friend, since the very beginning, when I recruited you into the company. I care for you, Jaxon. You have to believe me."

Hearing Evans' words caught Jaxon off guard. "What kind of employment were you targeting me for? If you knew I wanted out—hell, I faked my own death just to get out of the assassination game. What makes you think that I'll come back to that?" Jaxon asked.

Evans sized Jaxon up. "You know, you are really quite a mess right now. How long did it take for you to grow that beard? Did you just stop shaving the day that you and Gillette destroyed the space elevator?" Evans asked, a smirk on his face.

"What. Job?" Jaxon demanded, ignoring Evans' attempt to change the subject.

"In due time, my friend. We have a bit more in our journey before everything will be revealed. Please, why don't you follow Miles? He'll get you ready for departure. Also, we're fully aware of the open hit order on your life, so everything's pretty hush-

hush right now. We're not taking you back to the company quite yet, and the director will reveal everything to you personally. But we have to get to land first and then get you to the safe house. Once we're secure, the director will arrive and explain everything."

As Jaxon tried to remain focused on Evans' explanation, he couldn't help but notice a nervous tic in his demeanor. His eyes twitched as he avoided eye contact. Jaxon knew he was holding something back, but what?

Jaxon followed Miles back out and further down the corridor until they came to yet another stairwell. They descended another level down into a closed-in boat dock. Tendered at various points along the platform were half a dozen speedboats and small yachts. Miles led Jaxon through the docks until they arrived at a sleek titanium-colored yacht that Jaxon instantly recognized. He'd remembered training for a number of missions on that very yacht and believed that it was Evans' personal craft. It all started to make sense.

Miles stepped onto the boat and led Jaxon into the lower level and into a windowed cabin. "There's a change of clothes for you in the closet. You also have an en suite if you want to freshen up."

Miles started to turn and leave when Jaxon stopped him.

"Hey, sorry about back on the transport ship, but I didn't know ..."

"No worries, boss. I was just following orders. I knew you didn't belong in restraints, but my own hands were tied ... if you catch my drift."

Jaxon understood. "Good enough."

"Good enough," Miles said before walking out and closing the cabin door.

Within fifteen minutes, Jaxon felt the engines fire up, and the yacht disembark. As soon as the momentum shifted to a higher speed, he decided a quick shower and change of clothes was in order. As he shed his ragged clothing, most of which was covered in soot and debris from the grenade explosion on the moon's stairwell, he was happy to see that his wounds were healing quickly. He'd always been a fast healer and was pleased that that part of his life hadn't changed.

As he mindlessly washed under the hot, steaming water, his mind remained occupied with the only thing that mattered to him.

Who was his killer?

He continued hashing through his past, trying to figure out who it might be that had it in for him.

23

Seventeen years ago.

Brutus confidently strode through the streets of Guadalajara, despite having only been in the city a few times before. Being an American in a world filled with so many incensed natives would normally be suicide. He felt safe, though, because of his connections.

As he approached their arranged meeting location—a quaint café with both indoor and outdoor seating—Brutus wondered if enough time had passed since the assassination. He was taken by surprise for even getting called upon for an in-person meeting so soon.

Brutus would've preferred to sit outside, under a faded umbrella to enjoy the warm weather, but the now controlling heir to El Tonto was still reluctant to be seen out in the open, due to his facial disfigurement.

Stepping inside, Brutus walked past the barista without a word. He walked deeper into the café, toward the rear. Near a back hallway, most likely leading to private storage rooms, he found an inside corner booth that was almost completely out of the public view. There were three men sitting around the table, two wearing dark-colored sport coats and one in a light-colored polo shirt. Brutus reminded himself once again to not stare out of common courtesy.

"Sorry I'm late, Mr. Guzman, but your city continues to confuse my navigational skills," Brutus said, standing in front of the table.

The man in the polo shirt nodded silently to his companions, and they promptly left the booth for another table, just out of earshot.

"Please have a seat," Guzman said. "Perhaps if you'd learn the language of my people, you wouldn't be so easily confused."

Brutus smiled as he slid into the booth. "I've tried many times. But it's the verbs that continually trip me up," Brutus said, maintaining eye contact in an effort to not glare at the hideous wounds on the side of the man's face.

"You'd be surprised at what a little effort could do for your learning ability," Guzman said. "I trust your trip was pleasant?"

Brutus nodded. "Absolutely sensational, thank you. It was kind of you to send a car to pick me up at the airport. I'd almost certainly have been delayed even longer if I hadn't been able to get to the hotel in such quick time." Brutus chuckled.

Guzman nodded silently but maintained eye contact with Brutus.

"I am pleased to see you're out and about. Have you experienced any aftereffects due to your injuries?" Brutus asked, noting that he couldn't completely ignore the deformities on Guzman's face.

The man smiled and lightly touched the discolored scar at the side of his head where his ear once had lived. "Other than the unyielding hearing loss, I'll be fine. The doctors tell me that the scarring is going to be a permanent exhibit to my persona. And that is quite disheartening. I've only recently started stepping out into the public—the looks that are given to me are involuntary, but are still more hurtful than the recovery period has been."

Brutus nodded. Having never experienced such an injury, he had trouble finding the right words. "I can imagine. But, with the influence of your family, I'm sure those glances will diminish with time."

"Oh, yes. My family," Guzman said, his face turning red. "The stature of my dead father no longer has any ground. He was an ugly man that had committed heinous crimes on society. His power was that people feared him, and I was quite content distancing myself from that lifestyle. But, as you can imagine, the incident from a year ago has ... changed my perspective," Guzman said, touching his scarred face once again.

Brutus understood. He'd privately known the Guzman family for many years, long before the assassination, and at the time, everyone thought that assassinating Ignacio Guzman was the right thing to do. Nobody could have guessed the repercussions of that decision.

"Regardless of El Tonto's atrocities, he was still my father— he was still family. Since his death, my mother has been a complete mess. She's become more addicted to the drug that my dad once peddled through the streets of this very city. As much as I've tried to help her, she continues to resist. I've tried everything, and I fear that vengeance may be the only cure for what ails her."

"Vengeance? For an unknown assassin?" Brutus asked.

"That is why I called for you, my friend. I remember you and my father meeting many times through the years, and I know he respected you despite your position at the GSA. I'm here to ask—to plead for your help. If you can discover the identity of my father's killer, my family would be *very* grateful."

Beads of sweat began to materialize on Brutus' temples. "You have my full devotion, Mr. Guzman, but I'm not sure how much I can help. At the time of the assassination, we had no agents in your country, let alone at your location," Brutus lied.

"But couldn't you investigate? I know you and my father had an occupational relationship, and I would like to extend the same courtesy to any of your agents. I do not need quantifiable results, just the identity of the person who gave me this hideous scar. I will take care of things after that."

"Absolutely, Mr. Guzman. I'll look into it personally, as well as put my best man on the job. If you could just give me a month or so to develop an adequate cover story, things could move much smoother."

"It's Pablo. Please, call me Pablo," Guzman said, leaning forward with intensity. "Take the time you need, but not too long. I want this revenge not only for my mother's sake but for the sake of my people. Despite my father's drug dealings throughout the world, this is a small community, and everyone has felt a shift in power. It is my plan to regain that power my father once had."

Brutus nearly gasped aloud. "But what about law school? Weren't you recently accepted into Harvard? Think about the power that you could bring to the community with such a notable education and degree."

"I am done with the education system. My community needs me now, not in five years," Guzman demanded.

"I, um, I don't know what to say. Am I to assume that you'll also need the GSA to extend the same professional courtesies to you as we did to your father?" Brutus asked cautiously.

"Initially, no. Production has been at a virtual standstill since the day he was killed. It is going to take me some time, at least half a year, to reach those production levels again. As we move closer to that moment, I am sure you and I will have yet another conversation. But, until then, please devote your attention to finding my father's killer."

Brutus and Pablo continued their uninterrupted conversation well into the afternoon, with Guzman feeding Brutus as much information that he knew about his father's death. Which wasn't much. The cat and mouse game that Brutus hoped ended with El Tonto's assassination had just reared its ugly head.

24

After docking at a quiet mainland port, Jaxon was escorted from the yacht and quickly shuttled into a compact van with darkly tinted windows. He was accompanied by Evans, Miles, and another unidentified man. Having been off planet for nearly a decade, he'd anticipated a more modern approach to vehicular transportation, but that wasn't the case today. The van they were in was an older model vehicle, typical government transportation, that he remembered.

Miles and the other man sat in the front seat while Evans sat next to Jaxon in the back. Despite the hundreds of questions coursing through Jaxon's mind, he practiced restraint, opting to wait until they reached their destination. If he'd known the trip would take four plus hours, he might have disregarded the notion of self-discipline and bombarded Evans with all he had.

Instead, the road trip consisted of relative silence. The reticence caused Jaxon to doze in and out of consciousness most of the way, despite his efforts to remain cognizant of their location and direction. With each micro-nap, Jaxon ran through the last 48 hours in his mind. With every replay, the image of Gillette being murdered jolted him awake.

"We're close now, Jaxon," Evans said, looking out the window at a thicket of trees that dotted the edge of a single-lane dirt road.

Jaxon looked out his window, finding a similar view. They appeared to be deep inside a forest, and he cursed himself for not staying awake. Now, he was lost and in the dark, despite the shining daylight.

"How are you feeling, Jaxon?" Evans asked. "Having been off planet for so long typically has a drain on your energy. The gravitational differences between what's here on earth and what's simulated on a space station certainly will take its toll."

Jaxon hadn't paid any attention to the lag until Evans mentioned it. After a moment of introspection, he realized that despite his efforts to stay awake, it was a futile effort. He was exhausted.

"I'm doing okay," Jaxon lied. "A little discomfort but nothing that I can't handle."

Evans brow rose. "That's surprising. We've had people come back to Earth from extended space station excursions that have had to take nearly a week off, just to acclimate—"

"I'm not most people," Jaxon snapped. "So why don't you tell me why I am in the back of a dark van driving through an isolated forest heading to an unknown location? Why all the hush-hush?"

"It was a group decision actually. The director and I thought that keeping your reintroduction to society low key would be beneficial. As far as everyone at the company knows, Jaxon, you're still dead," Evans said. "Furthermore, we have reason to believe that there's a mole in the company, and only a handful of select people even know about this operation."

"That's understandable," Jaxon said with a slight nod. "But can you tell me this: why were you even on the moon base at the precise time that I was certain to die?"

"I'll admit, the timing of our arrival was exceptional. And once the director arrives, he'll be able to explain things much more clearly."

A look of surprise crossed Jaxon's face. "The director's actually coming here"—Jaxon paused to glance out the side window once again—"wherever *here* is?"

Before Evans could answer, the van slowed and turned onto a particularly rough dirt road that declined at a rather steep angle. A few moments later, the van pulled up to what appeared to be an abandoned mountain cabin.

The four men exited the van and Jaxon stretched his sore legs before following the other men up to the cabin door.

"This is one of the company's most remote safe house locations in the country. Only a select group of people know of its existence. You see, the director and I have been working in symphony all along and felt that this would be an ideal place to debrief you and fill you in on our current objectives."

Miles opened the door, and they all filed inside. Despite the rugged and deteriorated exterior, the inside of the cabin was far more modern than one would expect. Besides the plaid-patterned drapes at the windows, the rest of the decor was right out of an Architectural Digest spread. Fine wool rugs were scattered across the floor, and contemporary furniture filled the room. To one side, a hallway led to what were most likely a few bedrooms. On the opposite side, a modest kitchen sat next to a quaint dining area.

"So, tell me: why am I here?" Jaxon asked, slumping down onto a leather sofa.

"As I said, once the director arrives, all will be made clear."

Aggravation quickly took over, and Jaxon couldn't remain seated. He began to pace around the open floor plan, formulating his next question.

"Okay, then tell me this: at what point did you realize that I was still alive?" Jaxon asked.

Evans' eyes followed Jaxon as he paced. "We've known from the very beginning. Remember, we weren't very far off when the explosion occurred. A research team, led by yours truly, investigated, and when no bodies were discovered, it didn't take long for us to put things together."

Jaxon flinched at hearing his plan was actually a failure. "Then why didn't you come for me sooner? Or did it just take the company that long to locate me?

"Oh no, we picked up on your location quite early on. In fact, we had a man on the shuttle you used to get to Taloo Station initially. The company had you monitored quite closely. At first, at least. Then, once we realized that there was no threat of you revealing any sworn secrets about your past missions, or the company, we left you alone for the meantime."

"The meantime?" Jaxon asked, picking up on the inference quickly. "And what now?"

"And now, we hope to introduce you back into the company as an active agent," said a new man just walking into the cabin.

25

Jaxon froze and stared at the new man with a hint of recognition. He remembered possibly meeting him many years ago, maybe on one of his missions. But he couldn't be certain.

"Ah, you made better time than we did," Evans said, standing up to greet the new man. "Jaxon, this is the director of the GSA. Meet Alton Howe."

Howe stepped forward and extended his hand. "It's a pleasure, Mr. Rasner. Or should I call you Saber?"

Jaxon stared at the director's hand for a moment before accepting it. "Jaxon will be fine."

"All right, Jaxon. The assistant director here has briefed me on your most recent adventure in Luna City, and I first want to formally apologize that we didn't get to you sooner."

Assistant director? Jaxon mused. He made a mental note to ask Evans more about it later. "Apology accepted. Now, will somebody tell me what the hell I'm doing here?"

Howe moved to the sofa and motioned Jaxon and Evans to join him. "Please, let's sit and I'll try to fill you in as best I can."

Jaxon and Evans took the seats across from Howe and waited patiently.

"You see, Mr. Rasner ... er, I mean Jaxon, we've wanted to reach out to you for quite some time, but until now, you've been a relatively low priority. The company has maintained an unwavering approach to past and present agents. Our attitude toward any retired agent is that after a substantial debriefing of their missions, the agent is then processed through a memory altering program, wherein any classified information is *coaxed* out of their mind. The memories aren't erased, specifically, but they are ... overwritten through a process that our medical engineers have developed. When you and Gillette feigned your *catastrophic* deaths, my predecessor made the determination to leave you in play ... just as long as neither of you leaked any proprietary information. Trust me when I say this, Jaxon, we've had eyes on you the entire time."

Jaxon felt a pit in his stomach begin to grow. He knew Evans well, almost like a brother, but this character, Howe, concerned him.

"So, was it you that put out the kill order on me? There've been several attempts on my life over the past few days, and if the company knew about my location the entire time, it just seems a little ironic that—"

"Let me stop you here. I give you my word that the company has had no such orders in play. It's quite the opposite, really. We were about to approach you, to ask you to come back to the company. You see, there's a particular mission that's come along that warrants Saber's expertise."

Jaxon shook his head. "No. I walked away for a reason. I left because I was tired of being your private assassin. That's not why I joined the GSA."

Howe nodded. "Would it help if I told you that the GSA has become more of a kinder, gentler organization? Yes, the division you were associated with was notorious for covert assassinations around the globe. But, I assure you that each and every one of those missions were vital to the security of the world. If you can pardon my analogy, you were the rifle and your controller pulled the trigger. You were a mere tool for the GSA. Your record was particularly exemplary. As such, you were left to your own accord until you were needed. And here we are."

"Does this kinder, gentler GSA call upon me today to give someone a massage?" Jaxon asked sarcastically.

Howe laughed. "Not exactly. We'd like you to disable a particular drug production facility in the outer ring. You'll be authorized to use whatever force necessary to carry out your mission. If that involves killing one or two of the bad guys along the way, then so be it. The GSA has no preference on the matter either way."

Jaxon winced at Howe's cavalier attitude. Reading between the lines, he knew the directive was a sham because it left it up to him alone to determine whether or not someone should die. He almost preferred it when he was just given the directive to assassinate.

"I'm sorry. I'm not your man. Like I said, I left for a reason. If it's all the same to you, I'd rather take my chances on my own."

Howe frowned. Then his face contorted into an apologetic smile. "Perry thought you'd feel that way. So, we attempted to persuade you in with an alternative method. Unfortunately, that approach didn't quite work out as planned. Jaxon, I have a bit of bad news for you. You see, Assistant Director Evans and I formulated a plan that would enlist the assistance of Lily Abbott for your recruitment. As I understand it, you and Lily were quite an item while at the Academy. I'm also told that you and Lily produced a child, but never married. Are my facts straight?"

"Yes. Get to the point."

"We sent a team of special agents to talk Lily into helping us persuade you to come back to the GSA. Unfortunately, Lily was killed hours before our initial contact."

The blood drained from Jaxon's face. He stood abruptly,

nearly losing his balance from his fatigued muscles. He regained his composure and began to pace. "And what about Celeste?"

"Celeste is your daughter?" Howe asked.

"Yes. Is ... is she alive?" Jaxon asked, staring intently into Howe's eyes.

"The status of your daughter is unknown. When the team arrived at her residence, Lily's body was found lying on the living room floor, strangled to death. Your daughter was not on site. We assumed that she was fortunate enough to not be at home at the time of the invasion, but none of our efforts of locating her have panned out. For all we know, she could be simply staying at a friend's house—"

"How long ago?" Jaxon interrupted.

"This was two weeks ago," Evans said, chiming in for the first time since the director arrived.

Jaxon's head spun. "Two weeks? Two goddamn weeks and you're just now—"

"Listen, Jaxon. We're not sure who it was that killed Lily. We have a detachment on the scene. We have an additional team out looking for Celeste. Unfortunately, there is no trail to speak of, on either of their lifestyles. Lily, being a trained agent herself, knew how to cover her tracks. She and your daughter have lived for quite some time in obscurity. It took our internal investigators nearly a month to initially track them down."

Jaxon began to feel lightheaded. He retook his seat and rested his face on the palms of his hands. "Jesus. I've never even met my daughter. Well, I've seen her from a distance, but she doesn't even know who I am."

"Jaxon, I apologize for your loss. Sincerely, I do. I'm sure Lily was a great person and mother. But we're confident that Celeste is still alive, somewhere. She's a teen girl, and if she is anything like my own daughter, she'll no doubt turn up in a few days—"

"I've got to go find her," Jaxon said, more of a demand than a suggestion.

"I promise you, Jaxon, we have people on the task. The situation is being handled, and your expertise is needed elsewhere—"

"Right now, the only place I should be is looking for her. The rest of your plans can go to hell."

Howe smiled warmly. "I understand how you feel, Jaxon. I really do. But you have to realize that your assistance in the search would most likely cause more harm than good." Howe held up a hand, cutting Jaxon's interruption off. "Just hear me out. Although you are a highly trained agent, you've been inactive for the better part of a decade. You've been out of the public eye for nearly that entire time, at least down here on earth. In all that time, many things in society have changed. You'd be surprised how lost and disoriented you'd be if left to your own volition.

"The teams I have in place are earth-based and are highly trained. You have to trust me when I tell you that it's in everyone's best interest for you to let this be. Let them do their job, just like we let you do so many times in the past. You're too close to this, and your emotions would certainly cloud your judgment on your actions. Besides, there's still a kill order out for you, and until we know who's behind it, your life is still in danger. For all we know, Jaxon, whoever put the hit on you may have also killed Lily."

Jaxon sat in his chair, sulking. He hated to admit that Howe was correct, that he'd be completely useless if thrown back into the general population on earth. It pained him greatly to feel so lost and out of control.

"So, what? Do I just sit here and wait for you to find my daughter?" Jaxon asked.

"If we didn't have other pressing matters, that's exactly what we'd do. But there are circumstances in play that demand your attention. I offer you this, Jaxon. Agree to be read in on this highly sensitive mission and I am certain that you will understand the urgency. If you agree to the mission, upon its completion, you're welcome to return to the company and have the full resources behind you in investigating Lily's death and the location of your daughter, assuming we haven't found her by then."

Jaxon contemplated Howe's offer. He knew that his options were limited and that it was a slippery slope that he was on—risking the chance that they'd scrub his memory if he didn't agree. *That's how they normally got rid of agents,* as Howe himself said earlier.

The thought of being able to lead his own team again was appealing, and he knew the sooner that he completed the mission, the sooner he'd be able to be out there, looking for Celeste. The sooner he'd have his life back.

"Tell me about the mission," Jaxon said, leaning forward.

26

Howe leaned forward excitedly. "Do you agree to our terms? I need to hear you say it."

Jaxon sighed deeply. "It doesn't appear that I have any other recourse. So, it looks like you've got your man, director."

"Extraordinary. I have no doubt you've made the right decision," Howe said.

"Fine. Whatever. Just get on with it," Jaxon said, standing to pace once again.

Howe stood as well and began to stride alongside Jaxon. "The reason we felt that you were the best choice for this mission was because of your ties to a previous assassination. I'm not sure if you can recall—"

"Trust me, director. I remember every single assassination that you've sent me on. Vividly."

"This one goes quite a ways back. If memory serves, this was your first live training mission, and you were sent to assassinate El Tonto. It was in Ixtapa, Mexico and it was the summer of—"

"Yes. I remember. I inadvertently killed two men on that day, Ignacio Guzman himself and his son."

Howe nodded. "Yes, I suppose you would recall that mission distinctly. If it's any consolation, you only killed one person that day. El Tonto. You only maimed his son, but his injuries were severe enough that it looked as if you had taken his life."

Jaxon stopped in his tracks. "The company knew this the whole time? And nobody had the decency to tell me that I hadn't killed an innocent boy?" Jaxon asked, sensing his anger build once again.

"Relax, Jaxon. That information was withheld for your own protection. Pablo Guzman was an asset himself. His identity remained a secret, and if you had been read in on the entire file, you'd understand why."

"Then, what's changed? Why bring me up to speed now?" Jaxon asked, his impatience building.

"Because, Jaxon. It's Pablo himself that has changed. Shortly after that mission, he decided to sever all ties with the company and follow in his father's footsteps. At that point, the company elected to monitor his progress and only react when it was deemed necessary. For many years, the son struggled to equal his father's production levels, and we watched him stumble and fall many times. There were rivalries with other drug lord families throughout the region, and we hoped that natural selection would take over, and one of the other families would eliminate the target."

"Obviously, that hasn't happened," Jaxon said, filling in Howe's rhetoric, "otherwise you wouldn't need me to go after him. Am I close?"

"Precisely. Now, after years of struggling to reorganize the family business, Pablo Guzman has done something that no other drug family has been able to do in quite some time. He's developed a new drug that is quite different from anything that anyone has seen in our lifetime. The drug gives the user a euphoric feeling that is highly addictive. So addictive, in fact, that just a single dose of Whitetail is all that's necessary to cause severe dependency. Oh, and there's absolutely no side effects."

Jaxon's eyes widened as he listened to Howe. "How is that possible? No side effects at all? And with nearly instantaneous addictive qualities?"

"That's right. To make matters worse, the Guzman family has made those facts known and that it is basically a safe haven drug," Howe said. "Initially, they started selling it at a cost substantially less than any other drug on the market today. Then, around six months ago, a sharp price hike took the market by surprise. They've continued to increase the cost ever since, pricing it nearly twenty times more than heroin or cocaine. It's virtually priced out of nearly everyone's budgetary constraints."

"Why would Guzman do that?" Jaxon asked.

"Because he can. He knows the addictive nature of the drug will force people to pay, regardless of the consequences. Now, violence and terror have broken out in virtually every drug community in the world. The demand has skyrocketed, and Guzman has now reduced his production levels, continuing to drive the cost up. Actually, the man has devised a brilliant marketing technique, and if it weren't for the narcotic nature of his business, he'd probably win some kind of an award for his process."

"And your so-called chemists haven't been able to reverse engineer the drug? Find out what makes it so addictive?" Jaxon asked.

"There've been many attempts by some of the highest-trained chemists in the world, but each has been an epic failure. We feel the only solution to the problem is to eliminate the drug at the source."

"Kind of like cutting the head off the snake?"

Howe grimaced. "As I said before, we only want the production source to be eliminated. If there's a chance that you can remove the leader from the equation at the same time, that would be a bonus. But, let's be clear, that is not your main directive," he explained.

Jaxon stopped in front of a picture window that overlooked a pristine meadow surrounded by pine trees. The location they had chosen certainly was isolated. Jaxon stared out at the serene surroundings as he contemplated what the director told him. Of the countless assassinations that he'd been sent to carry out, it was that first one that remained so indelible. It was the only time an error had occurred throughout his illustrious career.

The news that the son had actually survived should have brought him joy. It did not. And now, the same company—the same organization that had sent him out to kill so many times before—was about to send him out once again. Jaxon smirked. He saw right through their bureaucracy about mission objectives. He knew the underlying order instantly, and it was to kill Pablo Guzman. Now, he really was in a no-win situation: accept the mission to kill a man that he'd already thought was dead, or refuse the mission and risk losing everything he'd ever known. Literally.

As he contemplated this, Jaxon wondered if the second option would be better in the long run. To erase the memories of every person that he'd killed had a certain appeal. But what else might he lose? The memory of Lily? Of Celeste? His parents? His childhood? When would it end?

"Jaxon?" Howe said, bringing him back to the present. "Is everything all right?"

"Yeah, I'm good. I was just ... thinking," Jaxon said. "So, what's the plan? Am I to go back to Mexico and cut the head off of the snake?"

"Not exactly. What we've been able to gather is that the drug is not being manufactured on earth. Our chemists have determined that the production cannot be replicated at our gravity level, so it stands to reason that it's being produced on a space station. Yet another reason we want you as our man," Howe said.

"Do we know which one or do you suggest I go gallivanting through space until I stumble upon the right one?" Jaxon asked, his words saturated with disgust.

"Ha. Perry said that you had a sense of humor," Howe said, smiling. "The answer to your question is both: yes *and* no. First, the no. We do not know precisely which station the facility is located on. We do, however, know that it is in the outer ring."

"Well, the outer ring was going to be my next stop on my run from the killers," Jaxon said.

Howe nodded his head. "The problem is that Pablo is known to occupy multiple stations in that region. His family business has grown since the development of the drug, and he's expanded his empire to cover prostitution, human trafficking, and gambling. You may or may not be aware, but there are at least a dozen casino and gambling houses scattered throughout the region. Your guess is as good as ours as to which station is being used to produce the drug."

"And you expect me to do this alone? It will take me months to track down the location."

"No, no. You'll have company. We'll be sending you with a team. Besides yourself, we've assembled three additional candidates to fill out your detachment."

"A single detachment to search through a dozen outer ring space stations? And all the while, I'll be avoiding a continual barrage of assassination attempts? Why not just send active agents that are already in the region? I know they exist; I was part of several detachments during my time with the company."

"In a perfect world, Jaxon, that's exactly what we'd do. However, Guzman has certain ... political ties around the world. Simply sending in a hit team in today's environment would be a bureaucratic nightmare," Howe said, dancing around the true mission directive.

"Exactly why I left the GSA. I was tired of being your weapon," Jaxon said, throwing the implied assassination back into Howe's face.

"Be that as it may, this is off book. Your team will consist of retired agents, along with a single chemist to aid in your search."

"So, I get an untrained scientist and two additional agents that are probably older than dirt? Am I clear on things?" Jaxon asked scornfully.

Howe stared at Jaxon impatiently. "The chemist who's going along has been fully trained as a field agent, although he has no real experience."

"And the two retired agents? Do I get to at least pick who I'll be working with?" Jaxon asked, Gillette's face flashing in his mind, as he would have been his number one choice. He cringed.

"Unfortunately, no. Your team has already been selected. As you might imagine, locating decommissioned agents that are suitable for field work is quite a challenge."

Jaxon nodded, fully realizing the gravity of the situation. The moment he saw Evans' face on that landing platform, he knew that he was screwed. Now, with everything that the director had just told him, he was confident in his initial gut reaction.

"Well, when do I get to meet my flunkies?" Jaxon asked, exasperated at the situation.

"Ironically, you've met one of them already. Miles Oliver has been fully briefed on the mission and is on site and ready to proceed."

"And the others? Besides the scientist, that is," Jaxon asked nervously. He sensed the director wasn't telling him everything.

"Ah, yes. The final member of your team is on her way as we speak."

A shocked look spread across Jaxon's face. "She?"

"Yes. I think you might even know her. The final member of your team is Camille Parker," Howe said, obviously aware of the implications of the past relationship.

"Sonofabitch," Jaxon mumbled. *Of all the people in the world, why did it have to be her?* Jaxon wondered.

As Jaxon digested this last bit of information, Howe retreated to his attaché and withdrew a commPad, a paper-thin communication and information device.

"The personnel files for your team are all on here. Give them a read through. And for God's sake, clean yourself up," Howe said, finally commenting on Jaxon's appearance. "You'll find everything you need in the lower levels of the facility. There's a barber on sublevel two that will fix you right up. After you've cleaned up, you can get outfitted on sublevel three. By then, the rest of your team should be on site, and you can begin planning your mission."

Jaxon lowered himself into a chair and stared blankly at the GSA logo emblazoned on the commPad. He contemplated how he would react when he saw her again. When he saw his fiancée—who, until now, thought he was dead.

After dropping his belongings off in his bunkroom on sublevel one, Jaxon proceeded to the showers to get cleaned up. Although he'd had a brief shower on the yacht, he could've spent hours underneath that showerhead, relaxing. He'd understood the effects of being off planet for an extended period of time would be substantial, but he was surprised at the severity.

When Jaxon felt that he'd used up the last drop of hot water, he reluctantly turned off the shower valve and dried off. Stepping out of the shower, he noticed that his clothing had been removed, and a pile of neatly folded fatigues had been left in their place. They were quite similar to what he'd worn when an active agent, but with some modern twists. The entire uniform seemed to fit him perfectly, and he questioned how they got his size so quickly.

His next stop was the so-called barber. He sat Jaxon down in the chair and went to work, cleaning up the rat's nest that existed on his head. Twenty minutes and eight inches of hair later, Jaxon was a new man. In addition to the drastic haircut, he'd gotten a close shave, saving a goatee at his request. Still, it was a drastic appearance change from what Jaxon had composed over the past eight years.

Back in his room, he stood in front of the mirror, continuing to analyze what would no doubt take some getting used to. The purpose of letting himself go, for so long, was no longer necessary. He didn't need to hide anymore, and he felt better about himself. His self-admitted admiration was halted by a knock on the door.

Jaxon opened the door to a friendly face. Evans stood alone, smiling. "Can I come in?"

Jaxon stepped aside, allowing the assistant director into his compact bunkroom.

"So. Quite an afternoon?" Evans said.

"I'll say," Jaxon said, taking a seat on his bed and glancing at the dossier for Camille.

"Have a chance to review any of that yet?" Evans asked, noting the file that was currently displayed.

"No, just got back a few minutes ago. I have to say, though, the team selection worries me a little," Jaxon said as he continued to skim through the pages of Cam's file.

"The director wasn't lying when he said that we had slim pickings. Most agents either die on the job or are promoted within the company. He's not about to pull some advanced agent out of some high-level office to give you assistance."

Jaxon nodded. "I get that, but Camille? Do you think she's the best choice, regardless of her qualifications? I'd almost be better off with a three-man team," Jaxon said as he got deeper into her file.

Evans remained silent as Jaxon continued to read.

Although fraternization inside the company was frowned upon, it was virtually inevitable in certain cases. Jaxon's case was one of them. His devotion to his job dictated that any outside relationships were fundamentally impossible. The company looked the other way when Jaxon and Camille became an item, electing to allow them a nominal semblance of a normal life.

"My God," Jaxon stammered. "They shut her down after the news of my death?"

"Well? What did you expect? She was in love with you, and she thought you were dead. You didn't think about cluing her in on your … departure?"

"I … I thought about it, but I didn't want to force her hand into something that she might regret. So, I felt it better for her to cope on her own." Jaxon let the commPad drop to the bed. "I guess I always thought that she loved the job more than she loved me, making the decision easier."

"Easier for her, or easier for you?" Evans asked.

Jaxon closed his eyes and leaned back. "Jesus, Perry, does she even know?"

"Not yet. When I reached out to her, she'd recovered surprisingly well from her mental breakdown. All she knows is there's a mission, and it's going to the outer ring. She knows it's a four-member team, but she's unaware of any individual identities. She'll be here in a few hours, and we'll have time to acclimate her to her new reality."

"Holy shit, a breakdown?"

"I was there when they told her about the explosion. She imploded instantly, not being able to cope with anything for quite some time. We gave her nearly nine months to recover, but she never did. She was able to function in society, but not to the level of an active agent. Not until recently, that is."

"What happened? Why the change?" Jaxon asked.

"Not sure. Perhaps it was just the passage of time."

Frustrated, Jaxon tossed the device across the bed. He glanced down at the display, and it flipped to the scientist.

"What about this one?" Jaxon asked, picking up the commPad again.

"Like the director said, he's a chemist, and he's green. In the sense of fieldwork, that is," Evans said, adjusting the lapels on his collar.

Despite being inactive for so long, Jaxon picked up on the

nervous tic instantly. "So, a scientist with no field experience. Great."

Evans glanced at his watch before continuing. "Well, it's as the director said. He's had simulated training, and we feel that he's a prime candidate for your team."

"What exactly about him makes him prime material for this mission?" Jaxon asked, noticing more signs of discomfort from Evans.

"He's a young, impressionable man. He's—"

"How young?" Jaxon asked as he delved deeper into the file.

"Compared to you and me? He's a child. He's twenty-three, but he's an accomplished scientist. He graduated from MIT with honors and came on to the GSA immediately. He's spent a few years in the research and development department of one of our subsidiary companies. About a year ago, the director brought him into our division, where he's successfully completed his training. He wants to make a difference, and both the director and I feel that with the right tutelage, he could develop into a talented asset."

Jaxon continued to observe Evans' suspicious behavior as he explained the attributes of the scientist. He began to wonder if his skills in observation were a little rusty, as his one-time handler quickly returned to his normal behavior. Then, right when he was about to dismiss the ordeal entirely, Jaxon noticed Evans look at his watch for the third time since coming in, and he was continually shifting his weight from foot to foot. *He's clearly holding something back regarding the scientist, but what?* Jaxon wondered.

"Yes. I think he'll do fine," Jaxon said, deciding to hold any further questions until later.

Jaxon closed the file on the chemist and opened the last one on the commPad. Miles Oliver. "What's the story on—"

Suddenly, the lights in the room flickered, and sirens began to blare. He studied Evans' reaction, and it was a cross between bewilderment and equal surprise. He was difficult to read.

"What's going on?" Jaxon asked, leaping to his feet.

"I ... I don't know. I'll find out," he said before stepping out into the hallway.

Jaxon shuffled nervously about his bunkroom, wondering if the assassins had somehow found out their location. With his advanced training kicking in, he quickly prepared for yet another bug-out. He grabbed his duffle and started tossing things in, beginning with his new environmental suit and helmet. Next, he threw in the commPad along with a number of other necessities that had been given to him upon his arrival. Within moments of completing his packing, the door burst open.

Evans looked at the packed bag and smiled. "Oh, yes. Your motto still stands, I see. Always be prepared," he said. "Looks like we have a change of plans. The compound is under some kind of attack, most likely more of the assassins coming after you. Sorry, old chap."

"Are you certain that's who it is? I've only been here for a few hours."

"Unknown. Very few people know this place even exists, so—"

"The mole? Did somebody leak that we were here?" Jaxon asked, slinging his bag over his shoulder.

"Again, unknown. There's a sport UTV in a storage shed at the back of the property. You and Miles need to get out quickly. As soon as you two sneak out the back door, I'll ... create some kind of diversion in hopes of drawing their attention away. Once you get on the road, head for the spaceport in New Mexico. Miles knows where it's at."

Jaxon knew as well, but it had been years since he'd been there. "Where exactly are we? Will the UTV have enough fuel for that distance?" Jaxon asked, concerned.

Evans rushed out into the hallway, leading Jaxon through the sublevel corridors. "Yes. We're only about a hundred miles away, and Miles has driven the route already. Besides, the quad is, how do I say it? Special? It has an energy drive system that doesn't require solid fuel. It's a new prototype that we've been developing for a few years. Trust me, you're going to have a blast," Evans said as he began to climb the stairs to the main level.

When they reached the landing, Miles had his duffel bag slung over his shoulder and was standing in an attack stance, his feet shoulder width apart. Jaxon nearly laughed out loud at how ridiculous the man looked.

"Relax, partner. We've got this," Jaxon said, then continued to explain the plan while Evans fumbled through a closet at the front of the cabin, looking for something in particular. A moment later, he called out to them.

"Okay, guys. On my mark, you need to move quickly. If this diversion goes as planned, you'll have a wide open window for at least several minutes."

Jaxon was not one to question Evans' motives. He'd learned to trust the man early on, and in situations like this, it paid off. "Ready."

Miles shuffled from side to side and simply nodded his head. Evans opened up the black box that he'd taken from the closet and pulled out an antenna. He flipped a couple of switches on the console, and a rumble could be heard out in front of the cabin. Jaxon's curiosity got the best of him, and he moved to a window and pulled a curtain to the side. What he saw caused him to smile.

"A remote-controlled decoy car?" Jaxon asked.

Evans returned his smile. It's a fully functional vehicle, with some added modifications from the company. If I drive the car away from the cabin, you boys should be clear to head in the other direction."

Jaxon walloped Evans on the back as he hustled toward the back door. He cracked it open, an inch at first, then a bit more, until he got a good view of the open field. From his vantage point, it was clear as far as the eye could see. But, for all he knew, there could be more killers in the forest beyond.

Exactly where they needed to go for their escape vehicle. Before stepping out into the open, Jaxon slipped his freshly issued energy pistol from his holster and flipped off the safety. "You ready?" he asked.

Miles nodded silently and pulled his own weapon out. Then, they stepped out and ran through the open field before ducking under the cover of the trees. Ten minutes later, they arrived at the storage shed, just where Evans said it would be. Once inside, they tossed their duffels into the compact cargo bed before they both moved toward the driver's seat.

"Sorry, pal. I'm driving," Jaxon said, slipping past Miles and into the seat. Miles huffed with disappointment and quickly moved around to the passenger side. Within moments, they were out of the shed and winding their way along a dirt road, heading for the unknown.

28

Unknown space station, located in the outer ring.

Pablo Guzman rolled over onto his back, panting heavily. "My Lord, Tosha. "Are you trying to kill me?" he asked.

The girl that lay next to him, less than half of Pablo's age, pulled herself up and on top of Guzman. "That was not my plan, Señor. But I can take you to the edge if you'd like." She leaned in and kissed Guzman passionately, driving her naked breasts into his chest.

It took all of Guzman's might to push her away, if only to give himself a moment to catch his breath. "Please, dear. At least let me rest for a few moments before—"

"What? Does this mean that you don't have what it takes to handle me completely?" Tosha asked with a pouty lip.

Guzman smiled and stared up into her hazel eyes surrounded by a deep cocoa complexion, and thought that he actually might be in love with this one. "Oh, I can handle you, my dear. In just a short time, I promise you that you'll be completely satisfied," Guzman begged.

Tosha sat up, straddling Guzman's naked body. She held herself upright by placing her hands on his chest then ground her pelvis over his. "Okay, Señor. I can wait a few minutes ... if you can," she said then giggled devilishly.

Guzman thrust his head back and closed his eyes in ecstasy. Every sensation in his body was heightened, and he was now quite positive that she was, in fact, trying to kill him with her sexuality. As his arousal returned rapidly, a knock came at the door.

"Wha ... What? Who is it?" Guzman asked angrily.

The door opened, and an armed guard stepped in. He looked at Guzman and Tosha, neither of them hiding their nakedness. Tosha smiled innocently as she rolled off of Guzman and laid along the edge of the bed, exposing her full frontal nudity to the guard.

"I, uh ... there is a call for you, Señor. It's from Brutus."

The anger in Guzman's eyes vanished instantly as he sprang from the bed. "What did he say?" he asked.

"Nothing, Señor. He's still holding and said that it's urgent," said the guard.

Guzman grabbed a robe from the bedside and quickly wrapped it around his shoulders before following the guard out into the hall. At the end of the hallway, a small room that housed three radio operators was open. Each of them monitored various communication sources.

"Give me privacy, dammit," Guzman snapped as he lowered himself into the chair in front of the computer terminal. He adjusted the headpiece and slipped it over his ear, placing the microphone in front of his mouth.

"This is Pablo. Brutus, are you there?" Guzman asked impatiently.

There was a slight delay in the transmission strength, due to the location of Guzman's space station in the outer ring. "Yes, Mr. Guzman. I read you. I know that direct contact is only to be used as a last resort, but I have urgent news."

"I only hope that the news you bring is that agent Jaxon Rasner has been eliminated," Guzman said, staring at a blank monitor. "And why aren't we on a vidphone? I want to see your face when you tell me this glorious message."

Another brief pause before the response.

"Unfortunately, a video connection at my present location is unachievable. And I won't be near a console for another few hours. We'll have to do this through voice only," Brutus said, hesitating between almost every word. "I, unfortunately, do not have the news that you wish for. Rasner is still alive, and our efforts to sidetrack his mission have failed. As I speak, the mission is proceeding as planned."

"Jesus Christ," Guzman yelled. "Your instructions were clear, and you continue to fail me at every step. You've known about his location for, what? A year and a half? And you disregard my advice to eliminate him before your prestigious company can assemble a plan to bring him back? And now, you tell me that the mission is proceeding?"

Guzman leaned back in the chair and cursed at the unavoidable delay in communication.

"I understand that you're upset, Mr. Guzman. But please know that—"

"I don't want to hear your excuses, Brutus. We've known each other far too long for lies. I want results. If you cannot handle my simple requests, perhaps I need to reevaluate who it is that I associate myself with in your GSA."

After a longer than expected period of silence, Guzman began to flip random switches in an attempt to clear the connection. "Brutus! Did you understand my last—"

"That won't be necessary, Pablo," Brutus said, using Guzman's first name, which he rarely did. "All is not lost."

"Yes, I'm listening," Guzman said anxiously.

"Although Rasner's team has been assembled and they are in route to their ship, their approach and plan have weaknesses," Brutus said. "First off, his team consists of only himself and three additional members. There will be no further support from the GSA. Secondly, the ship that he's been given is of a new design that might be of particular interest to you. It has been equipped with top of the line technologies that will make them virtually undetectable unless you're staring out a portal window."

"I understand your point about the small team, but you lost me on the undetectable ship. How is that a weakness?" Guzman demanded.

"You see, unless you have the specific code for their individual ship, it is very much untraceable."

"And you have this specific code?" Guzman prompted eagerly.

"Yes, of course. I have the code for their ship, along with the identities of the entire team. I'm unable to prevent them from departing, but once they've launched ... all an approaching ship would have to do is key the code into their targeting computer, and our problem can be eliminated," Brutus said, confident that his news was positive.

Guzman listened intently as Brutus explained the procedure. After jotting down an unfathomably long digital code, he folded up the paper and held it firmly in his hand.

"Assuming that the code is valid, you may have just avoided a very unpleasant *circumstance* for you and your family, Brutus," Guzman said, accentuating the mole's code name. "It would be quite unfortunate if our ongoing relationship was suddenly made public."

"I assure you, the code is valid. I presume you have a team in place?" Brutus asked.

Guzman nodded. "Yes, yes. Despite losing twelve men on Taloo Station, and an additional four in Luna City, I have plenty of warriors willing take their places."

There was yet another long pause before Brutus replied.

"Unfortunately, more of your men were lost on earth today as well. I was confident that the hit was to be a success, but unforeseen circumstances changed the outcome."

Guzman unfolded the paper and read through the information once again. He smiled. "Those were mere peasants. They were local workers from my home village, and the loss of their lives means nothing to me. All I want is my revenge. I want Jaxon Rasner dead!"

Guzman disconnected the connection without waiting for Brutus to respond. He dropped the headset onto the desk and walked out of the communications office. As he reached his bedroom, he slipped the folded paper into the pocket of his robe. He had plenty of time to deal with that later. First, he had unfinished business to attend to.

"Tosha," Guzman said playfully. "Where are you?"

29

After several hours of driving across mountainous terrain and finally into the vast plains, Jaxon could see the spaceport in the distance. They were about twenty minutes out, and his mind had not stopped thinking about the relentless attack on his life. *Besides Howe and Evans, who else had known about the location?* Jaxon looked sideways at his travel companion, Miles Oliver, but quickly dismissed the suspicion because he would hardly have known about the depths of his own cover. *Unless he was working with somebody else.*

"Hey, Miles. When did they recruit you for this … mission?" Jaxon asked, hoping to utilize their last bit of privacy in hopes of obtaining some information.

"A few months back, maybe?" Oliver replied, not taking his eyes off the road ahead of them.

"That a question? Or, are you just not sure about your own immediate history?" Jaxon asked, noting that his companion was not particularly wordy.

Oliver turned toward Jaxon, his face deadpan, and said,

"A few months back," annunciating the end of the statement.

Jaxon decided to let him be with the questioning but had another thought to get him talking. "Why don't you use that radio in the glove box and reach out to someone? I don't care who, but just find out what happened back at the safe house. I'd like to know if Evans and Howe made it out safely."

Oliver opened the glove compartment and withdrew the small, hand-held radio. He held it up to his mouth, but before pressing the call button, he looked at Jaxon.

"I'm confused," Oliver said. "Why do you want me to find out if the director made it out safely when he left the compound more than an hour before the attack?"

"That's news to me," Jaxon said. "I must have been down in the sublevels when he left. At least not everyone was in danger during the attack." As the words left Jaxon's mouth, he began to wonder if the timing of Howe's departure was a coincidence or something else entirely.

"Who else was at the compound?" Jaxon asked.

"Besides you and me, and the assistant director, I think there were a few staff members in the sublevels. But how many and who they were, I'm not sure. Do you still want me to call in?"

Jaxon downshifted as he came up on a tight turn then headed directly toward the spaceport. "Yeah, why don't you? Perry, I mean the assistant director, and I go way back. I'd like to know if he's safe. Ask about the rest of our team as well. Evans said that he'd redirect them to the spaceport. I'm just not sure if he got that message out or not."

Over the next 10 minutes, Oliver did as Jaxon asked, retrieving as much information about the incident as possible. At the end of multiple radio conversations, it was clear that the assistant director did, in fact, survive the ordeal. Oliver also learned that contact was in fact made with Francisco and Camille. They were also advised that the director had arrived at the spaceport just moments ago, surprising everyone on site.

Oliver tossed the radio back into the glove compartment as Jaxon maneuvered the vehicle into a parking stall along the perimeter of the security fence.

Grabbing their gear from the cargo bed, Jaxon and Oliver made their way to security, Jaxon's gut turning the entire time. He wasn't sure how Camille would react to his presence. He was relieved, however, that he could be present when she learned about his mortality.

Taking his ID back from the guard, they stepped through the gate and into the facility. Jaxon hoped that he'd be able to meet with her alone—before the rest of the team was assembled—to allow him time to explain the situation. But, with the director already on site, he doubted he'd have the opportunity.

As they rounded the corner toward their designated hanger, Jaxon caught sight of their assumed spaceship. The bay door was open, and just inside was the most advanced flying ship that he'd ever seen. It was aerodynamic and sleek in appearance. The surface was practically free of any screws or rivets. It was as it were formed out of a single skin. The color was charcoal gray and had a matte finish.

It took several moments for either Oliver or Jaxon to realize that they'd stopped in their tracks and were staring in fascination. "Pretty incredible, wouldn't you say?" Jaxon asked.

Oliver remained silent but nodded his head in agreement.

"You took the words right out of my mouth, Miles," Jaxon said with a smile.

As they walked into the hangar, Jaxon noticed several men in uniform surrounding the ship, assault weapons slung over their shoulders. At the base of the boarding ramp, Jaxon caught sight of Camille for the first time and his heart skipped a beat. Before he was close enough for her to notice he was there, she was already climbing up the ramp. Behind her, the director stood, solemnly, with his hands clasped behind his back. Jaxon and Oliver approached.

"Ah, you made it!" Howe said excitedly. "I understand there was a ... skirmish at the safe house. I'm glad to see that you two made it out alive."

"You'd think that by now, after countless attempts on my life, they'd realize that I'm a tough man to kill," Jaxon said. "And Miles here, well, let's just say that he appears to be equally indestructible," Jaxon said, slapping him on the back.

A blank expression remained on Oliver's face before he stepped up onto the ramp and disappeared into the ship.

"Strange, that guy," Jaxon said. "He's really the best that you could get?"

"Let's not recapitulate things that have already been discussed. How about we introduce you to the rest of your team?" Howe said, more of a statement than a question.

"About that, I was thinking—"

Before Jaxon could finish his plea of talking with Camille alone first, the director had already started up the ramp. Jaxon fell in behind him, taking a deep breath to prepare for what was certain to be an awkward situation.

J axon followed the director up the boarding ramp, which landed at what appeared to be the centermost part of the ship. The main hold. It gave access to all parts of the compact ship, much like a central hub. Along the perimeter of the oversized bay, Jaxon noticed multiple cargo lockers intermixed with various access doors. Opposite the boarding ramp was another ramp, leading up to what was most likely the control center of the ship. On either side of the ramp, ship's ladders dropped down to lower gangways. To the right and left of the boarding ramp, additional ladders led up to a metal grate platform that circled the entire holding bay. Off of that platform were several more doors, most likely leading to engineering and the weaponry. The entire vessel seemed smartly designed, and if it hadn't been for his bundled-up nerves about seeing Camille, Jaxon would certainly be giddy about taking the ship out on its first mission.

The director stopped in the middle of the hold and re-clasped his hands behind his back. There were nearly a half dozen other people working about, emptying supply crates or programming the various control panels scattered around the bay. Camille stood at the far end of the bay with her back toward them. She appeared to be in conversation with another man, who looked up just then and recognized the director standing, stoically, seemingly waiting for someone to call attention to his presence. The man broke off the conversation with Camille and cleared his throat, straightening his back. Camille noticed the change in his demeanor and turned to look at the source.

A sudden urge to vomit overcame Jaxon, but he swallowed hard, forcing the bile back into his stomach. He couldn't remember being this nervous in his entire life. He watched intently as Camille turned, her eyes first locking onto the director, then onto himself.

Jaxon had never forgotten how beautiful her tanned skin was, kissed from the sun above. After all those years of not seeing her, he was pleased to see that some things never change. The toned complexion, however, did not last. The blood drained from Camille's face as recognition set in. Camille remained frozen in place, unable to move.

"Good afternoon, everyone. I'd like to thank you all for your efforts in making this ship flight ready on such short notice. If you're not part of the crew, please exit the ship now," Howe said, watching Camille's reaction to their presence.

The cargo bay erupted into hushed murmurs and shuffling of feet as the various support personnel completed their tasks at hand and made for the rear exit way. As the final technician stepped onto the exit ramp, Director Howe continued.

"Fantastic. It looks like we're all here now. Unfortunately, Assistant Director Evans will not be able to see you off. He ... got held up back at the safe house, but he sends best wishes on a fruitful mission to you all."

Jaxon continued to gaze into Camille's eyes, Camille still frozen in time. The man standing next to her stepped forward, blocking their eye contact.

"This is our mission leader, I presume?" the man said,

moving toward Jaxon.

"Yes, that's right," Jaxon said, stepping around Howe. "I'm Jaxon Rasner, and you must be Clay Francisco?" he said, extending his hand.

Clay took Jaxon's hand and pumped it vigorously. "I am. But, your name? Is it—"

"Yes, I'm *that* Jaxon Rasner. Rumors of my death have been overly exaggerated."

"I ... I can't believe it. Is it really you?" Camille said, stuttering hysterically. "I was at your funeral."

Jaxon's nausea finally subsiding, he moved toward Camille. "It's me, Cam, and I know what you must be feeling right now."

"How? How can you even? How ... how are you even alive? You're dead, they said, they ... said you were dead." Tears brimmed in Camille's eyes.

Jaxon stepped closer, minding not to crowd her too soon. "I know what they said, and none of it's true. I'm here, and I'm alive. And—"

"Stop! Just stop it," Camille screamed and rushed out of the main hold, nearly falling in the process. Jaxon watched in horror as she vanished.

Jaxon took in a deep breath and exhaled slowly. He turned back toward the rest of the crew and was met with questioning eyes from both Francisco and Oliver.

"Jaxon," Howe said. "Would you like to delay departure until—"

"No," Jaxon said firmly. "I'll handle this. Is the ship ready to go?" He glanced at Francisco and Oliver.

"We're fully supplied," Francisco said.

"It's okay, Jaxon. We can launch tomorrow," Howe began again.

"No, that's not necessary. Is the ship fueled?" Jaxon asked.

Howe nodded. "It was completed moments before your arrival."

"Good. Now get off my ship and I'll take things from here,"

Jaxon said, turning his back on the director and heading to flight control. Oliver followed Jaxon's lead, walking by the director, silent as usual.

All that remained were Francisco and Director Howe.

"Well then. Good luck on your mission ... Francisco?"

"Yes, it's Clay Francisco. Do I need to show you the way out?" he asked.

"No, I'm quite familiar," Howe said then turned on his heels and walked off the ship.

Minutes later, the ship's engines fired, and it hovered out of the hangar before rising up into the sky.

In flight control, Jaxon sat at the pilot station with Oliver in the copilot. Jaxon requested authorization for departure, which the tower promptly granted. Severing communication, he looked at Oliver.

"Miles, think you can handle things for a while?"

Oliver looked at Jaxon apologetically. "Sure thing, boss. I'm sure you'll find her down in the crew quarters."

Jaxon smiled and slapped Oliver on the back as he moved out of the cockpit.

Jaxon knocked on the only closed door on the cabin level. He imagined the sound of tears emanating from the other side of the door but dismissed the thought due to the thickness of the titanium-skinned panel. He knocked again and definitely heard something after the second attempt.

"G-go away!" Camille yelled from inside.

"If you'd just give me a minute to explain," Jaxon yelled loud enough for her to hear.

"Not n-now," Camille said, stuttering.

Jaxon knew that unless they talked—the sooner, the better—the success of the mission could be jeopardized. Being familiar with the locking mechanism on the door, he pushed a series of buttons, and the door slid open.

"Can't you just leave me alone?" Camille sobbed.

Jaxon stepped in and closed the door. He lowered himself next to Camille, sitting on the edge of her bed. "I'm sorry, Cam. I ... I'm a horrible person for not telling you sooner."

Camille tucked her chin to her chest and closed her eyes. Jaxon could see she was hurting. He decided that silence right now was probably the best medicine, so he sat there, patiently resisting the urge to console her.

Jaxon thought back to the moment he'd decided to leave the company and his rationale for not telling her about the plan. At the time, they'd been engaged for only a few months, and although the relationship wasn't strained, it lacked the spark that he'd always figured would be associated with true love.

It wasn't until just then that he fully realized his mistake. "I won't lie to you," Jaxon began. "I faked ... well, Gillette and I faked our deaths to get away from the company. We'd seen what happens if you remain active for too long, and neither of us liked what we saw."

Jaxon paused to see if Camille wanted to hear more. Her breathing slowed slightly, quieting her tears. He continued. "I had already made the decision before we were engaged, and I even delayed things several times to try and figure things out. Then, something changed. Something in how we were. I think you felt it too, or at least that's how it seemed at the time.

"Anyway, Gillette and I were put on a mission that was particularly attractive for our departure, and I had no time to tell you of the plan. I'd always had intentions of reaching out to you and bringing you into the loop at some point. But the longer I was away, the better I thought you'd be without me."

"What gives you the right," Camille said, raising her head to look at Jaxon, "to make decisions for me? I was completely in love with you then, and I was so afraid I'd mess things up that I stopped reacting to every little thing. I didn't want to"—she broke into tears once again—"I didn't, I didn't want to scare you away by being too clingy."

Jaxon felt a lump in his throat grow. He'd felt horrible for a long time afterward, and he never thought it possible to feel worse. Until now. "I really am sorry. I know my words can't give you back the last eight years, but if you could at least understand why I did this, you might be able to find it in your heart to forgive—"

"Were you not listening to me? You want me to forgive you? Do you even know what I've been through since you selfishly removed yourself from my life? Hell no, I won't forgive you! I agreed to this mission, and I'll see it through. But if it's not mission related, I don't want to see you. Now, get out!"

Jaxon was startled by her candor. Her pain clearly was deeper than Jaxon ever thought. He listened to her wishes and stepped out of her room.

Jaxon walked back into the cockpit, reclaiming his seat at the pilot's station. As he slumped down, his mood was clearly visible. His brow dipped at the center, and frown lines pulled at his lips.

"Went that good, huh?" Oliver asked.

Jaxon glowered at his copilot, his frown lines growing deeper. "You know, Miles, we haven't known each other for very long. But, you know how you do that one thing? You know? That one thing where you're silent? Now would be a good time for that."

"Sorry," Oliver said, stretching out the syllable in his apology. He looked forward again and adjusted a setting on his control panel.

Jaxon regretted his words the moment they passed his lips. "Hey, I'm the one that's sorry. I was out of line. It's just that Camille and I have ... a history and—"

"It's all right, boss. No need to explain. We all have issues with the ladies from time to time," Oliver said, staring ahead.

"Regardless, I was out of line, and if we're going to be

157

successful on this mission, I cannot alienate anyone on the team."

"Apology accepted," Oliver grunted.

"So, what's our status? Are we in line for departure assistance?" Jaxon asked, studying the display on the control panel in front of him.

"No, sir. It's my understanding that the engines on this ship are some kind of prototype jobs that are strong enough to escape Earth's gravity unassisted."

"No shit? I thought we were still decades away from that technology."

"Well, you haven't exactly been around for the lion's share of the last decade, now have you?" Oliver asked pointedly.

Jaxon openly gawked at him, astounded by his quick wit. "You certainly got me there," he said, knowing instantly that he liked the man and looked forward to working beside him on the mission.

"So, what are we waiting for? Let's get on with gettin' on," Jaxon said, paraphrasing a quote his father used to say.

Oliver danced his fingers across the control panel and within moments, the thrust of the ship pushed Jaxon firmly into his seat. As the ship continued to accelerate, Jaxon watched the digital readout rapidly increase its speed. After several minutes of solid thrust, the forward momentum of the ship seemed to slow down, despite the rapidly increasing speed on the display. Then, the force that had pushed him into his seat just moments before relented even further as his body began to float up from the seat. He reached across his control panel and activated the artificial gravity generator, suspending the weightless feeling that was overtaking him.

"Why don't you set a course for the first checkpoint station, then we'll gather on the observation deck to discuss the mission with the entire team," Jaxon said.

Before Oliver could respond, Jaxon walked out of the cockpit—his mind elsewhere.

Finding his duffel bag in his sleeping quarters, Jaxon rummaged through to the bottom and withdrew his commPad before heading up to prepare for the team meeting. As he stepped out into the corridor, he contemplated checking in on Camille but remembered her last words to him: *I don't want to see you.* Wisely, Jaxon walked past her door and continued on to the observation deck.

When he arrived, Francisco had finished stowing all of their gear and even set up for chairs around a small but serviceable table. Jaxon pulled up a chair and activated his tablet. As he waited for it to boot up, there was a loud blast right outside the hull of the ship. Seconds later, the entire ship lurched to the side, nearly knocking Jaxon to the floor. The lights flickered then turned to amber as warning alarms blared throughout the ship.

"Jesus," Jaxon exclaimed as he bolted for the cockpit.

"Status," Jaxon demanded as he rushed in.

"Believe it or not, boss, it appears we're under attack," Oliver said, executing a series of evasive maneuvers.

Jaxon leapt into the pilot's station and fastened his safety harness. Not having adequate time to fully review the ship's operations, he was at a loss on how to activate the stealth device or even raise the shields. "I'm flying blind here, Miles. I don't suppose Evans or Howe gave you the rundown on the ship's operations?"

"No, not entirely," Oliver said as he increased the thruster speed and careened sharply to the left, narrowly missing a stream of laser blasts. "Just navigation and velocity—"

"What the hell's going on?" demanded Camille as she stepped into the cockpit, closely followed by Francisco.

"What's it look like?" Jaxon snapped. "We're under attack, and unless either of you know anything about the defensive aspects of the ship, this will be a very short mission."

Francisco stepped around Camille and sat down at the gunnery station, analyzing the display. "I … studied a bit of the weaponry while I was waiting for the rest of the team to arrive."

"Great. Find out who's attacking us and shoot something in their direction. Give us some time to figure out how to turn on the damn stealth device," Jaxon ordered.

Camille stepped up to the remaining console in the cockpit and accessed the station's display. "I'll get the stealth up. Howe had me analyze the system last week."

At least somebody knows what the hell is going on with the ship, Jaxon thought.

"How about shields?" Jaxon asked as he flipped through multiple screens at his own console. "Oh wait, never mind. I found it."

Jaxon activated the shields, but the ship had already taken several indirect hits, weakening the shield strength by nearly twenty-five percent.

Suddenly, a new set of alarms blared throughout flight control. Oliver projected the short-range sensor array onto the main screen. It showed their ship's position at center screen, surrounded by four other ships. One of which had just launched a mass accelerator cannon directly at them.

"Evasive maneuvers!" Jaxon yelled.

"Got it," Oliver said, adjusting the pitch of their ship and rolling down and to the right. The g-force nearly threw Camille and Francisco to the ground, as they hadn't fastened their safety harnesses yet.

"That was close," Jaxon said, staring at the developing ambush displayed on the view screen. "At such close quarters, I don't see how we can react any faster until we can get that stealth device up and running."

"Jesus, Jax, I'm working on it!" Camille said, using her old pet name for him.

Oliver continued to avoid most of the non-lethal attacks as everyone else watched the screen with anticipation.

"Almost there," Camille said as her fingers punched at the console in front of her. "And ... it's active!"

On the view screen, the image of their ship faded from

stark white to a barely visible gray, indicating that they were no longer visible to long or short-range sensors.

"Fantastic, Cam," Jaxon said happily. "Now, Miles, get us out of here."

Oliver punched in a new course and was about to hit ENGAGE when Jaxon stopped him.

"Wait! I have an idea," Jaxon said, taking over the ship's navigational controls. He promptly moved the ship so that it was right behind one of their attackers. All four of the attacking vessels continued to randomly fire on the spot where they were last visible.

"What are you doing, Jax?" Camille asked. "We don't have time for this! We need to put as much space between them and us before they catch on."

"Relax. Perry assured me that this stealth prototype is virtually undetectable. I want to test this for myself before we can fully trust its capabilities. We watch and wait."

The tension in the control room was palpable. The alarms had silenced, and it was eerily calm throughout the room. All four sets of eyes remained focused on the large view screen.

After a few moments, the surrounding ships ceased their attack, no doubt finally realizing that they were firing at nothing. The moments ticked by, almost painfully, for the team. Once it was clear that the attackers had no idea what just happened, Jaxon smiled and leaned back.

"See? What did I tell you? We're out—"

Suddenly, the ship they were hiding behind exploded without warning, launching debris in all directions. Seconds after the explosion, firepower from the remaining three ships once again focused on their location.

"What the hell?" Jaxon yelled. "They shouldn't be able to see us. Camille!"

"I don't know. It tells me the device is active, but it's clear they know exactly where we're at."

Jaxon's mind flashed back to the conversation he and Evans had earlier about a suspected mole in the company. He wondered if information leaked about their presence in the sector, and more importantly the technology of their prototype stealth device.

Jaxon unfastened his safety harness and quickly moved to Camille's console. "Is there a way we can restart the system? Perhaps they've somehow locked onto some device signature? I just don't know enough about the system to know how it works."

"I don't think we have enough time for that, but what you just said gives me an idea," Camille said as she accessed a submenu on her display.

Jaxon stood beside her as she scrolled through several settings. Finally, she slowed her pace and brought up the device code dialog box. The system cursor blinked rhythmically, waiting for a user input.

"Well, it looks like we can change our identification sequence. By changing this unique code, we should be able to assign our frequency, and, with any luck, confuse their targeting software."

"Do it. And quickly," Jaxon said, resting his hand on her shoulder.

Camille deleted the current twelve-digit code then typed in a replacement number. Completely random. She tapped the execute button, and several other settings on the display changed over the next few seconds. Once the adjustment finished processing, Jaxon returned to his seat.

"Miles, now, get us out of here."

"You want me to park behind one of the other ships?" Oliver asked.

"Hell no. Just put some distance between them and us. We'll know if they've adapted their frequencies if they chase after."

Oliver entered a new destination into the navigational computer and hit execute. The ship lurched ahead, speeding away from the ambush. Jaxon continued to monitor the sensor array. Waiting. The remaining ships continued to fire blindly at their last location until they finally stopped. Jaxon watched eagerly, waiting to see if they turned to follow. They didn't move.

"That did it," Jaxon said, turning back and seeing Camille's satisfied face. "Can you set it up so that the computer randomly changes that code every few hours? You know, just in case they have some other kind of access to our system? Another back door?"

"Yeah, I think I can. Let me—" Camille trailed off as she began typing new commands at her console.

Jaxon let her be as he contemplated their next move. He still needed to fill the team in on the full mission details, and then probably talk a bit about his own past and just who it was that was attacking them. If he'd only known.

"I think it's time you all know the full gravity of our situation," Jaxon began. "First off, after what just happened, I'm positive that there is, in fact, a mole in the company."

32

Jaxon remained seated at the pilot's station and swiveled around to face his team. Stunned expressions covered most of their faces, save for Miles. His outward appearance remained his usual indifferent blankness.

"What makes you think that?" Camille asked.

"First off, both Director Howe and Assistant Director Evans mentioned the possibility of the mole. They had no conclusive evidence about the accusation, but too many coincidences have occurred lately; this last one certainly reinforces the argument. To be specific, our departure wasn't technically scheduled for another day, possibly two. But because of the attack at the compound, which also seems far too coincidental, our schedule was hastily escalated. The list of potential suspects is very limited—probably around eight to ten people—that the mole could be, present company included."

"If it were one of us," Francisco said, "do you think we'd still be on the ship if we were trying to blow it up?"

Jaxon nodded. "Valid question, Clay, but there's a lot that I don't know ... about all of you. And frankly, there's only one person on the ship that I trust," Jaxon said, glancing toward Camille, "and the other two need to earn it."

An awkward silence filled the room.

Oliver continued to monitor the sensor array, cautiously, but remained in the conversation. "So, are you going to tell us all what the hell is going on? he asked.

"First off, what have each of you been told about our mission or about myself?" Jaxon asked.

Camille began. "I was only told about a top-secret mission, which would involve the Guzman drug family, and that's about it. There was no indication about you, or the rest of the team for that matter."

"Clay?" Jaxon asked.

"Same as Camille. I've been in the loop about the drug family for a few months now, but back then, they only told me that the team lead was still being recruited."

Jaxon looked toward Oliver.

"Obviously, I've known about your situation longer," Oliver said. "I was read into your situation about four weeks ago, and I was shipped up to the moon base a few days before your arrival at Luna City."

Jaxon pursed his lips as he contemplated how much information to share. If he wanted to gain the trust of the entire team, he felt that full disclosure was probably the best course of action.

"I'll first start with my own status," Jaxon began. "I was an active agent for the GSA for the better part of nine years. Toward the end of my term, my partner and I both realized that our future with the company looked grim. We'd watched too many top-shelf agents either die in the line of duty or be forced into a less than desirable retirement, some having their minds erased due to concerns of divulgence. We decided at the time that we'd rather go out on our own terms. We organized our own assumed deaths." Jaxon paused to study each of the expressions on his team's faces. Oliver was blank, as usual. Clay showed surprise, and Camille's expression was the worst.

She looked pained for having to endure the explanation again.

"That was eight years ago, and my partner Gillette and I were able to go our separate ways and live in secrecy until earlier this week. That's when a hit was taken out on my life. Out of the blue, a small army of assassins have been on my tail, trying to end me. Even now, it remains unknown who is behind the hit. According to the director, that is. The attacks on me began on Taloo Station and carried over into Luna City. The raid on the safe house is also in question. And now, I can only assume that the ambush just minutes ago is part of that same assault. Besides Miles here, I feel that the director has given you each a disservice for not explaining the entire situation before we left. For that, I apologize. Your lives have been put into certain peril until we can neutralize the kill order."

Camille's facial expression suddenly changed. It softened at hearing more of Jaxon's background. "Do you think it was someone at the company?" she asked.

Jaxon nodded. "That is certainly a possibility. It seems that our *prototype* stealth device wasn't as invisible as we were told. It's all too clear that our unique signature frequency has gotten into the hands of some very bad people. If that's not a clear indication of a mole in the company, then I don't know what is."

Oliver whistled softly as the implications of a traitor in their midst were fully realized. "Am I the only one not completely privy as to what our real mission is?" he asked.

"Okay, here's what I know. Pablo Guzman has developed a drug that has severe addictive qualities. Our directive is to track down the production facility located somewhere in the outer ring and cease its operations. Based on what I've seen of our ship and its capabilities, I think we take the easy way out. We locate the station where the drug is being produced, and we neutralize the operation from space. We blow it up."

Francisco gasped. "But what about all the innocent people that would be on that station? You'd be killing hundreds of people."

"We don't know that for certain, Clay. If my intuition is correct, the production facility won't be on any normal station. I don't think Pablo would be naïve enough to mix business with pleasure to that degree. I might be wrong here, but I think the information that has been given to us is only half true. I think the list of possible space station candidates is part of a ruse to keep us preoccupied long enough for a lucky assassin to carry out the hit on my life. Personally, I like living, and I'm not about to give them the satisfaction. It's my intention to shoot first and ask questions later. The sooner we get on with this mission and finish it, the sooner we can all get back to our normal lives. Any questions?" Jaxon asked.

Francisco raised his hand, as if a nervous school boy.

"Go ahead, Clay. We're not very formal here," Jaxon said.

"Well, it appears that I have a different agenda than you, which has also come down from the director himself. I'm supposed to get eyes on the factory and obtain their manufacturing procedures of the drug. If possible, I'm also supposed to round up as many samples of the drug as I can before leaving the station."

Jaxon contemplated Francisco's words. "If Evans or Howe has given you a separate agenda, then so be it. My mission is clear, and it is to stop the production of the drug by any means necessary. At the end of the day, the manufacturing facility will be destroyed, and all I can say is that you best be on the ship when the last explosion ignites, if you want a ride back."

Francisco's face showed shock, Oliver simply nodded, and Camille now read indifferently in her expression.

"Miles, how long until we get to our first outer ring space station?" Jaxon asked.

Oliver turned to his console and brought up the navigation computer. He entered in a few keystrokes, and the ETA displayed on the screen. "A little less than thirty-six hours, boss," he said. "But didn't you just say that we wouldn't find the factory on any of the listed stations?"

"Yes, that's right. But we need to start somewhere. We'll need to get onto a station or two and ask some questions. We don't want to rock the boat too much, but right now we're flying blind and we need to get intel on Guzman's operation."

The flight deck drew quiet as the team individually pondered what they'd just learned. Once it was clear that no more questions were being put forth, Jaxon stood and headed for the door. Before stepping out, he paused and turned to look at his team.

"I'll be in my quarters if any of you have any further questions. I suggest we get some rest and be ready when we get to station number one."

With that, Jaxon turned and walked down the ramp, disappearing from view.

33

Having frequented many of the outer ring space stations through the years, Jaxon knew what to expect when in the region. Through conversations with the rest of his team, it became clear that he was the only one that had that exposure.

Camille Parker, despite having been an active agent in the past, had never had the opportunity to step foot on a spaceship, let alone journey into the outer ring. Her region was earth based.

Clay Francisco was the youngest of their group and had the least amount of experience, having only been trained through simulation. Jaxon was very concerned about his role in the operation, as so much of what they did was improvisational. Francisco was a chemist, and his lack of field experience could very well put the entire team at risk.

Miles Oliver, despite his propensity for silence, possessed the greatest advantage of anyone else on the team. Besides Jaxon himself, that is. Oliver had been active for many years, but Jaxon still had his reservations. Mostly due to his dossier.

The majority of Oliver's final year as an agent had been redacted. In the hours before their arrival at the first station, Jaxon tried to broach the subject with him but was stonewalled with yet more silence. Regardless, Jaxon's gut instinct said he needn't worry about Oliver, but also to keep a watchful eye on him.

As Oliver docked the ship, Jaxon readied the team to disembark. "The first thing they're going to do is do a weapons check," Jaxon said, looking at each of the team members as he spoke. "Now is not the time to try and guess exactly where you could hide a knife or a pistol and have it get through their detectors. Despite the corruption that runs rampant in the outer ring, most of the stations are virtually weapon free, save for the security personnel throughout each station, who are typically armed to the hilt. We're just here for a bit of *entertainment*, right?"

Everyone nodded, while Jaxon held Oliver's eyes a moment longer. Satisfied that he'd made his point, he proceeded.

"All right. As we discussed, we'll work in pairs. It'll be Cam and I covering the bars and clubs while you two head to the pavilion," Jaxon said. "Just find out what you can, and keep an eye out for prostitutes, boys. Those women are trained professionals." Jaxon winked. "They'll easily remove you from your money and not think twice about it."

Jaxon resisted laughing out loud as the blood drained from Francisco's face. He looked petrified, but pairing him with Oliver was probably the safest bet. Or so he thought.

The airlock opened, and they stepped through the docking ring and into the space station. Jaxon led them aboard, handing his falsified travel documents to the attendant at the security line.

The man was dressed in a charcoal-colored jumpsuit with an orange insignia embroidered on his sleeves. After only a few moments of scrutinizing the documents, he handed them back to Jaxon.

"Next," the attendant said, dismissing Jaxon.

Jaxon hesitated briefly, but when it was clear that they expected him to continue on into the station before Camille could step forward, he reluctantly left her behind.

Jaxon wandered to the edge of the moderately sized atrium just beyond the security checkpoint. He looked up and saw three levels of casinos, bars, and restaurants, all located above the shopping district that meandered around the main level. It was all quite similar to the promenade on his own Taloo Station. Moments later, Camille joined Jaxon, having passed through security without protest.

"Listen, I didn't say anything earlier, but as long as you're paired with me, we'll have to be more alert because of the potential of another assassination attempt," Jaxon said.

Camille leaned on the rail, the warmth of her arm touching Jaxon's. "That goes without saying," she said. "If I had a problem with it, I would've asked to be paired up with Miles."

Jaxon breathed a sigh of relief, not knowing exactly what to expect from her. In the brief time that they'd been around each other, her emotions had been quite scattered, and he couldn't blame her. He could only imagine the emotional roller coaster that she'd been on recently.

"Wow. This is … not quite what I was expecting," Camille said, looking up at the many levels of flashing neon lights and scores of people living on the edge. "I assumed from all of the cautionary tales that both you and the director mentioned that the outer ring would be a dingy and dangerous place. This looks … quite fun."

"Yeah, it does have a certain fascinating feel to it. The ambiance certainly is welcoming, and the sounds from the casino of all the winning slot machines definitely promote frivolity. But it's all just smoke and mirrors," Jaxon said. "It's all just a guise to loosen your grip from your hard-earned money. There's more crime and corruption per square meter of this place than there is back on earth, all the states of the US combined."

"Huh," Camille muttered. "You'd never guess it."

After a few more moments of gazing up at the scenery, Jaxon said, "Shall we proceed?"

"But shouldn't we wait for the boys?"

"Meh, they're grown men. They know the plan, and Miles will no doubt be familiar with a place like this."

"Okay then. I guess I'll follow you."

Jaxon led Camille through the crowd of the shopping district, where they found a stairway leading up a level to the bars. Walking past several recognizable establishments, they crossed into an entirely different atmosphere. It was like walking from a world of safety and innocence into another, laced with danger and corruption, as they turned down a side street.

"Well? Do you have a preference?" Jaxon asked, motioning to the dozens of themed strip clubs along the walkway.

"One is as good as the next, right?" Camille asked, clearly out of her element.

Jaxon nodded and walked toward the entrance of the nearest club. The sign above the entrance flashed Diamond Bell Emporium in blue neon lights.

After paying a small cover charge, they walked into a dark, smoky hallway that opened up into a room lit with black lights on nearly every surface.

Once inside, there were two bars—one straight ahead, on the far side of the club, and one tucked into the left, just near the exit. It was no doubt to tempt the departing customers into having one last drink before they hit the road.

There were four dance tables arranged in a diamond shape throughout the club. Besides the immediate seating at those stages, there were a dozen or so smaller cocktail tables interspersed.

More neon lights decorated the walls for accent while several colored spotlights drew attention to the individual dancers. Music bumped throughout the club, giving the dancers something to gyrate too.

Jaxon led Camille to a small table just away from the

immediate crowd. It was situated near a curtained-off doorway, most likely leading to the private entertainment facilities.

Jaxon took a seat and motioned for Camille to sit to his left. Their backs were against the wall, and as soon as Jaxon could, he caught the attention of a waitress to bring them some drinks.

"You think it wise that we drink something being mixed out of our sight?" Camille asked. "I've heard stories about bartenders in places like this spiking the drinks with something, then the guy wakes up several hours later with empty pockets and an open fly, and no idea what happened."

Jaxon smiled and winked. "That's why we only order bottled beer. But you certainly paint a vivid picture."

As if on cue, a scantily clad waitress came by and took their drink order before disappearing to the back bar.

Camille leaned over to Jaxon to speak more discreetly. "So, how do we do this? Do we just ask the next person that comes by where we can buy us some drugs?"

Jaxon shook his head. "Unfortunately, it's not that easy. My bet is the real information will come from one of the strippers. They're most likely strung out as it is, and they'll be more likely to bleed the information out if we ply them with a handful of credits."

"So, what? Do we just go up there and ... give them money?"

"That's usually how strip clubs work. If we play it right, they'll come to us. The glory of the side table is that you can make eye contact with just about any one of the girls, and as soon as their set is over, they'll pay us a visit. If they're interested, that is."

Camille sat back up and looked across the club at the women dancing. She had a frown on her face. Not quite of disgust, but out of curiosity.

"What are you thinking?" Jaxon asked.

"I don't know. It's just ... how is it that these women become strippers in the first place? How is it that they're okay with selling their bodies to drunk, arrogant men?"

"I don't think these dancers are actually selling their bodies," Jaxon said in defense.

"Oh? These are dancers?" Camille asked sarcastically.

"Yes, they are, but not the kind of dancers at your ballet. These are dancers for hire, I guess. They're just selling an image of their body but not the body itself."

"So that makes it okay with you? To give these women money to show you their naughty parts?"

"Hey, don't blame me. Strip clubs have been around for hundreds of years, and I bet these women make more money than you or I did last year. Besides, it's a young woman's profession. After a certain age ..." Jaxon stopped, thinking about the path of the conversation, and decided to curtail it before he said the wrong thing.

Camille looked at him quizzically. "And? What happens when they hit that age limit?"

Before Jaxon had a chance to respond, the waitress returned with their beers and Jaxon paid her, giving her a handsome tip. She winked at him before continuing on to her next customer. Jaxon tipped his bottle back, drawing a cool stream of beer into his mouth.

After several moments of silence between them, Camille leaned over again and spoke. "So, tell me, Jax. Which of these ladies is your type these days?"

Jaxon surveyed the four dancers up on stage for several minutes. "I guess I don't really have a type. But if I had to choose, I guess I would opt for a woman that was fit, not too tall, but not too short. Perhaps with brunette hair, down just past her shoulders, and blue eyes if possible." Jaxon had just described Camille, almost to a T. "But then again, beggars can't be choosers in this market." He winked.

Camille continued to eye the various dancers, either electing to ignore Jaxon's description of herself, or simply scrutinizing the various women types in the club. "They certainly do come in all shapes and sizes," she said, resting her arm against his. "And ages," she continued. "Jesus, is she even thirteen?"

Jaxon followed Camille's gaze and found a very young girl on the far table. She had already dropped her top and was moving rhythmically to the music. Her breasts were clearly not fully developed, and it pained him to see the spectacle. As he continued to watch, his eyes rose up to her face, and he was startled at the similarities to that of his own daughter. Granted, to the picture of his daughter that was loaded on his commPad. It was clear that the girl wasn't his daughter, but what frightened him most was the fact that it very well could have been Celeste.

Suddenly, walking across the club, Jaxon saw another young girl. She was around sixteen or seventeen—about the same age as Celeste—who had more striking similarities to her as well. Jaxon leaned forward slightly, until he got a better look at her face. "My, God. It can't be," he said, his face white as a ghost.

34

The young girl turned toward Jaxon and smiled from across the room. As soon as they made eye contact, Jaxon thankfully realized that his mind was playing tricks. It wasn't her. He'd convinced himself that it was, simply because he was so powerless to help her. And, until they completed the mission, he would remain useless.

Jaxon drew his attention to the table closest to them. He wanted the image of his daughter out of his mind. Just the thought of the possibility that his daughter could be lost in a place like this caused his heart to race. He sat up and took another drink of his beer. He could feel his skin flush with anger.

"Jaxon, are you okay?"

"Yeah, it's … I'll tell you later."

Forcing himself to recover, Jaxon looked at the woman on the near table more closely. She was a tall blonde, with enormous double E breasts. Not at all his type, but they needed to make headway. He pulled out his credit stick and laid it on the table next to his beer, certain that she noticed his action.

Jaxon winked, and she smiled in return.

Jaxon leaned back and noticed that Camille was watching his every move. He leaned into her and said, "The bait is set," nodding to the voluptuous blonde that had just finished her dance set.

No words were spoken for several minutes as they waited for the stripper to approach. As predicted, she arrived at their table once she had gathered all the tips scattered across the stage.

The dancer, now redressed in a red, sequined mini-dress and crystal-clear, six-inch spike heels, smiled.

"Hi there, I'm Misty," she said. "Are you two looking for some company?"

"Absolutely," Camille said eagerly, then slid out the empty chair across from her and Jaxon.

As she sat down, she continued to eye Jaxon's credit stick lying on the table before them. "Are you two here for business or pleasure?"

Jaxon was about to respond when Camille cut in.

"A little bit of both. We had a conference earlier, but now we're out to have a little fun, before ... returning to our significant others back home," Camille said. leaning in close to Misty as if sharing a great secret.

Jaxon was taken by surprise at Camille's quickness in drumming up a believable cover on the spot.

"Hey now," Jaxon protested mildly. "Let's not share too much personal information with Misty. We just met her, and who knows who she might tell?" He winked.

"Don't worry, mister. I've heard it all. Your secret's safe with me," Misty said, returning his wink. Then she looked back to Camille, who had clearly captured her attention. Seeing a woman in such a male-dominated environment was not the norm. "Have you been to Alpha Station before?" she asked.

Camille answered Misty's questions as they settled into a nice conversation. As the ladies talked, Jaxon's training took over, and he proceeded to scan the club for questionable characters and exit pathways. It had been a few days since the last assassination attempt, and he wasn't exactly sold on whether or not they were out of danger.

Before returning his attention back to the girls, he noticed a new dancer stepping up onto the table where Misty just left. Jaxon's heart nearly burst at the sight of yet another young teen dancer. Jaxon was dumbfounded because this one looked almost younger than the first girl they saw on the other table.

"I don't want to sound too forward," Jaxon said, interrupting the girls' conversation. "But, is there any chance we can get a ... private performance?"

"Absolutely!" Misty said with excitement. "For you, or the missus?" she asked.

"Both," Camille said as she weaved her fingers into Jaxon's hand sitting on the table.

"All right," Misty said. "Just so you know, I'll have to charge a little more, seeing as we're making this a threesome, but I'm sure that won't be a problem, right?" she asked, her eyes falling on Jaxon's credit stick once again.

Jaxon was more than happy to dial up the extra credits on his device before tapping it onto Misty's credit receiver, which was disguised as a necklace pendant around her neck. *Her tip jar,* so to speak. Jaxon would've paid twice as much if it got his mind off of his missing daughter.

Misty smiled gleefully as she led Jaxon and Camille past the velvet curtain, practically dragging Camille by the hand. Jaxon followed and noted the light dimming as they stepped into the other room.

The atmosphere was similar to out front, but privacy and seclusion were prevalent. She continued leading the couple to the first unoccupied booth and motioned them in. Once they were in the booth and sitting next to each other on a tall back leather sofa, Misty stepped in and pulled the drapes closed.

The music could still be heard from out in the club, but it was much more subdued, allowing conversations to be carried out with ease.

"Okay, you've paid for one private dance, which lasts the length of one song. If you'd like to extend the dance, feel free to tap my pendant any time during the performance. Also, touching is frowned upon," she said, first looking at Jaxon and then shifting her gaze to Camille, "but I won't tell if you don't."

The previous song ended, and the next track started up. Just as the rhythm began to vibrate through the floor, Misty began writhing about. Within moments, her mini-dress had dropped to the floor, exposing sparkling body glitter that had been rubbed on her breasts. She turned around and bent over at the waist, touching her hands on the floor and shaking her bare butt in sync with the music.

Camille leaned over and whispered into Jaxon's ear. "Um, do you think we should stop her, and ask about the real reason why we're here?"

Jaxon chuckled. "What? And deprive her of performing her civic duty? She's a paid woman, Cam. We should wait—"

Camille shoved her elbow into Jaxon's rib cage, interrupting his chauvinistic thoughts before regrettable words were said.

"Ouch, I mean, Misty. As wonderful of a job as you're doing here, can we stop you for just a moment?" Jaxon asked.

Misty stopped her gyrations and turned to look at them quizzically. "It's your dime, mister."

"It's just that, our real reason for bringing you back here was to see if we could, I don't know, score a little medicinal entertainment?" Jaxon asked.

"What makes you think I have anything to sell?" Misty asked as she stood in front of them, completely naked save for her high-heeled shoes.

"Obviously, we'd never assume that you'd be the seller," Camille said as she reached out and caressed the side of Misty's thigh. "But if you could point us in the right direction, to someone who might have what we're looking for, I'm sure we could thank you properly." Camille slid her hand up and across Misty's abdomen, then in between her ample breasts, before she flicked her pendant.

Misty moaned softly. "Ooh. I like how you think, sexy woman. What is it that you're looking for? I might know someone that can help you two out."

"We'd like some Whitetail. Some for now and enough to bring home for later," Jaxon said, fighting the erotic distraction from all the touching between Camille and Misty.

Misty's enthusiastic smile and flirtatious demeanor changed instantly. Frown lines deepened on her face and she took a step back, dropping a hand in front of her pelvis as if to say *this entry is closed.* "I'm sorry. I … know nothing about that. Perhaps you two should look someplace else."

Before they could protest, Misty picked up her dress and bolted from the private booth.

"What do you suppose that was all about?" Camille asked.

Jaxon shrugged. "Beats me. She seemed pretty shaken up at just hearing the name. If I had to guess, she's probably running out there right now, telling some bouncer named Guido that we've been inappropriate with her. I think we should get out of here while we still can."

"Agreed," Camille said, stepping out of the private booth.

Once past the velvet curtain, they headed straight for the exit, not even pausing to see where Misty might have gone.

Francisco and Oliver walked into the control room of the ship and found Jaxon and Camille sitting next to each other on the flight couch.

"You two have any luck?" Jaxon asked.

"That's a negative, boss," Oliver said. "Found just one dealer in the entire two hours we were there, and he clammed up like a nervous oyster the minute we said Whitetail."

A curious look passed over Jaxon's face. "Strangely, same result with us. We had a lead on a seller, but as soon as we mentioned what we were looking for, she ran out of the private booth as if it was on fire."

Oliver's brow rose. "Private booth? Are you holding out on us, boss?"

"Not at all. Just running down our best options. Let's undock and get out of here, and then we'll regroup."

The team dispersed, and minutes later, they released the docking clamps and headed for their next stop.

"We're about two hours away," Oliver said as he engaged the autopilot.

"Great. Let's gather on the Observation Deck and discuss the next station," Jaxon said before he and Camille left the cockpit.

Thirty minutes into the flight, the team had concluded their abbreviated mission briefing and were each researching information at their own computer terminals. As the objective remained the same—gain information on Whitetail—the discussion was cut short and independent research prevailed. As Jaxon read through various details and capabilities of Beta Station, the ship's sensors picked up a disturbance directly in the path of the ship.

"Hey, boss. What do you make of this?" Oliver asked.

Jaxon closed the file he was reading and brought up the ship's sensor array. On the display, there were a series of small spacecraft, around seven in the thirty-meter range, directly in their path.

"Can you tell who they are?"

Oliver tapped at his control panel. "No, sir. It's like they're ghosts. No information whatsoever about their origination or their class."

"Just plot a new course. We don't need any more trouble right now," Jaxon said. "Is the stealth device still active, babe … Cam?"

All eyes focused on Jaxon as the flight deck drew quiet. Jaxon could feel his skin heat up because of his Freudian slip.

"Yes, puddin'," Camille said with sass. "The code randomizer that Clay and I created is working as planned."

Jaxon swallowed hard. It wasn't like him to flub any part of the mission, but this was no ordinary situation. Having Camille thrust back into his life was something that he'd never have anticipated in his wildest dreams.

"All right. I'll be in my quarters until we arrive if anyone needs me." Jaxon stood and practically ran out of the control room to avoid any uncomfortable questioning.

Beep, beep.

Jaxon was lying on his bunk, reviewing Camille's personnel file for the fiftieth time, when the intercom call interrupted him.

"Go ahead," Jaxon said, flicking the switch on the wall panel.

"Hey, boss? We've got a small problem up here. Care to join us?" Oliver asked.

Jaxon closed the file on his commPad when he saw the time. They were twenty minutes out, according to Oliver's latest estimate. "I'll be there in a minute," he said, dropping the tablet to his bunk. He was thankful for the distraction, as he was beginning to think his obsession with Cam was verging on the unhealthy side. He slipped his shoes on and headed for flight control.

When Jaxon walked in, Oliver was sitting at the navigation console. He glanced at tactical but Camille was nowhere in sight. Francisco sat opposite Camille's station, no doubt scrutinizing some random chemical compounds.

"What do you have?" he asked Oliver.

"I called in for docking procedures a bit ago, and they said that they were full up and that we can't stay docked at Beta Station for longer than ten minutes; long enough to drop off or pick someone up."

"Completely full? Really?"

"It's what he said. I gave him our IMO number, and that's when he told me it was a no-go."

Jaxon's eyes narrowed. "What are our options?"

"We've got two, boss. We can stop the Buddha in orbit around the station, and they can send a tender for us. Probably twenty minutes, round trip."

"Second option?"

"We could dock long enough to unload part of the team, but somebody would have to stay back to pull the ship away and wait."

Jaxon contemplated for a moment. He knew that if the whole team was on the station at the same time, they could cover twice as much ground. The drawback was that if something went awry, there wouldn't be an immediate means of escape. They'd have to wait for the shuttle to tender them back to the Buddha. At least with the second option, all they would have to do is call the ship and have Oliver pick them up if things went sideways.

"How far out are we?" Jaxon asked.

Oliver projected the navigation computer's readout to the main screen. "Twelve minutes to dock."

"All right. Miles, you and Camille will stay with the ship. Clay and I will do a quick pass of the station. I'm not comfortable splitting the team up right now, but this is one of the smaller stations compared to the others on the list. If it wasn't on Evans' list, I think we'd just pass it up."

"Roger that, boss," Oliver said.

Jaxon looked back toward Francisco, who was still engrossed in his computer terminal. "Clay?"

There was no response.

"Clay!" Jaxon said, raising his voice several octaves.

"Wuh ... what? Did you call me?" Francisco asked, rubbing his eyes clear.

"Yeah, change of plans. It's going to be just you and me on the station. There's a problem about docking, and only two of us are going. Camille and Oliver will stay back and come get us when we're through. Grab your gear and be ready to go. About ten minutes."

"Yes, sir," Francisco stood and walked out of the control room.

"Well, this will be fun," Jaxon muttered.

"Eh, the kid's not bad. He's a little nervous, but he means well," Oliver said.

"Yeah, it's that nervous thing that worries me," Jaxon said. "Can you fill Cam in on the plan change?"

"Yeah, sure thing, boss."

Jaxon left the cockpit and went to grab his own gear from his bunk.

36

Having passed through security with much less pomp and circumstance than the last station, Jaxon and Francisco headed for the bars. Initially, Jaxon felt that the strip club was a good approach, but with Francisco as his partner, he decided to keep it tame. Jaxon wasn't so sure if Francisco had even seen a naked woman in person, let alone talked to her openly about drugs. He figured the right bartender might have the information they were looking for.

As they walked along the much smaller pavilion streets, Jaxon and Francisco were silent. Jaxon instantly regretted not bringing Camille instead, because they at least had a history to pass the time. With Francisco, he was cut from a different cloth.

Passing by the first few dive bars, he came to a particularly dark saloon. The wall had a saying below: *a rare place where high and low rub elbows*. Without hesitation, Jaxon stepped in, followed closely by Francisco.

The mangy establishment was almost empty. Save for a few locals shooting pool at the back and a few daring businessmen, the place was a ghost town. Exactly what Jaxon was hoping for.

He walked up to the bar and took a seat. Francisco sat next to him, closer to the exit door. Jaxon smiled internally at Francisco's nervousness.

The solitary bartender was dropping off drinks by the pool table, giving them a few moments of silence before he would return. Francisco chose that time to speak.

"You don't like me," he said. "But, if you just give me a chance, I—"

"I don't think that's necessarily the case, Clay. I'm sure you're a fine man, it's just how this team was assembled that has me off center," Jaxon said, flagging down the returning bartender.

Before Francisco could continue, he'd arrived.

"What'll it be?" he asked in a gruff voice, completely selling the dive bar aura.

"Two whiskeys, neat," Jaxon said, tapping his credit stick on the receiver at the edge of the bar.

"But I don't drink whiskey," Clay said nervously.

"Well, kid, today you do," Jaxon smiled and gave him a wink.

The bartender didn't go far, pouring their drinks right in front of them. Before Jaxon could ask anything further, the bartender retreated to the far side of the bar to tend to one of the businessmen.

After a few moments of lingering silence, Jaxon continued. "I'm just a little frustrated at Howe and Evans for how they threw this team together. They gave me a trained agent with limited field activity, Camille. They gave me a recently deactivated field agent that had half of his personnel file blacked out. And then there's you. You've had what? Twelve hours of simulation training?"

"Well, it's closer to fifteen hours but—"

"And there's my point. You can't train an agent in a simulator in less than sixty hours. I just don't know what Howe was thinking—"

"But I've been tasked with this mission for almost a year. I know exactly what to look for when we get to the right place. I'll know whether they're trying to pass off something else that's not Whitetail. I'll know what to look for in the production facility. You see, there's more to being an agent than just being able to shoot somebody up and defend yourself," Francisco said.

Jaxon took a sip of his whiskey before swallowing the rest of the glass in one gulp. He looked at Francisco then at the glass in front of him.

Francisco picked up his glass and repeated Jaxon's every step. Sip—pause—gulp. He nearly retched as the lukewarm liquid burned its way down his throat.

"See? It's good, ain't it?" Jaxon asked. He tapped his glass on the edge of the bar and waved at the bartender. He held his fingers up for another round.

After several deep swallows of saliva, Francisco slid his empty glass forward, reluctantly, just as the bartender returned to pour them each a new drink. Before the bartender left, Francisco slipped his own UNEX pod out and tap it out the edge of the bar. "This round is on me."

Jaxon picked up his glass and held it in his palm, warming the liquid from the heat of his hand. "Much obliged. But in the end, Howe is the one who's buying the drinks today."

The bartender turned and left after filling the glasses. Francisco held his hand up as if to ask him a question, but the gesture went unseen. Then he looked at Jaxon. "Should we ask him?"

"In time. It'll look too suspicious if we come and have a drink and then go straight to asking about buying drugs. Even though this is the outer ring, there's still a semblance of order that needs to be respected."

"So it's a game then," Francisco said, trying to decipher it like it was a code.

Jaxon sniffed at his scotch. "Yeah, kind of. I've been in my fair share of bars just like this and have seen many atrocities. Coming in here and just asking for some drug isn't really top-level spy kind of stuff, but regardless, it needs to be handled appropriately. Besides, we're looking for more than just buying the drug. We're looking for the source. If we play our cards right, we should be able to get both."

Jaxon tossed back his whiskey in one gulp and savored the oaky inebriant in his mouth for a long moment before swallowing it down. Francisco chose not to imitate Jaxon again and just sipped at it, as he rightfully should have the first time.

As the two of them sat at the edge of the bar, silently, Jaxon noticed two men walk in. They were clearly not regulars and were dressed in black jumpsuits with no identifiable insignia anywhere. Each of them wore heavy canvas belts at their waist, supporting a number of compartments.

"Don't look now, but it looks like we might have company," Jaxon said, tapping his drink at the edge of the bar once more.

Francisco took another sip, and as he set the glass back on the bar top, he nonchalantly looked toward the entry and saw the men. He returned his gaze to Jaxon, showing no signs of panic. Jaxon was certain it was there, just below the surface, but was proud of Francisco for trying.

"Why don't you go call the Buddha and have them meet us at the dock in forty-five minutes?" Jaxon said, maintaining a forward stare.

"Do you expect trouble?" Francisco asked.

"Don't know," Jaxon shrugged. "But better be safe than sorry."

"What about you? Are you going to—"

"When you leave, hopefully, the friendly visitors there will tail you, giving me a chance to talk to the bartender," Jaxon said.

Francisco tossed the rest of his drink back and winced slightly. He placed the glass on the bar, and said, "See you shortly, boss," then walked away. Jaxon remained looking forward, but with the mirrors behind the bar, the reflection gave him a view of the front door. As Francisco walked out, he gave the two security men a courtesy nod but avoided direct eye contact. Within minutes, the two men turned on their heels and followed him out. *Perfect,* Jaxon thought.

37

A few minutes later, the bartender returned, holding the bottle of whiskey. "Another?"

Jaxon smiled. "Sure, just one more. And then, maybe a bit of information?" he asked, dialing up a few hundred credits on his pod, allowing the bartender to see the amount.

He tipped the spout into Jaxon's glass and added two fingers to the bottom. "What kind of information?"

"I'm looking for Whitetail," Jaxon asked bluntly. "Before you get amnesia, I'm not a cop, and I'm not looking for any trouble. Just looking to buy a few doses."

The bartender returned the whiskey bottle to the shelf behind him and turned back to Jaxon. He leaned on the back edge of the bar top and stared right into Jaxon's eyes. Their gaze remained locked for several moments. Jaxon contemplated what the bartender might be thinking, but decided to remain stoic in hopes of obtaining the needed information.

The bartender sniffed briefly then wiped his nose with the

back of his hand. "Funny thing, that Whitetail. It's quite elusive these days. If you'd been here a month ago, there'd been ten guys standing along the streets selling you all they had. But, something happened a few weeks back. Whitetail just disappeared. All the dealers in town have gone dark. Not sure what's going on, but it's clear that the market is changing."

Jaxon pondered this new information. "It just dried up? Anybody know why?"

"Not a clue," the bartender said. "Personally, I'm happier that it's out of here. I've heard some bad things about it as I'm sure you have too. Listen, I'm usually a pretty good judge of character, and you don't seem the type. I'm sure there's something else that's more to your liking."

"Thanks for being honest. To tell the truth, you're right. It's not my bag either. But I've got ... personal reasons behind my request," Jaxon said as he dialed up a few hundred credits more on his pod and held it over the edge of the bar. "Any information about it would be greatly appreciated."

The bartender looked down at the large three-figure credit on Jaxon's pod display. He nodded, and Jaxon tapped the pod at the bar, zeroing out the display.

"You can't get any on Beta Station, or the next two closest stations either. Word is you can get it on Delta Station, but you'd be a fool if you went there looking for it."

"Why is that?" Jaxon asked, downing his third whiskey.

"Delta Station isn't quite what it appears on the surface. Not only is it the largest station in the outer ring, there are some questionable activities going on there. One minds their P's and Q's, if you know what I mean."

Jaxon understood. After many years in the field, he'd learned how to read a person's character. If Jaxon's skills of interpreting were still sharp, he thought his new friend had had some type of formalized training in his past. Much like his own.

"Much obliged, sir. Looks like my next stop is Delta Station."

A look of surprise flourished on the bartender's face. "You must be desperate. Maybe you didn't get exactly what I was saying. It's a dangerous place. They have the highest level of security of any station in the ring, and trust me when I tell you, it's not worth it."

Jaxon nodded. "I understand. My hands are tied, and I need this."

"Well, then, here's some free advice. When you get there, you'll have two choices. One is a female casino dealer that has the right connections. The other is an exotic woman working for Madame Elina at The Pleasure Gauntlet. Try one of those two, and be sure to watch your six."

"How about names?" Jaxon asked as he began to dial up his UNIX pod again.

"Put it away, friend. I don't have names for you, but I can give you some descriptions. The casino dealer will be hard to miss. She'll be the one with fire engine red hair. As for the hooker, she's quite the buxom beauty with auburn hair ... or was it a blonde?" the bartender asked himself.

"Red hair in the casino, blonde on the hooker. Got it."

The bartender stood and cleared the two whiskey glasses from the bar top. "Good luck, you're gonna need it."

With that, he turned and walked away. Jaxon sat for a moment longer, digesting everything that he'd just heard. He was nearly giddy with excitement, being almost certain that they found the facility so quickly. He'd anticipated having to visit nearly all of the dozen or so stations in the belt before they found what they were looking for.

Gleefully, Jaxon dialed up a few more credits on his pod and tapped it on the bar top.

Jaxon left the dive bar, retracing his steps through the pavilion. Before making his way back to the ship, though, he decided to hit a few shops along the way. He had a budding idea for a new plan, and picking up a number of items now would make all the difference.

After thirty minutes in a few clothing shops, Jaxon

finished his path back to the docks, where he found an eager Francisco waiting.

Oliver sat at the pilot's station with his seatback reclined and his feet resting on the edge of the control panel. Mindlessly, he stared at the ceiling. The hiss of the door opening and closing brought him out of an unimportant daydream. He looked up and saw a Camille walking groggily toward him. She sat down in the copilot's chair and smiled.

"How long have I been out?" she asked, rubbing the sleep from her eyes.

Oliver glanced at the clock. "Few hours? Give or take," he said.

A look of panic flashed in her eyes. "Jesus, what about Beta Station?"

"Changed. Couldn't dock, so boss and Francisco went out while you and I stayed back. Felt it was better to let you rest as opposed to waking you and—"

"Damn him," Camille said. "How long have they been gone?"

"Thirty, maybe, forty minutes? We're just sitting a few

hundred meters away from the dock, waiting. They shouldn't be long. They said they were going to check out a few places and then we'd move on to the next station," Oliver said, returning his gaze to the ceiling above.

Camille grumbled under her breath before mimicking Oliver's stance. "I guess there's not much else for us to do—"

"But stare at the ceiling," Oliver said, completing her thoughts.

As Camille relaxed in the chair, her mind tried to analyze Jaxon's thoughts. Why did he go on station without waking her? Was he hiding something? And what about bringing Francisco? Surely he should have at least brought Oliver instead. There had to be some reason.

"So, tell me, Camille. What's your story?" Oliver asked.

"Come again? I don't follow," Camille said.

"You know, between you and boss? There's clearly some kind of history, and he seems to revert to a schoolboy mentality when you're around."

Camille exhaled. She'd known the questioning would come around at some point, but she'd hoped that she'd be able to sidestep it. At least they were alone, and Jaxon wasn't around to contradict either of their histories with his own words.

"Jaxon and I go way back. More than ten years."

Oliver whistled.

"Actually, we were engaged," Camille said, expecting another surprised whistle out of Oliver, but there was just silence. She leaned her head to the side and saw him sitting upright in his chair, a look of complete surprise on his face.

"What? People get married all the time," Camille said defensively.

"Then, what happened?" Oliver asked, returning to his relaxation position.

"I'm not sure. We were living together eight or nine years ago, and things seemed to be okay, then Jaxon just … died. I thought he really died. And now he tells everyone he just faked it all."

"That son of a bitch. How could he leave such a wonderful woman like you in such a predicament?"

Before Camille could respond, an incoming communications alert echoed throughout the cockpit. Oliver accepted it.

"… This is Francisco, calling Buddha, over."

"This is Buddha. We read you."

"Jaxon is requesting dock pick up in thirty minutes. Over."

"Copy that," Oliver said. "What's the status? Over."

Francisco paused before replying. "Unknown. Perhaps cautionary, but I'm not certain. Just hurry. Over."

"Roger that. Over and out."

"What do you think that's all about?" Camille asked.

"Don't know. Just gonna follow orders," Oliver said.

The two remained sitting comfortably in their chairs for several minutes without any words. Oliver finally broke the silence.

"What were we talking about? Oh, yeah. The douche bag boss we have. He left you in—"

"He had his reasons. He's talked to me about some of it since we left and he really does feel terrible about it. There's more to it, and at some point, I'll get the rest out of him. But for now, I'm choosing to be the bigger person here and focus on the job."

Oliver didn't respond initially. He leaned forward and executed an auto-docking maneuver on the ship's control panel. He then turned back to Camille. "You are a bigger person, that's for sure. I'm just saying, if I was in his shoes, I'd have done things a lot differently."

"The thing is, Miles, I think I still love him, regardless of what he's put me through. Jaxon is a very unique man. And please, let's keep this between us. If he wants to share with you all, let that be his decision."

"Mums the word, boss," Oliver said as he continued to monitor the docking procedures.

Having been able to orbit so close to the space station

dock, they were clamping down within minutes. Jaxon and Francisco walked into flight control promptly after.

Jaxon walked up and leaned in between Camille and Oliver. He lowered himself down onto the edge of the control panel and crossed his arms.

"Well, boys and girls, it looks like we have our first bit of tangible information. I've got a location and a couple of potential contacts. As soon as we get underway, I'll fill you all in. We're going to Delta Station," Jaxon said excitedly.

39

A knock came at the door. Jaxon contemplated ignoring it, not wanting to carry on an awkward conversation with Francisco, but decided otherwise. He hoisted himself off his bunk and opened the door. It slid open, revealing Camille standing in front of him, her arms crossed and frown lines between her eyes. *Oh shit,* Jaxon thought.

"Come in?" he said questioningly then stepped aside.

Camille walked past him but refrained from taking a seat. She turned and stared at him with disappointment. "What the hell?" she asked.

"I don't follow," Jaxon said. He knew what she meant but decided not to immediately address his decision to leave her behind.

"I thought we were a team, and you let me sleep. I could've been useful on the station. Francisco told me a little about what happened and—"

Jaxon held up his hand to silence Camille. "It's okay. We took care of things and now we're here. We got some good information, and I think, all in all, the trip to Beta Station was a success."

"But, Clay? You couldn't have taken Miles, or myself, for God's sake? He's just a boy, Jaxon."

"He's a man and he's made it very clear that he's ready for whatever the mission can throw at him. We should give him a chance," Jaxon said, sitting on the edge of his bunk, motioning for Camille to do the same.

"Is that what this is really all about? Or was it something else? Were you afraid that I was leaving again and wouldn't return?" Jaxon asked, knowing exactly what was going through Camille's mind.

Camille looked away. "Can you blame me? You have no idea the pain I suffered after I thought you died." Camille took Jaxon's hand but looked away.

"I know that I haven't done anything yet to regain your trust, but you have to believe me. That's all in the past. I had my reasons and what's done is done. If I had it to do over again, I—"

Jaxon's words were cut off by a ship's communication.

He reached over and opened the channel.

"Go ahead," he said, gently squeezing Camille's hand.

"Hey, boss. There's a … call for you. Director Howe is on a secure channel and wants an update," Oliver said.

"Thanks, Miles. We'll be up in a min … I'll be up in a minute," Jaxon said, fumbling his words.

"I? We?" Camille asked.

"Oh, come on. I just didn't want him to think we're fraternizing or something behind closed doors," Jaxon said nervously.

"So what if he did?" Camille asked, maintaining a grip on Jaxon's hand. "It's not like we can just forget about our past."

Jaxon remained on the edge of his bunk. "I suppose you're right. And honestly, I don't think I ever want to forget what we had. I wish …"

"I know," Camille said then leaned in and kissed his lips. "We can talk later. Best not keep the director waiting."

Camille stood and left Jaxon's quarters. A moment later, Jaxon took in a deep breath and headed for flight control.

As Jaxon took his seat at the pilot's station, he brought up the communications panel and tossed the open channel onto the main screen. As the image of Director Howe materialized, Camille walked in and took a seat next to Francisco.

"Ah, great. The whole team is there," Howe said, smiling widely. "Do you have a status update for me?"

"Well, director, it's not going as well as we'd hoped. We've been to a handful of stations already, and we continue to get stonewalled at every turn. It's like they've stopped production, or perhaps your intel is out of date?" Jaxon asked, choosing his words very carefully.

"No, no. I'm positive that the drug is being manufactured in the outer ring. It's also been reported that Pablo Guzman himself is currently in the region, no doubt overseeing the operation personally."

"Guzman's here? When did this happen?" Jaxon asked, frustrated at the surprise information.

"We just found out. You'd already left, so we felt it best to wait and brief you now. Our sensors indicate that you've been on autopilot for the last hour. We figured that now was a good time." Howe looked off screen and nodded then returned his gaze to the camera.

"Yeah, well, we are heading to another station as we speak. Thanks for the Guzman information," Jaxon said, calming his temper.

"Any problems so far?" Howe asked.

"Nope," Jaxon said plainly. "Just a lot of *deer-in-the-headlights* when we bring up the drug. But I'm certain we'll find something on one of the next few stations. I feel pretty good about that," Jaxon said. noticing the strange looks from the rest of his team.

"Is there anything I can do from here that might help?" Howe asked.

"To tell the truth, it really is hampering us on not having

tech. It would be great if you could get us at least earwigs so we can communicate with each other when we're on station."

"Jaxon, we've already covered this. This is an unsanctioned mission, and you cannot be in possession of any gear designed or implemented by the GSA. We've given you each several thousand credits on your pods to obtain any of your needs along your way. Or did you forget?"

"No, we got that. Unfortunately, the few stations that we've stopped at had no communication devices to speak of. Sure, they had walkie-talkies, but for Christ's sake, we're in the twenty-second century. It amazes me that PCD's are so scarce."

"Trust me, Jaxon. I sympathize," Howe said, appearing compassionate. "But you'll have to do your best with what you have, and I know you can." Howe looked off screen once again and shook his head at something being said back on earth. "If there's nothing else, we'll reconnect after your next station stop."

"I don't. Anyone else?" Jaxon looked around the control room. Blank faces stared back.

"Nope, looks like were good. On another note, is there any word on that other ... situation?" Jaxon asked, wishing he was in a private conversation now.

"Listen, Jaxon. We're doing our best. The team at Lily's residence hasn't found any clues on who the killer was. And as for your daughter—"

Gasps of shock lingered in the flight control.

"—she's still missing. We've been trying to track her, but that's something that you shouldn't be worrying about right now. You have to focus on your own mission, and then you can return to help. Understood?" Howe asked sternly.

Jaxon's anger returned two-fold. "Got it," he said as he terminated the communication.

The room was silent.

J axon leaned back in his chair, staring at the blank video screen for several minutes. Oliver finally broke the silence.

"So ... boss? Are we changing course for the next station?"

"No. Maintain course to Delta Station," Jaxon said.

"But didn't you just tell the director that—"

"I'm aware of what I said. I'm just not sure who we can trust right now. With the attack right after we took first orbit, and with what Clay and I ran into on the last station, it seems like somebody's been ahead of us most of the way. Until we can determine who the mole is, we'll need to be cautious." Jaxon paused to turn and face the rest of the team. "For all we know, the director himself could be feeding us false information. Furthermore, he may even have eyes and ears on board this very ship." Jaxon glanced from Oliver to Francisco, and then to Camille. "I'd rather keep this between us for the time being. If I'm right, the assassins will be camped out on or around Gamma Station, waiting for our arrival within the hour. By the time they realize that we're not there, we'll be just about to dock at Delta Station. Anyone have a problem with that?"

Jaxon continued looking from face to face with no obvious reaction.

"Great. If there's nothing else," Jaxon began.

"There is something, boss," Oliver said. "What's this other mission that you asked the director about? Something about an ex-wife and a daughter?" he asked, quickly glancing to Camille then back to Jaxon.

"Not ex-wife. We were never married. She was ... a girlfriend from years ago, and we had a child together. A daughter; her name is Celeste. About a week ago, there was an attack at their house and Lily, my ex, was killed. It'd been more than ten years since I last spoke to her and I've never met my daughter."

"My God," Camille exclaimed. "Why didn't you tell us?"

"Well, I didn't know if there was anything to tell. I would really rather be on earth looking for Celeste than here on this goddamn ship, hunting down another crazed drug lord. But Howe assures me that he's on the situation. A team looking into Lily's death, as well as one looking for Celeste. There's no trace of her at the house, and nobody has seen or heard from her since."

Jaxon looked at Camille, and her face was full of pain and sympathy. Jaxon had told Camille about Celeste before they were engaged, and the reasons for not wanting to make her aware of his existence. It was for Celeste's protection and nothing more. Now that he'd been out of the company's grasp for this long, there was nothing more that he wanted to do than hold his daughter in his arms, and show her that he could protect her.

"I don't know, boss, but I think the company's feeding you a line."

"What makes you say that, Miles?" Jaxon asked.

"I, uh ... have had some questionable dealings with the GSA in the past. Let's just say I don't trust them any further than I can spit," Oliver said.

"Speculation will get us nowhere. All I know is that as soon as I'm done here, I'm getting back to earth and finding my daughter."

"If you haven't met her, how will you know what you're looking for?" Francisco asked.

"Howe gave me a file before we left. In it were several images of Celeste and Lily, that were fairly recent—within a year or two." Jaxon turned to his control panel and brought up the pictures that he'd loaded into the ship's computers, then displayed them on the main view screen for all to see.

"She's beautiful, Jaxon," Camille said sincerely. "How old is this?"

"I'm not sure, maybe earlier this year?" Jaxon said. flipping through several other photos.

"Anything we can do to help, boss, just give the word," Oliver said.

"Thanks, Miles. Means a lot. Now, what do you say about changing things up a bit? Let's talk about Delta Station and a new approach," Jaxon said, hoping a change of subject would take his mind off Celeste.

Murmurs echoed about the cockpit as Jaxon cleared the view screen.

"First off, we're going to try and go in disguise. Back when we were on the last station, I picked up some accessories that should help us along with the plan."

Jaxon spent the next hour explaining his thoughts on entering Delta Station. He was unsure if they'd be receptive to his plan and was happy that they all agreed with every detail.

At the end of the hour, they each returned to their own quarters to prepare for docking, which was another thirty minutes away.

Jaxon was first through the security and was surprised that the level of scrutiny for his travel papers was virtually nil. He was moving about the front lobby of the station within a few minutes.

Camille was through shortly after, an irritable glint in her eyes.

"Everything okay?" Jaxon asked.

"I'll be fine," she huffed. "Just a few wandering hands by one of the security goons."

"Which one was it?" Jaxon asked, motioning toward the security fence.

"I'm fine. We have more important things to worry about," she said, looking around the vicinity. "Let's not stand around like tourists."

Camille led Jaxon further onto the concourse that surrounded the large casino floor below. As they waited for Oliver and Francisco, they overlooked the crowd of degenerate gamblers and card sharks in silence.

It was nearly twenty minutes later when Francisco and

Oliver stepped up next to them and peered over the rail. "Which way to the hookers?" Oliver asked dryly.

Jaxon chuckled. "I think you'll find what you're looking for down those stairs and through the lower promenade."

"What was the holdup?" Camille asked, ignoring the bravado flowing freely between Jaxon and Oliver.

"Nothing that we weren't prepared for. After getting the third degree about our reason for visiting their pristine space station, Clay actually saved the day with his naïve question: 'Is there a wide selection of women in the Hooker Shop?'," Oliver recounted.

"You didn't!" Camille asked.

Francisco's face turned red, but he didn't deny it.

"Honest to God. Those were his exact words," Oliver said, looking at Francisco admirably.

Camille rolled her eyes and smiled. "Clay, I can't believe you let Miles corrupt you so easily."

"Okay, boys. Time to get to it," Jaxon said. "And watch out for Madame Elina. She's a known pickpocket, and she's quite good at it."

Oliver nodded and headed for the stairs. Francisco trailed, terror beginning to fill his eyes.

"Madame Elina, huh?" Camille asked. "It sounds like you've been here a few times," she said, holding her nose up in general disdain.

Jaxon smiled gleefully. "Oh, I've been here before. But I have no idea if there's a Madame or a Messieurs or what have you. I just said that to keep Francisco on his toes."

Camille chuckled. "You are incorrigible," she said, sliding her arm into his. "Shall we?"

"Lead the way, my lady," Jaxon said as they made their way to the grand staircase that led to the center of the casino floor.

As they reached the lower landing, they approached a money cage and exchanged a few thousand credits for two large stacks of casino chips. He gave one stack to Camille and slipped his own stack into the breast pocket of his sport coat. As was typical with Jaxon's irregular visits to the local gambling hall on Taloo Station, he led Camille throughout the entire casino floor, surveying the various tables and exit paths. He also noted that each of the four exit doors was manned by two armed guards. On their second pass through the casino floor, he paused at the side of a half full table that was playing Calypso poker. "Shall we?" Jaxon motioned Camille toward the table.

Confidently, Camille stepped up to the table and took the seat at the far right. Jaxon sat down next to her and organized his stack of chips. Camille did the same and had her initial bet out before Jaxon completed his account. He looked at her, surprise on his face. She just smiled.

The attractive dealer swiped her hand across the felt in a half circle, then began dealing out cards. Each player received three cards, and the goal was to beat the dealer, but also to beat everyone else at the table.

Jaxon looked at his hand, and he had a pair of three's with a king kicker. He waited for action, and when it got to him, he called Camille's fifty credit bet.

There were three others at the table and they each folded. The dealer, who showed two of her three cards had a Jack and a nine face up. Any face card in the dealer's window indicated that she must call.

The dealer nodded at Camille, the initial better. Camille gleefully turned over a three card straight. Seven, eight, nine.

Jaxon turned over his hand and said, "You got me." He then looked at the dealer's cards as she turned over her blind card which happened to be a second Jack.

Swiftly, the dealer cleared Jaxon's cards and chips, reallocating them in front of Camille. She then matched the stack once again out of the dealer's tray before shuffling for a new hand.

Jaxon eyed Camille questioningly.

"What? Beginner's luck." She giggled.

After a few dozen hands, and more tragic losses than great victories, Jaxon was almost through his initial stack. Camille, on the other hand, had more than doubled what she initially sat down with and appeared to be enjoying every moment of it.

As much as Jaxon would've loved to continue living their playful cover, he figured it was time to start getting down to business. He looked around the casino to see if one of the pit bosses was near but didn't spot anyone. He then leaned over the table slightly and spoke to the dealer, admiring her crimson hair.

"We're here on kind of a second honeymoon, and were wondering if"—Jaxon paused again to look around for any prying ears—"we're wondering where we could get some chemical entertainment. We'd love some Whitetail, to be specific." Jaxon winked and leaned back in his chair.

The dealer, whose name tag said Felicity, didn't even pause from her card shuffling. "I'm sorry, sir, but this establishment does not condone that sort of activity."

Jaxon portrayed an image of disappointment as he exhaled in defeat. Then he noticed something. Felicity winked at him then began dealing out the next hand. After she had dealt the third card all around the table, Jaxon picked up his three cards and found that he had a seven of diamonds, a three of clubs, and a card that had a name and a five-digit prefix on it. The name was Ziggi, and the number was 50961.

Startled, Jaxon looked up at the dealer, and she winked at him again. He promptly folded and nudged Camille.

"Well, dear, I think we should give some other people a chance to win. Let's cash out."

Disappointment was clear on Camille's face as she folded her last hand and promptly scooped her poker chips off the table.

As they moved away from the casino floor, Camille spoke. "That was abrupt. Did you sense trouble?"

"Not exactly. After the dealer shot me down on asking about Whitetail, she dealt me a card that had a man's name and what I assume is his room number. It's 50961, and Ziggi appears to be the man to ask for. Let's cash in our chips then go see what we can find."

The promenade was lined with numerous dive bars and strip clubs; a man stood out in front of each dingy establishment, urging the passing patrons into their clubs. Francisco stayed close to Oliver as they moved past the first half dozen bars.

"What, what are we looking for again?" he asked.

"Boss said to go talk to some prostitutes. Something about what he learned back on Beta Station," Oliver said.

Francisco remembered the mission briefing, but by the appearance of his pale skin, he wasn't exactly thrilled about their part of the plan. Oliver either didn't notice or chose to ignore the uneasiness that had overcome his partner.

The two continued their path through the promenade, ignoring all the pleas along the way. At the very end, they came to a pair of massive oak doors with a red neon sign above that read The Pleasure Gauntlet. "Looks like we're here," Oliver said.

"Do you think Jaxon actually meant for us to hire a prostitute?" Francisco asked.

"Why'd you think he gave us each three thousand credits? We can't just ask the Madame exactly where she buys drugs for her whores," Oliver said before stepping through the elaborate entrance.

The contrast in environments was drastic. The promenade was filled with glitz and glamour, and flashing lights were everywhere. Inside the brothel, things were much more restrained. The cold, steel floor present outside was replaced by a plush, mauve-colored carpet. The walls were lined with a wainscot of stained wood with decorative wallpaper above. There was a crystal chandelier at the center of the ceiling, providing ample yet subdued light. There were a series of velvet-covered armchairs, arranged in groups throughout the modest antechamber. At the far corner, there was a podium, similar to that of a maître d's station of harbor, situated in front of a wide, curtained doorway. There were several men in the vestibule, sitting, waiting in the various chairs, but the Madame was nowhere in sight.

"Does this mean that we should come back later?" Francisco asked, obviously uncomfortable in the environment.

"No, this means that we wait. I'm sure the lovely ladies will parade themselves around any minute."

Oliver took a seat where he could see the entire room's layout. Francisco took the adjacent seat. They sat in silence, and as the time passed, Francisco appeared to relax. Then, as Oliver had predicted, a number of sensually dressed women paraded into the room. They were followed by a heavyset woman wearing more makeup than a circus clown.

"You think that's Madame Elina?" Francisco asked.

Oliver ignored Francisco's question, as he was previewing the women for hire.

"What's that?" Oliver asked, forcing his eyes back to Francisco.

"Is that Madame Elina?" Francisco repeated.

"Might be. Why don't you go find out? I'm going to go over and talk to those lovely ladies," Oliver said as he moved toward the gathered prostitutes.

Francisco waited several moments before making a move, cursing his own lack of confidence. When he'd joined the GSA, he'd never had any intention of becoming a field agent, opting for the scientific aspect of the job instead. That would've allowed him to maintain a much lower profile and stay in the shadows, which he preferred. Initially, when the director approached him about this particular mission, Francisco thought it would be a great opportunity to move up into the advanced departments he'd envisioned. Now, as he sat watching Oliver effortlessly converse with three attractive women, he began to wonder if he'd made the right decision.

Realizing that unless he got a move on, he'd suffer ridicule for his inaction, Francisco reluctantly stood and headed for the Madame.

Oliver approached the three harlots that had gathered near a previously unnoticed fireplace. Having visited similar establishments many times in his ignominious carrier, he had no reservations about approaching the women.

"Hi there. Could either of you direct me to the nearest monastery? I seem to have wandered off the righteous path," Oliver said, grinning widely.

Two of the women giggled uncontrollably, while the third wasn't as amused by Oliver's dry humor. She smiled nonetheless.

"Just how far have you strayed, mister?" a salacious blonde asked. The other two women, both brunettes, stood silently next to the stone hearth.

"Just far enough that I fully realize that I've done some very, very bad things," Oliver said. Then he threw out an exaggerated wink and moved closer to the blonde.

"Well, I'm not sure about redemption, but if you'd like to further your adulterous path, I'd love to show you the way," said the woman. "My name is Gigi. And you are?"

"Ryan," Oliver said, stating his agreed upon cover name prior to leaving the Buddha. "Very pleased to meet you."

"Tell me, Ryan," Gigi said as she slipped her arm into his. "What would you like me to do for you?"

Oliver smiled and nodded to the remaining two women as Gigi led him to a pair of chairs nestled out of the way. "I don't have anything in particular in mind. Do you have a specialty?"

"I have lots of specialties, darling, but each of them are valued differently. How much would you like to spend? I can tell you what's on the menu."

"Well, I've got a pocket full of credits, so the sky's the limit. To tell the truth, I've been out of touch for so long, I'd love to have an open menu, and if you have any … additional recreation, I might be obliged to partake in that as well."

Gigi's eyes brightened. "Well, you've come to the right place. Let's get a deposit in place with Madame Elina then we'll move into the back for a little privacy."

Francisco nervously stepped up to the podium where the Madame stood. She looked up with her sky blue eyeshadow and Merlot-colored lips and smiled. "Hi there, sugar. You see something you like?" she asked.

Francisco could feel beads of sweat began to build at his temples. He scanned through his mind, trying to pick out the words that he'd just rehearsed moments before. Unfortunately, he stood there, tongue-tied and completely embarrassed at his inability to function properly in the field. Visions of fight or flight passed through his mind, and as he was about to take the second option, he felt a firm slap on his back.

"Well, Drake, you almost beat me to the punch," Oliver said as he stepped up to the podium with Gigi on his arm.

"I, uh, yeah," is all that Francisco could get out.

"Well, I'm here now. I think I have what we we're looking for." He nodded his head toward Gigi. "You're okay with a threesome, right?" he asked her.

Gigi's nearly perfect smile wavered slightly, but returned

with gusto. "Yeah, sure," she said excitedly. "If Madame Elina is okay with it."

Before the Madame could respond, Oliver pulled out two thousand credits and dropped them on the podium. Everyone's eyes watched as the universal currency settled on the mahogany surface. Greedily, the Madame scooped up the credits and stuffed them into her brassiere then stepped to the side. "You three have a good time now, you hear?"

Gigi led the boys back into a dimly lit corridor, which was lined with several doors on each side. As they moved along, moans and groans could be heard. Toward the end of the hallway, Gigi turned to the left and a new corridor appeared, along with a new series of doors. About halfway down on the right, Gigi stopped and opened the door. She gestured for the two men to enter. Francisco entered first, followed by Oliver. Gigi stepped in and closed the door, startling Francisco.

"What do you two boys have in mind?" Gigi asked as she began to untie her sheer robe. Before either Oliver or Francisco could protest, she dipped her shoulders slightly and the robe dropped to the floor, revealing her naked body. "Do you want to go individually? Or would you rather all three of us go at it at the same time?"

Oliver glanced at Francisco and resisted laughing out loud at the stark white appearance on his face. "If you don't mind, it's been a long trip, and I'm not sure about Drake here, but I'd like a little something to ease my mind, if you know what I mean."

"Absolutely," Gigi said, moving to the bureau on the far wall. She slid open the drawer and withdrew a slim black box with some indistinguishable insignia etched on the cover. "What's your pleasure?" she asked.

Oliver stepped up to Gigi and noticed the hieroglyphs instantly. He recognized them from the research files back on the Buddha, being related to the Guzman family. He knew they were in the right place. "I'm not sure. Like I said, it's been a while. I've heard about this new drug, but I can't remember what it was. Something like white … hip? White … nose?"

"Ah, yes. I think you mean Whitetail. Unfortunately, you'll find none of that here, at least not today. I have some of these blue pills, if you need extra support, or if you really want to get crazy, I have some Ex, or—"

"No Whitetail?" Oliver asked, portraying disappointment. "A friend of mine said that if I'm ever in the outer ring, I've really got to try that, and I've had my heart set on it. Any chance you could—"

"Like I said, not today," Gigi said sternly then returned the black box to her bureau. When she turned back around, her smile reappeared and she moved to where they were standing.

"Now, if you wouldn't mind, I think we should all get down to business," Gigi said as she slipped her hand into Oliver's trousers while she kissed him to keep him from protesting.

Francisco stood, his mouth agape. "I, uh, I'm not feeling very well," he said, backing toward the door. "Hey, Mi … I mean, Ryan, I'm going to go wait out front."

Oliver only grunted.

Francisco closed the door behind him as he stood alone in the dimly lit hallway. Overwhelmed by the situation, he tried to recall the direction they came in, but he couldn't remember a thing. He looked to his left and then to his right, but both routes looked identical. He had a fifty-fifty shot of making the right decision and he turned to the right. At the end of the corridor, he came to a T. To the left was another long hallway. To the right, he found an opening that was draped with a velvet curtain. He remembered first coming back, and was almost positive that he passed a similar curtain, but could've sworn that they took more turns along the way. He stepped up, parted the curtains and walked through.

Once through the passageway, he stood in a small vestibule that had a single armchair with a broken leg, causing it to teeter to the left. Next to the chair was a door unlike the others in the establishment. All of the others featured pink diamonds at the center of charcoal-colored ovals. This door was titanium and looked more like an exit door than anything else.

"Ah, a backdoor," Francisco mumbled before pushing through.

On the other side of the doorway, Francisco froze. He stood in a long, narrow room that was barely illuminated. From what he could see, there were a dozen or so steel wired cages along each side of the room. In each of the cages, scared, bloodshot eyes stared back. He felt along the wall for a switch and flicked it on. Bright light flooded the room and the horror set in. Each of the pairs of eyes belonged to a different girl. From what he could see, the girls' ages varied from young teens to grown adults. Each of the women were completely naked and some were malnourished. Their wrists were bound behind their backs, and they all wore ball gags at their mouths.

Petrified at the sight, his first thought was to free them and escape the facility. As he rushed forward and began opening the first cage, his analytical mind stopped him. He knew that freeing the girls now would certainly spell doom for their mission, and the livelihood of his entire team. He paused for a moment, trying to decide what he should do. He looked down at the woman in the cage. She was a teen, probably fifteen or sixteen, her auburn hair tied back in a ponytail. Her blue eyes looked up at him, filled with fright. Her pale cheeks were stained with dried tears and grime.

"I'm sorry. I wish I could help you, but I can't right now. I want to help all of you," Francisco said, addressing all of the women. "But I'm outnumbered at the moment."

One by one, each of the women began to sob softly.

"Wait, wait. Please don't cry. You have to keep quiet. If you don't, someone will hear and who knows what they'll do? Hush, please."

Painfully, Francisco re-latched the lock on the cage and retreated to the door. He flicked off the light once again and stepped back through. He retraced his steps down the hall, passing the doorway that Gigi had led them to. At the other end of the corridor, he turned right and saw the familiar cordoned off doorway. Beyond it, Madame Elina stood, her back toward him. He took several deep breaths for courage then walked out.

Madame Elina looked at him and smiled. "Well, aren't you a quick finisher?" she said.

Francisco puffed out his chest and smiled as confidently as he could. "Well, some people say it isn't a race, but, you know," he said as he sauntered out into the promenade.

43

Jaxon and Camille waited for the elevator to arrive, hoping that it was empty when it did. As they stood in silence, Camille leaned her head onto Jaxon's shoulder, sliding her arm around his waist. Jaxon was unsure how to react. Since having her thrust back into his life, he'd fully realized what a terrible mistake he'd made abandoning her. He wondered, though, if her actions were for their mission's disguise, or if she harbored the same feelings for him that he did for her.

When the elevator opened, the car wasn't empty, but the man aboard stepped off and around them, uninterested. Stepping in and looking at the panel of buttons to the right, Jaxon noticed the familiarity in its layout, as it was similar to his own space station's design, mixed use floors above and residential floors below, and at the very bottom of the panel, there was a button labeled 50. They were on level M, probably representing *Main.*

"Shit," Jaxon muttered. *It had to be all the way at the bottom.*

Camille pushed the button, sending the elevator car down to what they hoped was a lead worth the risk. After several minutes of descent, the car slowed as the crimson digits above the door rolled over to their desired floor.

The doors parted, but neither Jaxon nor Camille moved right away. They stared out into a stark white corridor that carried away from them. At the far end, there was an unremarkable door.

"Well? What do you think?" Jaxon asked.

Camille remained silent for a moment before cautiously stepping out. Jaxon followed, then the doors closed. The sound of the elevator whisking back up hummed quietly.

"Okay then. I guess we're checking it out," Jaxon said, stepping ahead of Camille. When they reached the door, they found that it had no distinguishable markings whatsoever. Curiously, there wasn't even a door handle present. Jaxon looked at Camille then shrugged. He reached out and rapped on the door.

Boom, boom, boom, the sound echoed in the stark corridor.

They stood, quietly, for several moments before either of them heard a noise. Suddenly, a high-pitched whining echoed throughout as the perimeter of the doorframe began to glow red. At the same time, the center panel of the door transitioned from the color of the door skin into a kind of LCD display with five empty boxes across the top, and a 10-digit keypad below. There was also a timer displaying 0:60 present. Then, the red glow at the doorframe began to flash in one-second intervals, in sync with the clock ticking backward. Fifty-nine, fifty-eight, fifty-seven ...

"What do you think?" Jaxon asked.

Camille narrowed her eyes on the keypad and reached out to enter the code given to them.

"Hold on a sec," Jaxon said. "Suppose we enter the wrong code?"

"Well, there's only one way to find out," Camille said,

holding her hand just millimeters away from the screen.

Before she touched the display, Jaxon looked over his shoulder, and his facial expression turned to shock. Camille saw his change and followed his eyes.

"Jesus," she exclaimed. "I guess if we don't get it right ... we're as good as dead," she said, staring at the machine gun that had lowered from the ceiling, pointing directly at them.

"Yeah, pretty much. Either that or ..." Jaxon paused and looked toward the elevator itself and was further discouraged to find that another blank door had suddenly appeared halfway down the hall.

"Or what?" Camille asked.

"Look," Jaxon said, pointing past the machine gun.

Camille exhaled dramatically.

"My sentiments exactly," Jaxon said, refocusing his attention on the display. Twenty-five, twenty-four ...

Without hesitation, Camille reached out and touched the keypad.

Five, zero, nine, six, one.

Nothing happened.

A few seconds later, the timer stopped, and the flashing red doorframe turned blue. A faint mechanical grinding noise could be heard from the other side of the door. Then, a click as the door popped open.

"Well, there you go," Jaxon said as he looked back at the machine gun. It was gone. It had retracted back up the moment they entered the correct code.

"Shall we?" Camille asked, moving toward the open door.

Jaxon reached out and gently tugged on her arm, pulling her back.

"Wait up a minute," Jaxon said. "Maybe we should rethink this. Maybe only one of us should go in, and the other should go check on the boys."

"Split up? Now? But we're so close."

"I know. But if this goes south, and they close us in again," Jaxon said, motioning toward the now visible elevator door, "we'll both be trapped down here. But, if you go back up now, you'll at least know where to come get me if something happens."

"But why you? I might have a better chance of persuading whoever is behind the door to give us what we're looking for," Camille said convincingly.

"Like you could actually talk your way out of a risky situation better than me."

She smiled, leaning into him closely, pressing her breasts against his chest. "Yes. Because I have lady parts, and you don't. Men are suckers for a nice rack."

Jaxon's heart rate increased momentarily at the closeness of Camille. He could smell her delicate scent, and he longed to touch that which was pressed firmly against his body.

"I don't know, Camille. Suppose it's a woman? She might be looking for a man just like me to sweep her off her feet."

"Oh, I'm sorry, what was the name on that card again?" She winked.

Jaxon sighed. "It's Ziggi, but I still think it's you that should head up. I've had nearly a lifetime of fieldwork, and I don't want to see you get hurt. Besides, you can use your lady parts to control the boys if they get out of line."

Defeated, Camille closed her eyes and nodded. "Point taken," she said. A moment later, she leaned in close to his ear and whispered. "At least let me track you," she said before kissing him on the nape of his neck. With her right hand, she reached up behind his left ear and pressed firmly, activating his implanted tracer module.

A moment later she slowly pulled herself away from him and sauntered back toward the elevator.

Jaxon waited until she was on the elevator and the door closed before he moved forward.

Pushing the door fully open, he stepped into another long corridor. One that carried on in opposite directions perpendicular to the one that he'd just exited. As he looked right, he could see it curve further to the right until it was out of sight. When he looked left, he saw the same thing, curving and disappearing to the left. Based on assumed space station design, he was most likely at the outer wall of the facility, and the hallway ran a complete circle. Without hesitation, he turned to his right and began looking for something, or someone.

"Ziggi, where are you?"

44

The elevator door closed, and as soon as she pressed M, the elevator car began to rise, taking her further away from Jaxon.

"Dammit. Dammit, dammit, dammit," Camille exclaimed. Why did she let him talk her into splitting up? she asked herself. Deep down, though, she knew he was right. About everything. His practical experience far outweighed anything she had to offer, and getting trapped down below while the rest of the team remained unaware of the dangers was not good. Regardless, she remained upset about leaving him in such troubling circumstances. She only hoped that it wasn't as bad a situation as her mind seemed to be telling her it was.

A moment later, the elevator arrived back at the main level. She stepped out and was instantly assaulted by the bright lights and hectic sounds echoing in from the casino. She knew right then that she was not cut out for that kind of lifestyle. She much preferred the peace and quiet of her old life, back on Earth.

She crossed through the casino and out into the

promenade on the far side. She followed along, outright ignoring the solicitors trying to lure her into their grainy establishments. When she reached the end of the promenade, she stood in front of the brothel and wondered if the boys were still in there. She contemplated returning to the ship to see if they returned early. If she did, and they weren't back yet, she'd have wasted all that time going through security for nothing.

"Dammit all to hell," she muttered.

Exasperated, she stepped up and was about push through and into The Pleasure Gauntlet when she heard a voice from behind her.

"Camille?" came the familiar voice.

She let go of the door handles and turned to see Francisco walking out of one of the pubs along the promenade. "Oh, thank God," she exclaimed.

Francisco walked right up to Camille and hugged her tightly.

"It's all right, Clay," Camille said. "Is something the matter?" she asked, pulling away.

"No, yes ... I mean, no. I think everything is fine, but—"

"Relax, Clay. Explain to me what happened. Is Miles okay?"

Francisco smirked. "I think Miles is doing just fine. We were in one of the hook ... I mean prostitutes' rooms and we were asking about the Whitetail. She got kind of weird about it and said that there was no drug like that on the station today. Then she and Miles kind of ... well you know."

"You mean sex, Clay? You do realize you were in a whorehouse, right?" she asked.

"Well, yeah, but I didn't think we were allowed to ... do that," Francisco said, blushing.

Camille laughed. "It's certainly something I don't agree with, but Miles is his own man, and if he felt that sleeping with a prostitute could get him more information, then who are we to disagree?"

"Yeah, I suppose. It was just kind of ... awkward, you

know? We sold our cover as two guys looking for a threesome, and I was there in the room when she stripped naked and was all over Miles' mouth."

Camille fought back more laughing as she saw Francisco's face and neck turn red from embarrassment. "It'll be okay. How long ago was that?"

"Maybe thirty minutes ago? But that's not the worst of it," Francisco said, doom filling his eyes.

"There's more?" Camille asked.

"Yeah, lots. Maybe we should have a seat while I explain," Francisco said, leading Camille back into the bar and to a table in front of the window. Over the next ten minutes, Francisco explained to Camille about his escape from the prostitute's room and then finding that horrific chamber with all of the women in cages. He explained everything in great detail, leaving nothing out. When he was finished, he leaned back and took a swig from his longneck bottle of beer.

"My God," Camille said, shocked at hearing the details of what Francisco had witnessed.

"What are we going to do?" he asked. "We have to save them, right? I know that if we call this in, they'll tell us to leave it alone because it has nothing to do with our mission. But, come on. We just can't leave them there, can we?"

"Well, let's wait for the rest of the team to gather before we make a decision. I agree, something has to be done. But ..." Camille paused as she thought about where she left Jaxon.

"But what?" Francisco prompted.

"Well, it's just that Jaxon is in a pretty difficult situation himself. He's some fifty levels down in the space station as we speak. He had a strong lead when we decided to split up."

"So you found the production plant?" Francisco asked, eager to find out more.

"Not sure," Camille said. "Once we got down there, we got cornered inside a virtual mouse trap. It was lucky we had the right code, or otherwise, the team would be minus two members."

It was Camille's turn to explain. She described the entire ordeal in equal detail, maintaining Francisco's attention throughout.

"So, here we are. I think what we need to do first is get Miles out, and then we need to return to the ship."

"But what about all those girls?" Francisco asked.

"We'll deal with them after we get our team back together. Right now, that's our priority, and then once Jaxon returns, we'll see what our options are."

Francisco nodded and finished off his beer, his face somber with disappointment.

"Now, let's go get Miles," Camille said, leading the way out of the bar and right toward the doors of The Pleasure Gauntlet.

45

Jaxon walked along the gently curving hallway, trying each door that he came to for access. Each one was locked, and there was no response to the repeated knocks. Finally, when he felt that he'd circumnavigated the entire space station, he caught sight of a different styled door coming into view. Cautiously, Jaxon slowed his pace and contemplated whether he should go into agent mode and strife along the wall, or continue on as if he was there for a purpose. Seeing as the casino dealer upstairs gave him the information freely, he felt the second option remained his best one.

Jaxon walked up to the door and knocked three times. A few minutes later, a woman opened the door and stared at him curiously. She was a short Asian woman wearing an orange jumpsuit, a dust mask hanging loosely around her neck.

"Felicity sent me. I'm looking for Ziggi," Jaxon said, keeping the conversation to a minimum.

"Door down hall," she said in broken English and pointed to the right.

Jaxon nodded. "Thanks," he said, peering into the room

behind her. From his vantage point, he could see at least nine other women in similar orange jumpsuits, also wearing dust masks. They were lined up along several banks of countertops, sorting what appeared to be Universal Credit bills. As he attempted to see further into the room, the Asian women stepped back and slammed the door.

At least he was heading in the right direction, Jaxon thought. As he continued through the corridor, he reviewed what he just saw. Ten women wearing jumpsuits very similar in color to the standard medium of exchange in the outer ring, splattered ink covering their fronts. If he didn't know any better, he'd have sworn that they were counterfeiting in that room.

No, he thought. *Not my mission. I need to find Ziggi and ... Whitetail.*

Finally, Jaxon came to another door that bore the number 961. Jaxon knew instantly that he was in the right place, as the room number was part of his five-digit access code. He knocked, and without waiting, threw open the door.

Not knowing what to expect, Jaxon stood in the open doorway and stared into a relatively small, cluttered room. It couldn't have been more than three or four meters wide and deep, and the ceiling wasn't much higher. At the center of the room sat an industrial-style desk with a metal top and drawers. There was wire shelving stacked floor to ceiling around the perimeter of the room. The room was vacant.

Jaxon leaned back into the hallway and peered as far as he could see in both directions. He was alone.

He stepped in and closed the door, then began rummaging through the contents of the shelves. He wasn't exactly sure what he was looking for, but with the name Whitetail, he figured the pills, assuming the dose was in pill form, would at least be white in color.

On the first stack of shelves, he found several plastic bins with cellophane bags filled with a dingy white substance. Figuring it was either heroin or cocaine, he moved on. The next set of shelves was filled with bottles of pink and black pills, and they at least had the label X in some designer font.

Jaxon continued rummaging through bin after bin, shelf after shelf, finding every imaginable drug known, and some unknown. Nothing jumped out at him, saying: *Hey, look. I'm Whitetail!*

The last wall of shelves had only boxes. He began flipping open the tops and found proof of his earlier suspicion. He found banded stacks of freshly minted universal credits. He combed through several stacks and found that their printing numbers had consecutive serial numbers.

All this, and no Whitetail, Jaxon thought. Perhaps Ziggi wasn't the man that he needed to talk to after all.

Jaxon returned the stacks of credits to the box and put it back on the shelf. A second after he released the box handle, the door swung open and in stepped a tall, rather spindly man.

"Who are you?" he demanded, shutting the door behind him. As he waited for Jaxon to respond, his hand rested on a weapon strapped to his waist.

"Hi there. Name's Graham. I was just up at the casino, and Felicity sent me down here and said I could talk to Ziggi. Are you him?" Jaxon asked, trying not to appear threatening.

"I am. But you shouldn't be here, certainly not alone," Ziggi said, maintaining contact with his weapon.

"Hey," Jaxon said, holding his hands up in protest. "I'm just looking for a good time. I asked Felicity where I could score some Whitetail, and she gave me your name with the number 50961. So? Here I am. I have—"

"No Whitetail here. I'm calling security now," Ziggi said, moving to the corner of the desk, where a small communication device sat.

"Listen, Ziggi. I'm not looking for any trouble. I'm really not. My wife and I are just looking for something new and fun, and all of my friends said to give this Whitetail a try. Honestly, I don't know what they're all talking about, and we're here on kind of a second honeymoon and ..." Jaxon stopped, as he'd moved closer. He shot his hand toward Ziggi's throat, his fingers rigid. He could feel Ziggi's trachea snap upon contact.

Ziggi fell to the floor in agony. He dropped the communication device and clutched his throat as he fought for air. His gasps for life quickly turned to gurgling.

"Now, listen here, Ziggi. I'm going to ask you this just once. I'm looking for Whitetail, and I need to know where I can find it. Do you understand?" Jaxon asked, placing his hand firmly on Ziggi's shoulder, holding him down to the ground.

Ziggi nodded, his gurgling turning to wheezing.

"Great. Now, tell me what I need to know. Can I find Whitetail here on Delta Station?"

Ziggi shook his head slowly, the pain evident with every movement.

"If I move on to Upsilon Station, will I have any luck finding Whitetail there?" Jaxon asked.

Again, Ziggi shook his head from side to side.

Jaxon exhaled loudly. "Oh, Ziggi. Perhaps I impaired your voice too soon. I so wish I could just ask you where we could find it, and you could just tell me, isn't that right?"

Ziggi nodded, and he attempted to speak. A gurgling yelp passed his lips before he spat blood to the floor.

"Well, I guess we are going to have to do this the slow way." Jaxon gripped Ziggi by the back of his shoulders and yanked him to his feet. He thrust him against the side wall before he bounced down behind his desk. Forcefully, he sat Ziggi in his office chair and scanned across the desk for a pen. Finding what he was looking for, he placed it in front of Ziggi and said, "Write. I want you to tell me the closest station where I can find Whitetail. Then, I need you to write down the location of where it's being made. Do you understand?"

Ziggi picked up the pen and began to write. Jaxon stood behind him, holding his neck firmly as he read the words coming out of Ziggi's pen.

Omega Station. Then Ziggi dropped the pen to the desk.

"What's this? Is this where it's made or where I can find

it?" Jaxon asked.

Ziggi quickly picked up the pen and wrote out the word *Made*. He looked up at Jaxon, his eyes pleading for mercy.

"Well, Ziggi, that's quite extraordinary. I really would like to thank you for your assistance here. But I'm not sure if I'll be able to make it out of here if I leave you alive. What do you think, Ziggi? Do I have to enforce your silence permanently?"

Ziggi vehemently shook his head, fear spreading deep into his eyes.

Jaxon didn't recall seeing Omega Station on the list from Evans. He wondered if Ziggi was telling the truth or if he was leading him into a trap. As Jaxon contemplated this, Ziggi's hand disappeared beneath his desk, and by the time Jaxon noticed, it was too late. The warning alarm began to blare throughout the station. He knew then that he wouldn't be leaving the station of his own volition.

Aggravated by the battle that was certainly ahead of him, Jaxon raised his arm high above his head and brought it down firmly, connecting his elbow and forearm hard on the back of Ziggi's head. Ziggi slumped over his desk, unconscious.

Jaxon rushed to the door and bolted out into the hallway before sprinting toward the elevator. He figured that if the alarm had just sounded, it would take a fair bit of time before security realized where the danger really was. He hoped that'd give him enough time to at least get into the elevator or possibly find a back stairway.

As he continued sprinting through the curved hallway, he flew by the printing room; thankfully, the door was still closed. Jaxon continued to be astonished at the meager level of security on the level, especially with all the illicit activities occurring. Then he remembered the automatic machine gun that lowered from the ceiling. He knew instantly that there would be no way for him to get through that final corridor and into the elevator without getting shot by the automatic defense system. He stopped in his tracks and decided to backtrack to possibly find another way out, anything that would prevent him from moving through that main entrance to the level.

Jaxon ran in the opposite direction, and as he approached the printing room again, he noticed the door open, and he quickly flattened himself against the side wall and strafed up to the edge of the opening. As he ducked his head in, a fist came directly at his face, connecting firmly on the bridge of his nose. First, his vision turned red as the blood gushed. Then it turned to darkness as he fell to the ground, out cold.

C amille burst through the oak doors of The Pleasure Gauntlet, anger in her eyes. She continued past several barely dressed hookers, and their soliciting customers, heading directly for the Madame.

"Where the hell is my husband?" Camille demanded. "We were supposed to be here on our honeymoon, and he said he was coming down to the promenade for a drink. I've been asking all day, and everybody keeps telling me he came in here!"

A look of confusion and worry spread across Madame Elina's face. "I'm sorry, Miss, but I cannot be held responsible for the behaviors of men. What they do with their own lives is their business. Perhaps if you had a stronger relationship with your husband?" Madame Elina said sternly.

"Listen, you bitch. Tell me where I can find my husband this very instant or there'll be hell to pay," Camille said, portraying the role of a jealous spouse.

Madame Elina looked Camille up and down before speaking again.

"Listen, Missy. I'm not completely dispassionate to your pleas. I, too, was once a woman scorned. But you have to understand, of the hundreds of men that come through my door, only a small fraction of those are men that wander. I can't have you coming in here, making wild accusations. Perhaps if you describe your husband, I can tell you whether or not he's even here."

Camille stepped up to the podium and looked Madame Elina in the eyes. "He's just short of three meters tall, black hair, grayish eyes, and somewhat stocky. His name is—"

"I don't need a name, sweetie. Besides, we like to keep things anonymous. I remember seeing your man. He and another gentleman went back about forty minutes ago. Something about a threesome?"

"I think you're mistaken. My husband would never partake in anything so … unthinkable," Camille said, pouring on the naïve wife role thick.

"Regardless of what you think, I'm telling you what I saw. They left me two thousand credits as a retainer on her services and walked through that doorway," Madame Elina said. "Strangely, though, the younger gentleman that went back with them came back out shortly after. I don't think he was back there for even ten minutes."

"Well, tell me which room and I'll go get him myself."

"I don't think that's wise," Madame Elina said. "I should send somebody else back. You know, privacy concerns and all."

Camille stood in front of the podium, staring at Madame Elina. Although she'd hoped that she might be able to catch a glimpse of the horrors that Francisco described for herself, she knew it was a long shot being allowed back into the catacombs of the brothel on her own. Finally, not seeing any other resolution, Camille nodded.

"Okay, fine. But just don't tell him I'm out here. Make up something else, because I want to see his lying and cheating face when he sees me standing here," Camille said, confident that she sold the story well.

Madame Elina smiled scornfully before disappearing behind the velvet curtains.

Camille anxiously paced around the plush foyer of The Pleasure Gauntlet, fighting the urge to rush back and see the atrocities that Francisco had described.

After several minutes and no sign of Oliver, she began to think something might have gone wrong. She couldn't imagine what would cause such a delay getting Miles dressed if he, in fact, was in the sack with the hooker.

Suddenly, the dimmed lights brightened fully, and a strip of red began to flash at the junction where the wall met the ceiling. Faintly, she could hear a repeating alarm, honking on and off. Then, the entry doors burst open, and the sound level increased dramatically.

"What did you do?" Francisco asked, stepping in.

"I didn't do a thing," Camille pleaded. "I ... just told her a small fallacy to give her a little motivation on getting Miles out here."

"What did you say?" Francisco asked, concerned.

"Wasn't anything big. I just said that I was his wife and that I was irate that he was in here screwing one of her whores. See? Just a little lie."

Francisco whistled with astonishment. "Couldn't you have just said ... I don't know, maybe that you're colleagues, and the ship was getting ready to leave?"

Camille sulked and nodded in agreement. "Yeah, I suppose. But my story had much more pizzazz."

"Not if she just called security on you for being a crazy, jealous, whack-job of a wife," Francisco pointed out.

"Yeah, well ... just wait outside and we'll be out in a minute ... hopefully." Camille hoped that she didn't jeopardize the mission with her antics.

No sooner than Francisco closed the front door, Oliver came stumbling through the curtains, followed by Madame Elina.

"... and I don't care if you were finished or not. The party's over!" Madame Elina said as she continued to chase after Oliver. "This him?" she asked.

"Yeah, that's my man," Camille said sullenly. "Did you sound the alarm because of me?"

"What? Oh, no. I don't know what that's for. Probably some brawl going on in the casino or who knows where else," Madame Elina said. "Now you two just get out of here. And honey, do yourself a favor and keep control of your man if you don't want him wondering back in here on his own."

Oliver looked at Camille with a confused look.

"Later," Camille said as she grabbed him by the collar and dragged him out into the promenade.

As soon as they were out of Madame Elina's sight, Camille released Oliver and gave him a wink. A few moments later, Francisco joined them, flinching at each sound of the alarm.

"What's going on?" Oliver asked, tucking in his shirt.

"Not sure. We thought the Madame sounded the alarm after I came in asking for you. But ..." Camille said, trailing off. "But I think it might be something to do with Jaxon."

"Weren't you two supposed to be together?" Oliver asked.

"Yeah, but we split up after a fairly frightening ordeal. I'll explain later. Right now, I think we should get to the ship and activate his tracer."

"You activated his tracer?" Francisco asked. "You didn't tell me that."

"Slipped my mind," Camille said as she started toward the other end of the promenade.

Despite the loud sirens and the flashing lights, most of the patrons along the sidewalks were either oblivious to the impending danger, or they knew something that the team didn't know. Regardless, the grating sound caused just a bit more urgency in their step.

As soon as they made it to the grand staircase, the emergency must have been taken care of, because the lights returned to normal, and the blaring alarm ceased completely.

"Dammit," Camille said. "I wish there was a way we could

communicate with Jaxon."

"I don't know. I think he'll be fine," Francisco said. "I know I've only known him for a few days, but … I think he knows how to take care of himself."

Camille chuckled. "And sometimes, that's all he takes care of."

They climbed the stairs and made for the docking bay. Not surprisingly, the security getting out of the space station was nearly as strenuous as it was getting in. They each got a full pat down and body scan. Once they were cleared, they cycled through the airlock and were back in the Buddha.

"Clay, I need you to start tracking Jaxon's tracer. How sensitive is the reading?" Camille asked.

"If I remember my training well enough, I think it's based predominantly on proximity to the receiving device. If we're close, the sensitivity is tighter. Within a meter or two. But at a distance, I think we can scan for him up to a few thousand kilometers. But then, the accuracy is scaled proportionately."

"Great. I last left him on the fiftieth floor below us. We'll maintain dock until he's on board. But I want you to watch his every movement."

Francisco nodded and disappeared into the control room.

"Miles, I want you to get through your preflight check. Get everything ready to go, so the moment Jaxon comes aboard you're releasing the docking clamps. Something feels … wrong. I can't put my finger on it, but I think … I feel that we're in trouble."

"You got it, boss," Oliver said, following Francisco up the ramp.

Camille stood in the main hold for several minutes, contemplating her next move. She was reluctant to follow through with her next action, but she knew that she had to. She had to call this in.

She retreated to her quarters and withdrew a compact, long-range radio and fingered the mic.

"Bluto, come in. This is Olive Oil, do you read? Bluto, come in."

47

Jaxon began to stir, and when he opened his eyes, he only saw darkness. He blinked several times, hoping to clear his vision. As the rest of his senses returned, he determined that his eyes were fine, but he had a hood draped over his head. He tried to pull it off, but his arms were bound behind his back.

Shit. Not this again.

Determined, Jaxon dropped his head between his knees and worked his leg pressure in concert with the strategic twisting of his neck until he was able to work the hood loose. Once enough slack was at the top of the hood, he was able to pinch just enough of the cloth between his knees to pull it all the way off.

With his sight returned, he looked around. He appeared to be in a bunkroom quite similar to the one back on the Buddha. There was a single bed along the wall and a small desk opposite it. There was a small portal halfway up the wall, looking out into space.

"Mffer," Jaxon tried to say, but the ball gag strapped to his mouth prevented any legible words from escaping.

He swung his feet to the ground and looked at them, expecting to see shackles. Thankfully, he thought, he was only bound at the wrists, with a gag to keep him silent.

He stood and wobbled about from sudden dizziness. He sat back down until he regained his balance. As he waited for the room to stop spinning, he took stock of the rest of his condition. His head throbbed, and various parts of his face ached. No doubt from the last thing he remembered—being punched in the face. He looked down at himself and saw that he was still wearing the tuxedo he'd purchased on Beta Station.

After several minutes, Jaxon stood, slowly, and began walking in circles in the small bunkroom. He'd always thought better when he paced, and thinking was exactly what he needed. He began to determine the depth of the shithole he was in.

First, he was clearly no longer on Delta Station, made obvious by the spaceship bunkroom. Furthermore, when he leaned his head against the bulkhead, he could sense a gentle vibration caused by the ship's engine.

Thoughts of escape flooded Jaxon's mind, and he knew that he'd be fighting an uphill battle with his hands tied behind his back. He knew what he had to do, and his stomach tightened at the thought.

Slowly, Jaxon bent over at the waist and pulled his left arm tight against the restraints. Once he felt the resistance at its extreme, Jaxon jerked his head hard to the right, dislocating the left shoulder. The pain was severe, but it allowed him to loop his arms down past his lower back and legs. Finally, Jaxon leaned back and fell onto the bunk as he lifted his feet in the air, allowing his bound hands to pass over freely.

Perspiration began to flow as Jaxon stood once again, his left shoulder slumping unnaturally. He walked to the bulkhead and raised his left elbow so that it was perpendicular to his torso. The position was painful, but he knew it would be over soon enough. Once his position was set, he rammed his shoulder back into its socket by driving his body sideways. The pain was most severe at that moment, but it subsided quickly once everything was back in its proper place.

Jaxon craned his neck from side to side, cracking his vertebra in the process. *Much better,* he thought.

He reached up and touched the skin beneath his ear and felt his tracking module still in place. *At least they didn't take everything,* he thought.

With a sense of clarity returning to him, he went to the portal and peered out, hoping to see something, anything, remotely familiar. There were no space stations or other ships in sight. All he could see was darkness. A moment later, the door to his bunkroom whisked open.

Jaxon turned and saw a familiar face, but he couldn't quite place him. After a few seconds, though, the battle injuries on his arm and face gave it away. He was one of the killers on Taloo Station, an obvious survivor from the grenade barrage he'd unleashed just outside his apartment door.

"You're up," the disfigured man said as he stood at the threshold. "Come with me."

The man grabbed Jaxon firmly by the shoulder and shoved him out into the corridor, slamming him into the adjacent wall. Jaxon was prepared for the hit and twisted his body at the last moment, avoiding a face-first collision.

The killer followed after Jaxon and continued to thrash him forward, down the corridor and into a large holding room, quite similar to the one back on the Buddha. Strangely, the ship's layout was actually quite similar to his own.

As Jaxon tumbled into the main hold, there were two other men, both dressed in the same black ninja suits that he'd seen on every other man or woman trying to kill him. At least he now knew who his captor was. All he could think about was how he could get away.

"I'm sorry, Mr. Rasner. You are, no doubt, thinking of a way out of your situation, but I assure you, there will be no escape for you today," came a voice from the control room door.

The man walked down the ramp, his hands neatly clasped behind his back. He maintained eye contact with Jaxon.

"Who are you?" Jaxon asked from the grasp of the killer at the center of the main hold.

"My name is Theodore Johansson, and I'm so very pleased to meet you," he said as he walked right up.

"I'd say likewise, but ... all I know is you guys have been trying to kill me for—"

"Don't hold that against us, Mr. Rasner. We were only doing

our job. It really wasn't anything personal. Besides, the assassination order on you has been retracted now that we have you in custody."

"Well, there's that at least," Jaxon said sarcastically.

"Ah, yes. They've told me that you are a positive thinker. Always looking at the bright side of things. I find that endearing in a man, and I think more people should think like that. Don't you agree, Mr. Rasner?" Johansson asked, clearly looking for an answer from Jaxon.

Who is this guy? Jaxon wondered. *As far as I know, I haven't had a tremendous amount of positive thinking lately.*

"Yeah, sure. There's a bright side to everything," Jaxon said.

Johansson paid no attention to Jaxon's reply. "Well, I just wanted to introduce myself. Your time here on the Calliope is about to come to an end. I trust the ride was smooth for you?" he asked condescendingly.

Jaxon ignored the question and asked his own. "Where are we docking?"

"Yes, that's right. It's my understanding that you've been looking for Mr. Guzman's secret hideout. Is that correct?" Johansson asked.

Jaxon shrugged but remained silent.

"Well, you'll be happy to know that your search will be over momentarily. I just came from the control room, and we're approaching Mr. Guzman's station as we speak."

"Guzman's here?" Jaxon asked, startled.

"Why yes," Johansson said. "He's the one that put the hit on you in the first place. Well, Pablo *and* his de facto cohort at the GSA, that is. Isn't it wonderful how two distinctively different organizations can function as one?"

The moment Johansson's words hit him, Jaxon began to put the pieces together. Obviously, the mole inside the GSA worked for Guzman. Current mission planning had been in the works for many months, giving Guzman enough time to hire mercenaries to prevent Jaxon from carrying it out. Everything began to make sense.

"Cat got your tongue?" Johansson asked.

Jaxon kept quiet and just glared at Johansson.

"Suit yourself," Johansson said as he turned toward the control room. "I assure you, though, our conversation would have been far more civil than what you're about to experience with Mr. Guzman himself."

And then he was gone.

"Clay, I need you to take over my console. Continue to monitor the stealth frequency," Camille said as she entered the cockpit.

"No problem, Camille," Francisco said, "but isn't that automated now?"

Camille walked past him as she headed for the pilot station. Jaxon's chair. "Yes, that's right. But I have reason to believe our efforts might be all for not."

"Then should I just change them manually? Or is that futile as well?" Francisco asked.

"Unknown. If we remove the subroutine, perhaps we'll be able to stay ahead of them. It's worth a shot at least." Camille turned to Oliver next. "Miles, can you program the navigation computer to follow a frequency beacon?"

Oliver nodded. "I don't see why not. You can program it to follow a specific number of waypoints and even tell it to avoid certain regions, whether it's spatial radiation or gamma rays, so I don't see why it would be any different to follow something specific."

"Okay, great. Why don't you get working on that and as soon as we can locate Jaxon's tracking device, be ready to enter it in."

"Sure thing, boss," Oliver said, getting to work. "Where should we set our heading for until then? We've just cleared the restricted idle zone around Delta Station. But we're not exactly heading in any specific direction."

"Leave it be for now," Camille said as she activated the long-range sensors on her display. "I'd hate to go too far in the wrong direction until we locate Jaxon's tracer."

The next several hours passed by wordlessly as each of the remaining team members focused on their individual responsibilities. Camille continued to analyze the readings of the sensors, trying to locate Jaxon's signal. Not having adequate training on the ship's systems or even a marginal understanding of what exactly she was looking for made the effort that much more difficult.

When a new signal blip appeared, she highlighted it in zoomed in, only to find out that it was some random freighter ship heading in the opposite direction. She knew enough about the transponder frequencies that once she found it, it would be obvious. But it was still like finding a needle in a haystack.

After what felt like an eternity of benign starts, a new signal blip entered the top of her screen. As she zoomed in and highlighted the signal, the frequency initially read out of range, but after a moment, the frequency readout changed, displaying exactly what she was looking for. It was Jaxon's transponder.

"Got it," she exclaimed. "He's on the far edge of our sensor range, and it looks like he's ... hold on." Camille paused as she analyzed the signal data for its trajectory. "At zenith: Longitude, 113° 00' 37.7". Latitude, +0° 57' 42.2". Distance, 697,384 kilometers."

"Got it," Oliver said, entering the coordinates into his control panel. "I see it, but it's—"

"It's what?" Camille asked, prompting Oliver to continue.

"It's just there. There's no ship on our sensors—just the

signal. They didn't eject him out into space, did they?"

Camille cringed at the thought. Not exactly sure who they were dealing with, she couldn't discount it either way.

"Lord, I hope not," she said. "Are you sure your readings are correct?"

"Positive, boss. It's like he's just zipping through space all by himself."

Camille pondered the situation. At his current speed, he had to be assisted by some kind of thruster or impulse drive. If he'd just been ejected into space, there'd be no way he could reach that velocity on his own.

"Maybe he's on some kind of cloaked ship or one that has a stealth device like ours."

"Could be. Only way to find out is to get eyes on it."

"Right. How long until we can intercept?" Camille asked.

Oliver tapped in a few computations in his computer and waited. "At maximum speed, we could be there in a little over thirty minutes. That's assuming they don't increase their speed in the meantime."

Camille thought about the attack on the Buddha earlier, and how they somehow got through the stealth frequencies. She was concerned that it could happen again.

"No, I don't want to crowd them. If they can somehow see us coming, which I suspect they might be able to, I don't want to provoke a confrontation. Let's go at half speed, but not on a direct course. I want to plot an undulating course, keeping Jaxon's transponder on the edge of sensor range. With any luck, if they can see us, they'll think we're just some kind of mining vessel."

Oliver entered Camille's instructions into the navigation computer and engaged the engines. The ship banked left swiftly, and they were under way. "ETA, fifty-eight minutes," Oliver said.

As the familiar clank and whine of the ship's docking clamp engaged, Jaxon's disfigured guard pulled him up from his flight chair and thrust him toward the airlock. Stepping through the docking ring and into the space station, Jaxon glanced back and discovered that they were on a ship identical to the prototype that the GSA had provided for him and his team. Jaxon wondered just how deep the deception ran.

The guard continued to guide Jaxon through the corridors of the space station, which were more like a military installation than the pleasure station that he'd known until now. As they moved through bleak hallways, they passed several men and women wearing white lab coats hustling about.

After numerous twists and turns through the corridors, Jaxon was led down a particularly wide hallway that was lined with glass walls. Because of the transparency, it was clear that they were some kind of chemistry labs, but not the production facility that he'd been looking for. Jaxon attempted to slow his pace to try and glean as much information as he could, but the guard continued thrusting him forward.

Finally, after even more stark hallways, Jaxon was shoved into a small holding cell, and then the door slammed. The door was solid, save for a small window peering out. Inside the room, there was a fold-out cot on the side wall and a combination sink-toilet directly next to it. Unfortunately, the guard did not remove his restraints, so he was still limited in his escape potential.

Jaxon sat on the cot and considered his situation. He only hoped that his tracking device was still functioning and that Camille was on her way. Next, Jaxon thought about the links between the company and his captors. The *prototype* ship was clearly provided to both Guzman and the GSA, no doubt giving Guzman full knowledge of its stealth capabilities and weaponry. Jaxon was honestly surprised just how far he and his team had gotten, considering how underhanded they'd been the whole time. Or perhaps that was the plan all along— get them this close before Guzman swooped in and snatched him away.

Jaxon's thoughts were interrupted as the door clanked open, and in stepped Pablo Guzman himself.

"Well, if it isn't Jaxon Rasner in person," Guzman said. "Let me tell you, you're a tough man to kill."

"You're behind my assassination attempts?" Jaxon asked, already knowing the answer, but he wanted to hear it from Guzman himself.

"Yes, that's right. I am the monster that you created ... when you killed my father all those years ago."

"But I didn't—" Jaxon began but was interrupted.

"Do you deny being in Ixtapa eighteen years ago? Do you deny shooting him from the hotel room across the plaza?" Guzman asked. "Do you deny maiming a young man—a mere child?" Guzman turned his horrifically scarred face toward Jaxon. "Do you deny being a coward?"

Guzman's anger radiated through the small cell. With each

accusation, he became angrier, causing redness to flourish across his olive-colored skin.

"You should have been murdered years ago for the pain you've caused my family," Guzman said, relaxing his angry grimace into a pleasant smile. "But if I'd known that this moment would be so glorious, seeing your face in person, I would've never put the hit out on you as suggested by Brutus."

"I'm sorry," Jaxon said, "but you have me at a disadvantage. Who is Brutus?"

"Ah, Señor. Brutus and I go way back. Actually, Brutus goes so far back that I'm not even sure you were born yet when he and my father agreed to help each other with their various *complications*."

"So, Brutus is your mole? Does he have another name that I might—"

"Silence!" Guzman demanded.

Jaxon followed the order. He recognized the instability in Guzman and knew that if he wasn't careful, he could in fact cause the man to lose control completely and exact the revenge that was surging through his veins.

"Good, that's good, Mr. Rasner," Guzman said as he paced back and forth in front of Jaxon's bunk. "Who I associate myself with inside your company, your *GSA*, is none of your concern. If I were you, I would worry more about how exactly you are going to die." Guzman leaned in close to Jaxon's face. "And let me tell you, it will not be a pleasant experience. I will not afford you the same consideration that you gave my father all those years ago. It will be slow and painful." Guzman spat with each word, causing Jaxon to nearly gag at the stench coming past his lips.

"But," Guzman began, standing upright, "before we get started, I think we first need to neutralize the rest of your traveling companions. Tell me, Mr. Rasner, where exactly are they hiding? I had hoped that I could capture all of you in one, solitary swift motion. But then again, I should have figured otherwise—you're all trained agents, after all. It was wise of you to split up."

Jaxon was elated to hear that the rest of the team was still out there. As much as he wanted to throw it into Guzman's face, he remained silent and only smiled confidently.

Guzman watched Jaxon's expression, waiting for an answer. Unfortunately, it was too late for Jaxon to retreat before he recognized Guzman's insanity surface. Guzman reached behind his back before whipping his hand across Jaxon's face.

Jaxon had been beaten many times throughout his career, and normally a backhand offense would only have a momentary sting, but something was different. Something was more severe with Guzman's assault. Jaxon ran his tongue across the front of his teeth and tasted a metallic residue. He leaned to the side and spat a mouthful of blood. He looked up at Guzman, who was smiling back. He held his hand up in front of Jaxon, displaying the brass knuckles resting on his palm.

"I have to tell you, Mr. Rasner. I am so very delighted that you are here with me. Our next few days are going to be such sensational fun. Well, fun for me—not so much for you. Or your friends for that matter. To tell the truth, I don't need anything from you. I was only asking as a professional courtesy before I kill them. What do you say? Would you like to watch—possibly even participate?" Guzman asked before removing his brass knuckles and opening the door. He nodded to the guard and then motioned toward Jaxon. The same disfigured killer stepped in and grabbed Jaxon firmly before throwing him out into the corridor, and off to a new location.

Jaxon's transponder signal maintained its speed and trajectory for an additional twelve minutes before it abruptly stopped. The sudden halt caused Camille to stare blankly at the screen for several moments. Not sure what to expect next, she looked at Oliver.

"Yeah, I see it. Either his giddyup ran out of gas, or they reached their destination. Still nothing on the scope."

"Still no ship? What about its location? Is there a station or perhaps another ship in the area?" Camille asked.

Oliver compared his sensor results with the known entity maps on the ship's computer bank. After a series of back and forth views, he responded. "Nope. There's nothing on any of the sky maps. It's like he just stopped in midair. Should we continue on our course?"

Camille considered the situation. "How long until we intercept?"

Oliver was bringing that information up as she asked. "Less than fifteen minutes. Assuming he doesn't deviate from his current position and we maintain our staggered approach."

"What if we change course and head directly for him at our best speed?" Camille asked, evaluating all her options.

As if Oliver was on Camille's same mind track, he had the stats already up on his display. "We could be there in six minutes."

Camille sighed heavily then mumbled quietly. "I hope to hell you know what you're doing, Jaxon."

"Come again?" Oliver asked.

"Change course. Let's get there fast and see if there's anything he needs from us," Camille said. "Clay, when was the last code change done on the stealth device?"

"Last cycle was ... twenty-three minutes ago, and the next change will be in seven."

"Okay, be ready for it. I also need you to do whatever you can to increase the defensive shields. I have a feeling we're in for a battle."

"I ... I don't think it's possible to increase the strength—it's at minimum power as long as the stealth device is active. It's not quite a one or the other scenario, but it's certainly close," Francisco said.

"Okay. Do your best then. Any sign of attack, throw the shields up to full strength and ditch the stealth device."

"Understood," Francisco said.

The silence on the bridge was practically audible. The moments ticked away as the Buddha narrowed the distance to Jaxon's position.

"We're still a few minutes out, but we should be able to see his location via external cameras," Oliver said.

"All right. Let's see it."

The main screen flickered from the long-range sensor array to what appeared to be a still image of outer space. At the center of the screen, there was a bright, metallic object increasing in size. Within seconds, the indistinguishable shape began to take form. The exterior surface was charcoal in color with a matte finish. There was virtually no reflection from its skin. The shape of the structure was cylindrical in nature, with two perpendicular shafts intersecting at the middle.

It was a space station.

There were no ships anywhere in sight, assuming that the station had external docking ports in the first place.

"Holy shit," Oliver exclaimed. "It's an undocumented space station. This shouldn't be here."

"I've got a bad feeling about this," Camille said. "How could they have built such a structure without alerting the GSA?"

"Theoretically, it's impossible. Extensive detailed drawings need to be submitted, and approvals must be secured prior to any construction," Francisco said.

"Well, it's right there, and none of our sensors can pick it up. The station must have its own stealth device installed."

The Buddha slowed before it began to orbit the station. Now fully visible on the screen, it appeared to be about a quarter the size of a standard entertainment class space station typically found in the outer ring. The closer Camille scrutinized the design, the clearer it became that the station was more like a fortress than anything else. On first glance, there were no visible view panels and only two cargo bay doors large enough to permit docking ships. On the other hand, there were at least a half dozen torpedo cannons and railguns at various points on the station. Camille's heart skipped a beat as she watched one of the cannons continually track them as they drifted by.

"Not good. Not good at all," Camille muttered.

51

Jaxon sat in a cold metal chair with no padding whatsoever. His arms were bound to the armrests, and his ankles were shackled to legs that were bolted to the floor of what appeared to be an oversized airlock.

The airlock was bright white and had various gauges, controls, and peripheral connections throughout. Straight ahead of him was a rectangle door with a small view portal at the center. He tried to peer out from his position, but could only see faint darkness. Above and to the right of the door was a large view screen displaying various technical information.

"I presume that you are comfortable, Señor?" Guzman's voice said over the intercom in the airlock.

Jaxon looked up and around, as if to locate the source of the voice, but didn't answer. He wasn't entirely sure words would help him one way or the other, as he looked perilously toward the airlock door in front of him.

"Can I assume that with your distinguished career at the GSA, you know precisely the effects caused by the vacuum of space?" Guzman said. "If not, let me give you a firsthand demonstration."

Jaxon somehow knew what was about to happen well before Guzman began to ramble on. He took in several deep breaths—exhaling fully in between—before taking a final breath. With his lungs full, a warning light flashed at the perimeter of the airlock and the door opened up to the vacuum of space beyond. Every cubic meter of breathable air vented out of the chamber. The sound of the air escaping was nearly deafening. As the last volume of life passed out into space, silence took over, and Jaxon involuntarily expelled his own last breath. Panic and fear overcame Jaxon as he fought for the air that wasn't there. He thrashed against the constraints holding him in place. His vision quickly began to cloud over as darkness seeped in. The mere seconds that passed seemed like an eternity, then he noticed the airlock door closing and the display screen beginning to turn from red to green as air was being replenished.

As Jaxon gasped for air, Guzman spoke. "Tell me, Mr. Rasner. What are you feeling right now?"

Guzman paused, but after only a few moments of silence, he continued. "More importantly, how do you think it feels to suddenly have your breath taken away from you?" Guzman laughed. "Ha, ha. I know that's a rhetorical question, seeing as you just experienced that firsthand. Perhaps I need to be more precise with my question. Do you think it feels the same when your breath is taken away as it feels when a loved one is ripped from your life?"

Before Jaxon could answer, he saw the door light flash again as the airlock cycle began. Unfortunately, Jaxon had no time to prepare for the second assault on his lungs, and there was scarcely any air left in his chest. The screaming of the air vacating the chamber was deafening. Dizziness and darkness took hold on him much quicker, and just as he was about to pass out, the airlock closed again.

Jaxon gulped at the air as it refreshed the chamber, and although he had training for rapid decompression in space, he was always inside of an environmental suit when it happened. The drills were an exercise to quickly patch a leaky suit. There was no preparation for what Guzman was doing to him now. As Jaxon regained control of his breathing, he gasped out loud.

"Stop. Please, stop," Jaxon begged.

"So. He still can speak," Guzman said, chuckling gleefully. "Why exactly should I grant your request?"

Jaxon continued to breathe deeply, feeling the burning sensation in his chest dissipate. He held a finger up as best he could despite his restraints. Finally, when he felt that he could speak coherently, he began.

"You ... don't have to ... do this. I'm sure that ... if there was something ... I could do, we could ... work something out," Jaxon said, breathing deeply as he spoke, preparing to fill his lungs once again at the first sign of another airlock cycle.

"That's the thing," Guzman said. "I don't need anything from you. As a matter of fact, I probably know more about your mission than you could ever imagine. For instance, I've known that you were on your way to visit me for at least a week. And before that, I knew that you were being sought for active duty several months before you did. Oh, Mr. Rasner. I know so much more, and I could go on, but to tell the truth, I'm actually quite enjoying seeing you suffer. Perhaps the pain that you're now experiencing can come close to the pain you caused me when you took my father from my life."

Who the hell was feeding him his information? Jaxon wondered. His mission to assassinate El Tonto was only known to a few people. And the knowledge of his existence on Taloo could only have come from one or two people at the company. *But who was it? Who was the mole? Who was Brutus?*

"Ah, I see that your mind is like a mouse on a wheel. It's running and running and running, but you're getting nowhere—the answers just won't come. Isn't that correct, Mr. Rasner? You're asking yourself right now who is my inside man at your precious GSA?"

"You're right, Guzman. You've got me beat. If you just untie me from this chair, I'll be happy to call off the half dozen reinforcement ships that are heading this direction as we speak," Jaxon said, hoping that a different approach would delay the inevitable that deep down he knew would come.

There was silence for several minutes as Guzman was either checking his resources with the company or scanning the external sensors.

"Ha, ha," Guzman laughed. "You almost had me there, Mr. Rasner. It's highly unlikely that what you say is true. There will be no reinforcements. Otherwise, Brutus would've warned me long before now. You see, it's just you and your three team members. That's it. Your mission was set up to fail from the start. I've known about you all from the very beginning." He paused, and Jaxon could hear papers rustling in the background. "Mr. Miles Oliver, for instance. He is probably the most formidable foe of the group. He has the most recent activity with the company, but his personal philandering crossed the line one too many times."

Jaxon was shocked that Guzman had more information about his team than what was given to him by Director Howe. The majority of Oliver's file had been redacted.

"Then, there's Mr. Clay Francisco. He's the child of the group, is that correct? He's on task to discover what makes Whitetail so addictive. Rumor has it that he may, in fact, be a double agent."

Francisco? A double agent? Jaxon thought back and realized that he may have been tainted by somebody else inside the company. Francisco was the obvious mismatch for the team.

"Finally, Mr. Rasner, we come to your FiFi. She's ... special to you, isn't she?"

"Leave them out of this. If you want to exact revenge, focus on me and no one else," Jaxon demanded.

"You're in no position to demand anything."

Suddenly, the viewscreen flashed from the safety green circle to a view of outer space. As Jaxon deciphered what he was looking at, the blood drained from his face. He saw the Buddha circling the space station.

52

Several minutes passed as Jaxon watched the Buddha cross through the view screen. It was slowly drifting through space, most likely looking for a point of entrance to the station.

"What is it you want?" Jaxon begged. "Whatever it is, just leave them alone. I'll give you anything."

"I want nothing from you, Mr. Rasner. Well, nothing that you can physically give to me. What I want is retribution and that will only come from seeing you suffer."

"Then take it out on me and leave them out of it. They're just following orders. They mean nothing to you," Jaxon yelled.

"Oh, contrary to that statement, they mean everything. They mean everything to you and if I remove them from your life, you will begin to experience even more so what I felt nearly 20 years ago."

The speaker in the airlock cut off as Jaxon continued to watch the view screen. He hoped that Camille was wise enough to not stay in any one position for too long. Then, the screen flickered from the floating Buddha to a new display, showing the familiar layout of a close proximity sensor array. From what he could tell, the scanning region was void of any contact, as a teal-colored radar sweep rotated around the space station.

Suddenly, a dialog box appeared on the screen, and a multi-digit hexadecimal code was entered in. The dialog box disappeared. Then, a new one displayed, saying: SEARCHING FOR FREQUENCY. Jaxon inhaled sharply as he hoped that the subroutine that Camille installed was continuing to function. Within moments, an error displayed on the screen: NO SIGNAL FOUND.

Jaxon exhaled slowly, satisfied that at least one thing was going for the team. Then, a new dialog box appeared that read: SYSTEM OVERRIDE.

Jesus, Jaxon thought. *How much more does Guzman know?*

His question was answered promptly, as Guzman entered in the direct access override code for the Buddha and hit execute. The screen flickered and turned black before the display that Jaxon was familiar with appeared. It was the control panel layout from the Buddha itself. Guzman now had full access to the ship's controls. He watched in horror as the selection indicator hovered over the stealth device menu. Jaxon inhaled sharply, but Guzman didn't access the system as expected. Instead, he dropped the selection down to ship's defenses and brought up a new screen, displaying the status of the shields.

"God, no," Jaxon exclaimed.

Suddenly, the screen flickered back to the view of space. Seconds slowly ticked by, turning into minutes. Painfully long minutes passed until the ship came back into view. Jaxon caught his breath at the sight and knew the inevitable was about to happen.

Then, without notice, the airlock door flashed as it began to open, once again vacuuming the breathable air out into space. Jaxon breathed in deep and fast, taking in what would most likely be his last breath. Strangely, though, the door halted with only an inch-wide gap between. The air continued to escape, but at a much slower pace. He could still feel the pull on his lungs, but it was a manageable resistance that he could bear.

Siding with caution, Camille had ordered everyone to don their environmental suits at the first sign of hostility. Seeing the space station's gun turrets trained on the ship certainly justified that action.

As Camille stepped back onto the bridge, her two companions had already changed and were back at their stations.

Sliding back into the pilot's chair, she asked, "Status?"

"No change. Still no apparent point of entry, and the station's weapons continue to track our movement. I think it's safe to say they know we've arrived."

"Francisco?" Camille prompted.

"Stealth device active and frequency changing every five minutes, but I think I have to agree with Miles. Shields are up and are at the maximum level allowed considering the stealth device's demands. Perhaps we should divert all power to ship's defenses?"

Camille pursed her lips as she contemplated the suggestion. Not having any quantifiable field experience in battle scenarios, Camille questioned her own ability to lead the team, let alone make a decision about whether or not to maximize the shields. *What would Jaxon do?* She continued to speculate his thought process when Oliver called out.

"Hey, boss. What do you think about this?" Oliver synchronized his display with the main view screen. The ship's camera was just coming around the edge of the station, and a small light source began to splash out into space.

"Tighten in on that," Camille said.

Oliver did so, and as the lighted portal filled the screen, a faint mist could be seen rushing violently out into space.

"What do you suppose that is?" Camille asked.

"It appears to be an airlock of some sort, and the atmosphere inside that chamber was just vented out into space," Francisco said.

"Perhaps it's a malfunction on the station, or they are venting some kind of noxious gas that might be a byproduct of the manufacturing of the drug."

As they watched, the hatch opened fully before re-closing within moments. The Buddha maintained its snail's crawl in orbit around the station, and the forward cameras drifted out of view of the hatch.

"Hold on," Oliver said. He rapidly tapped at his control panel and then re-synced his display. The rear-facing cameras on the Buddha picked up where the front cameras left off, and all three of them continued to watch in silence at the first sign of entry to the space station. After several minutes of inactivity, and just as the portal was about to leave the camera's range, the whole process started over. The door cracked open, and atmosphere rushed from the chamber. Before the cycle could complete, the cameras drifted out of view.

"Can we get it back?" Camille asked.

"We're in a slow orbit around the station. We'll be back in range in just a few minutes. The front cameras should pick it up in just a bit," Oliver said.

Camille took control of the view screen and replayed the

image from the cache on the computer. There was something about what she saw that caught her attention. It was faint, but she could've sworn that she saw a person's foot just inside the door, only visible for a split second. She continued to replay the image, trying to convince herself of what she saw.

Suddenly, Francisco interrupted her concentration. "Something's up," Francisco exclaimed. "I've just lost control of the ship's defenses. Wait! I just lost access to the stealth device as well. Oh, shit! Both the stealth device and the shields are down."

Camille tried to access both displays on her own control panel, but they were locked out just the same.

"Navigation?" she asked.

Oliver entered several commands at his station then balled up his fists, slamming them onto the armrests of his chair. "Locked out."

Camille began to think about the next move when suddenly, on the screen in front of them, the airlock hatch came into view again. Just as it did so, it appeared the door was cracking open again, but then it stopped. Wisps of oxygen could be seen exiting through the crack. Then, suddenly, collision alarms blared throughout the bridge.

With a quick motion of her hand, Camille activated the sonar array. A missile launched from the space station was heading for the tail end of the Buddha. "Brace for impact!"

The initial collision of the rocket was substantial, knocking everyone from their chairs. The bridge door seal remained intact. More alarms blared, indicating a hull breach and other system failures throughout the ship. She glanced once more at the main view screen and knew that they only had moments before their fate would be sealed.

"Boys, grab your helmets. Looks like we're going for a walk."

" **N**ow, Mr. Rasner. We will see just what you are made of as you watch the destruction of your only escape. Mind the air, because it is most likely the last breath you'll ever take."

As the Buddha was almost across the display, a small projectile entered the screen at the lower left corner. It shot across the view, and an instant later, it made contact with the ship. As the missile hit the Buddha's tail section, a small explosion brightened the display. It took several moments for the initial debris to clear before Jaxon finally saw the Buddha again. It was tilted and drifting unfavorably. Sparks and flames jetted out of the hole made by the missile. After nearly a minute, the Buddha exploded.

As the blood drained from Jaxon's face, his thoughts went to Camille and how he'd just lost her all over again. The fight to maintain his last breath weakened. Just as he was about to spew the last bit of oxygen from his lungs, Guzman spoke again.

"Where are your reinforcements now, Mr. Rasner? Where

is this backup team or your cavalry that you spoke about? Your team and your ship have now been destroyed. There's no one left to save you. It's just you and me now, and I'm about to exact my revenge completely. It's time for you to die, Mr. Rasner."

Anger and terror tore through Jaxon. The rage-induced adrenaline pumped through his veins as he tried to free his arms from his restraints. It was useless, and he knew it.

Suddenly, the airlock door began to move. Jaxon, still holding onto his final breath, watched in terror as the door opened fully. Within seconds, Jaxon lost his fight and his lungs emptied uncontrollably.

"Goodbye, Mr. Rasner," Guzman said. "When you get to where you're going, be sure to say hello to your Lily and your new FiFi, because you're about to see them both again."

Lily? Jaxon thought as he wished he had his last breath back. He closed his eyes tight and thought about what Guzman just said. *Say hello to your Lily and your new FiFi*—did he know Lily was dead? And now, so was Camille. He must have been behind Lily's death—and what about Celeste? He didn't say Celeste. My God, she was still alive!

Without any air to replenish Jaxon's lungs, he began to convulse and his vision clouded over. Images of Celeste came to the forefront of his mind. He only wished that he could hold her in his arms just once. Now, that likelihood was whisking away, just as the air wafted into space right before him.

When he thought all was lost and he could no longer focus, his mind began to play tricks. With his consciousness dwindling, he could have sworn that he saw someone coming in through the airlock.

Then, there was darkness.

Holding onto the edge of the door with one hand and covering her eyes with the other, Camille waited for the repercussions of the exploding ship to dissipate. As the last vestiges of the turbulent waves faded, she dropped her hand and saw Francisco still shielding himself from the catastrophe, blocking any of the ship's debris that might fly their way. Oliver, on the other hand, was calm and collected, and was already about to enter the open airlock.

"It's clear, Clay. Let's get a move on," Camille said, tugging at his environmental suit and pushing him toward the airlock hatch.

Francisco followed Oliver in with Camille bringing up the rear. As they stepped into the airlock, the artificial gravity took over and their feet dropped to the floor instantly.

With weight once again at her soles, Camille focused on her surroundings. The room was an oversized airlock that was brightly illuminated. She took a step forward but ran into the backs of Francisco and Oliver, who were both staring ahead, frozen. She tried to lean around them to see what had their interest when she finally noticed Jaxon, tied to a chair in the middle of the room.

"Jaxon!" Camille said as she barreled past her companions. When she approached Jaxon's lifeless body, his eyes were strangely fixed on the video screen on the wall. Right as she reached him, his eyelids dropped shut.

"Ah, yes. And you must be the cavalry," came a voice over the speaker. The three of them looked around for the source of the voice, but there was no one there.

"Unfortunately, your friend has just expired. So sad. As I can see by your expressions, you're all terribly torn up about it. So, so sad," the voice said.

Camille turned toward Oliver and Francisco and studied their faces. With just one look from her, they both nodded and proceeded to take action. Oliver turned his attention to closing the exterior airlock, while Francisco attempted to gain access to the station's computer system, hoping to terminate the camera feed in the room.

Camille turned her full attention to Jaxon. She knelt next to him and quickly pulled her auxiliary breathing mask from the lining of her suit and held it over Jaxon's face.

"Come on, dammit. Breathe."

Jaxon showed no signs of life. Camille checked her suit's information display and brought up the status of her air supply. She diverted ample supply to the auxiliary breather then checked for a pulse on Jaxon. Unfortunately, the action proved difficult through her gloved hand. She thought she could feel a sporadic pulse, but she wasn't sure if it was Jaxon's pulse or her own out-of-control heartbeat, causing interference.

As she continued to hold the mask over Jaxon's mouth, she began working on freeing his restraints. With her free hand, she fumbled with the thumbscrews holding Jaxon's arms to the armrests.

"Come on, you sonofabitch. I'm not about to let you walk out on me twice in one lifetime," Camille said, wishing her words could be heard by Jaxon.

"Ah, yes. Young love," the voice said through the speakers. "If it's any consolation, Miss FiFi, I am sure Mr. Rasner's last thoughts were of you ... and that of his dead ex-girlfriend. Ha, ha, ha!"

Camille turned toward Francisco, her eyes fuming. "Clay?"

"Almost in."

"First thing you do is shut that bastard up."

"Gladly," Francisco said as he continued to breach the computer.

With Jaxon's right arm free, Camille switched sides so she could work on his left. As she pivoted for better access, she saw the airlock begin to close.

"Oh, thank God," she gasped.

As she awkwardly fumbled with the remaining thumbscrews, she felt something touch the back of the hand holding the mask for Jaxon. She stole a quick glance up and saw Jaxon's own hand on hers.

"Jesus, you're alive!" Camille said, her raging fear jackknifing into righteous joy at seeing life fill his eyes.

Jaxon tried to speak, but could only mumble inside Camille's auxiliary breather.

Camille's eyes momentarily blurred from the tears of joy. "Dammit," she said, knowing that there was no way to wipe them away.

"Miles?"

"Fifteen seconds, boss," Oliver said calmly.

Camille turned to him as he strode confidently toward the opposite airlock door—the door that led to the rest of the space station.

"Hold on a second, baby," Camille said, her voice trembling.

The voice over the speakers blared once again. "I assure you, that regardless of your efforts, you will all die just as—"

"Got it!" Francisco exclaimed. "All communications are severed between the rest of the space station and us."

Just then, a mechanical grind echoed throughout the airlock as the hatch closed and tightened its seal. Seconds later, air could be heard whisking into the airlock, equalizing the environment.

Camille pulled her auxiliary breather from Jaxon's face, and he smiled faintly. He tried to speak, but Camille held her hand against his lips.

"Hush for now. You're in no condition. I'm gonna let Francisco get you out of these restraints while I help Miles."

Camille stepped to the side, allowing Francisco space to begin freeing Jaxon's ankles. Jaxon and Camille's eyes locked, as if life were reaffirming its grip on their existence together.

Camille moved to Oliver, who was working on gaining access to the rest of the space station. "What's our play?"

"Well, assuming that I can get this door open, I expect a fair amount of resistance on the other side."

Camille nodded and took in a deep breath. She finished stowing her emergency breather before withdrawing her plasma gun from its holster. She thumbed off the safety and placed her hand on Oliver's back. "Whenever you're ready."

Oliver slipped a cylindrical device from his side pocket and thumbed the activator, causing alternating red lights to flash all around its edge. Then, he opened the door.

56

The two guards stationed by the door were momentarily caught off guard. The mechanical seal grunted its release and the door cracked open, but just a few inches. Before either of the guards could react, a grenade dropped to the metal floor and the door reclosed. A quick four seconds later, the amount of time that Oliver dialed in, a muffled explosion reverberated through the airlock.

Oliver dialed open the door once again and found the two guards sprawled across the floor, motionless.

"Are they dead?" Camille asked, more out of curiosity than anything else. She wasn't necessarily leery of seeing corpses, but it was a new experience.

"No, just incapacitated," Oliver said, stepping over the bodies. "It was just a concussion grenade. More bark than bite. However, these have a little extra *juice* to them. They'll knock you out if you're within range. Otherwise, they normally cause temporary blindness and loss of hearing. They'll recover, but we'll be long gone before that."

Camille followed Oliver's steps down the narrow corridor.

They strafed along the wall, prepared for more guards. Guards that never came.

When they reached the first intersection, Oliver eased to the edge and peered around the corner. It was clear. Without pause, Oliver lurched ahead in the direction that he hoped they'd find the source of the voice over the intercom.

A few meters down, they came to a closed door. The plaque next to the door read: airlock control center.

"He's gotta be in here," Oliver said.

Camille stepped around Oliver and was about to press the console button when Oliver grasped her arm.

"Let me, boss. I have a bigger frame than you and can take more of the potential hits. Hang back, but come in a few seconds after and clean up what I don't get on my first pass."

As eager as Camille was to eliminate the putrid man responsible for nearly killing Jaxon, she saw the logic in Oliver's thinking and stepped back.

Oliver keyed the console, and the door whisked open. Plasma bursts instantly blasted out of the opening. Oliver dropped to the ground and rolled to the side, pointing his own plasma gun into the room. Three quick blasts from his pistol and the commotion halted. Oliver stayed on his back, his pistol pointed into the room. Several moments of silence passed before he grinned.

Camille, taking Oliver's smile as a good sign, tilted her head around the corner and into the control room. There were two more guards on the ground, dead. There was a third man in the room who was seated in the only chair. He had dark skin, was in his mid-thirties, and wore green combat fatigues and a beret tilted to the side. His face was pockmarked from years of acne, and the left side of his head was badly mutilated. It was Pablo Guzman.

Camille brought her pistol up to the side of his head in a quick motion as she stepped into the room. "You sonofabitch," she blurted as she slid her finger over the trigger. "Give me a reason, asshole."

The look on Guzman's face was at first stunned, then placid acceptance. "Oh, my dear. I shall not give you a reason, for you will die before that happens. You see, I have already triggered the silent alarm on my station, and an army of a hundred men are on their way here right now. You and your team will be dead soon enough."

Anger pulsed through Camille's veins, and she hauled off and smacked Guzman across the face with the butt of her gun. "Try again, asshole. Call off your rabid dogs and I might let you live."

Guzman soothed the side of his face at the point of impact. He looked up into Camille's burning eyes and laughed out loud. "I know why you're here; Brutus already told me. You came here to put a stop to my operation and to take my life. You're here to complete the mission that Jaxon Rasner failed to do twenty years ago."

"But I didn't fail," Jaxon said, stepping into the room. "You were never part of my mission. It was all about your father and you know that."

"Won't you just die?" Guzman asked, staring incredulously at Jaxon. "It has taken me years to find my father's killer, and you continue to rob me of my revenge."

"Heh, I aim to please," Jaxon said with a smirk.

"It doesn't matter. As I just told your FiFi, I've already activated the silent defense alert for the station and your time is now limited. Mark my words, you will all be dead real soon."

Jaxon looked at each of the team members in the room. "We still have a job to do," Jaxon said, "and less time to do it. Miles, why don't you go see what you can do about stopping our hosts from ending the party too soon? Clay, why don't you and Camille go get the research that you need and then find us a ride off this station?"

"What about you?" Camille asked.

Jaxon stepped up to Guzman and placed a firm hand on his shoulder.

"Me? Oh, I'm going to get a little more acquainted with our

new friend here."

Jaxon dragged Guzman from the chair and threw him out into the corridor. He continued driving him toward the airlock he'd just left.

Blood caked the side of Guzman's face where Camille had struck him, yet he didn't make an effort to wipe it away. "You know, Señor, there is nothing to be gained from doing this," Guzman said as Jaxon fastened the restraints at Guzman's wrists.

Jaxon only smiled as he kneeled down and tied his legs to the same posts where his had been a short time ago. "You're probably right, but experience dictates that I have to at least make an effort."

With Guzman tied in place, Jaxon returned to the doorway leading to the rest of the space station. He keyed the door open and slid a supply crate into the door's path, forcing it to remain open. Next, he stood at the control panel and began deactivating the safety settings.

"What exactly is your plan, Señor? I assure you that no matter the torture, I will not divulge anything that you're after. Besides, my security will be here in—"

Jaxon ignored Guzman's attempts to dissuade him from proceeding. After he'd completed the reprogramming of the exterior airlock, he turned to Guzman and smiled.

"I wouldn't be so sure, Pablo. I've only been with my team for a short period and let me tell you, they are far more resourceful than you could imagine. I'd wager that Miles is preoccupying your crack security team as we speak."

"Oh, I think it's you who's mistaken, Señor. You underestimate my control on this station. It's quite impenetrable, and that's only due to the dedication and resolve of every man on board. They are my family. They will not relent until I am safe."

Jaxon shrugged and threw his hands in the air in a gesture of surrender. "Okay then. You have me. Should I just stand here and wait for them to handcuff me again?" Jaxon asked sarcastically.

Guzman scowled. "You jest, but just wait."

"Well, while we wait, there's no harm in you giving me a little information. Seeing as you're going to capture me again and kill me and all that, what do you have to lose?" Jaxon asked.

"Let me guess. You want to know who Brutus is?" Guzman asked.

"That would be a start. It seems like whoever it is, he's been in your back pocket for quite a while. I have my own guesses, but I would like to know for certain, so I know who's going to die next."

"Ha, you amuse me, Mr. Rasner—"

"Please, Pablo," Jaxon interrupted. "I feel we've known each other long enough; I think you can use my first name."

"You amuse me, Jaxon." Guzman said his name with Spanish flair. "You still think you're going to get out of this alive, and I think we both know that can never happen. Not since you've seen my secret lair."

"Brutus. Who is he?" Jaxon asked, tiring of the mindless chatter with Guzman's overinflated ego.

"Let's just say that he's a powerful man and he would not be very happy if I divulged his identity. You might say he's quite untouchable. He's in an absolutely sensational position, really."

Jaxon smiled. He knew Guzman would never reveal Brutus' true identity. Besides, he already had enough information to track down his hunches.

"Fair enough," Jaxon said, moving back to the control panel. He pivoted the display away from the wall so that he could see Guzman's face as he activated the exterior airlock. With just a few quick motions on the touch screen, the door to outer space began to inch open.

"Wha-what are you doing?" Guzman asked, his confidence vanishing.

"I just thought I'd open a window to get some fresh air in here. Isn't it a little stuffy in here?"

Guzman craned his neck around and saw the crate keeping the door open. "You're crazy! If you open the door, you will kill us all. If you haven't noticed, we removed your environmental suit when we brought you on board."

Jaxon shrugged. "No matter," he said as he paused the opening of the door. He adjusted the setting on the panel until the door reclosed, quieting the hideous whistling sound of the air rushing out into space.

"If you're trying to scare me into giving you the information, you might as well give up now. I'm not going to betray Brutus."

"Oh, but you have already. I know exactly what I need, and now for the next question. Your answer will be the key to your survival," Jaxon said, hovering his hand over the control panel.

"I don't know what else you want from me," Guzman said, watching Jaxon intently.

"You said earlier that it was your team that was sent to take my life. You also said that Lily's death by your command."

As Jaxon built up his question, Guzman appeared to know the direction of the interrogation and began to nod his head.

"So you know what I'm looking for? You're a smart man,

Pablo. Why don't you just tell me?"

Guzman smiled broadly. "That's what you've always wanted to know. From the very beginning. Since the moment you stepped on this station, isn't it? You want to know about your daughter. Isn't that right, Señor?"

"See? I knew you had intelligence. Tell me where she is and I will not open the door."

"Before I tell you, Señor, you need to untie me first. You killed my father and maimed me at the same time. How can I trust that you won't still kill me?"

Jaxon triggered the airlock again, the hiss returning as air began to escape. Once the door was just a few centimeters open, he halted its movement.

"Listen, Guzman," Jaxon said, getting in the face of his hostage. "Tell me where she is right now or I will simply walk away, leaving you here to die."

Jaxon stared into Guzman's fear-riddled face. Sweat began to bead up on his face, glistening on his hideous scars.

"How do I know you won't just leave me anyway?" Guzman asked, his eyes once again darting to the blocked open door.

"You have to trust me, Pablo. Tell me what I want to know and I will let you live. If you fuck with me, I will kill you. Just like I did your father." Jaxon stared intently at Guzman, assuring him that he was done messing around.

"B-B-Brutus. It's Brutus. He was supposed to kill her and your girlfriend, but he kept her for himself," Guzman pleaded.

"Looks like we're back to square one. Who is Brutus?"

Guzman sighed heavily and averted Jaxon's stare. He dropped his head and looked at the floor. "Brutus is—"

Suddenly, warning sirens blared throughout the space station, followed by an automated voice.

"Warning: Hull breach detected: level six. Hull breach detected: level seven. Hull breach detected: level eight."

"Well, I guess that's my cue," Jaxon said, standing upright and striding toward the blocked open door.

"But, Señor!" Guzman screamed. "You said you wouldn't

kill me."

Jaxon paused at the door and contemplated Guzman's words. He turned toward the drug lord and smiled. "But I haven't killed you. You've killed yourself."

Jaxon pressed his shoulder on the edge of the door, releasing the pressure on the crate. In one swift motion, he kicked the crate to the side and stepped through the closing door. As soon as the airlock sealed, the howling whistle ceased. Unfortunately, the warning sirens continued to blare.

58

As Jaxon walked away from the airlock, he could hear Guzman's faint screams for several meters. Jaxon forced the pleas out of his mind and rushed forward, beginning to retrace his steps through the facility. He thought that he could recall each of the turns they made when entering the labyrinth of corridors, but he wasn't completely sure he didn't get turned around somewhere between the holding cell and the airlock. Only time would tell, and he could only hope that his path to the docking bay wasn't somehow blocked off.

Passing by the airlock control room, he continued forward with his weapon at the ready. At the end of the corridor, he came to a T where he had to make his first decision: go left or go right. The incessant blaring of the alarm clouded his senses, he couldn't use sound as an indicator of direction. Only pausing for just a moment, Jaxon chose the path to the right and didn't look back.

Suddenly, the corridor began to turn to the right, almost certainly following the path of the exterior wall of the station. He tried to remember if they'd gone down a corridor like that earlier, but he was confused. Had he? Or was it from Delta Station? Everything kind of blurred together.

Regardless, he stayed on the path and increased his pace incrementally. As he reached the end of the corridor, he found a solitary door that did not look even remotely familiar. He briefly contemplated turning around and heading in the other direction, but decided it was too late for that and proceeded forward. He opened the door and barged in, hoping to catch the occupants in the room off guard.

The room was brightly lit but vacant; it was apparent that whoever occupied the space had heeded the warnings and was already looking for a way off the space station. As he was about to turn and head back out into the corridor, he noticed a door on the far side of the room. Next to the door was a large plate glass window overlooking an enormous multilevel chamber.

"A lab," he muttered. He faintly recalled passing by such a facility on his initial arrival. He rushed to the window and peered out. The window overlooked a two-story laboratory that was also vacant. The door accessed a balcony, but the railing blocked most of his view from inside the room.

Wasting no time, Jaxon opened the door and stepped out, his pistol leading the way. Once at the edge of the rail, he looked straight down and saw a lone security guard with his plasma rifle pointed to the opposite side of the lab. Jaxon followed his sight and saw the top of a person's head ducking behind a laboratory table. At that moment, Jaxon realized it was one of his own. It had to be either Francisco or Oliver. Otherwise, why would the security guard be pinning down one of the other space station inhabitants?

Before Jaxon could act, the guard fired several plasma bursts in the direction of the hiding man, trying to drive him out into the open. With each blast, he could see the man inch closer and closer to the edge, and worse, into full visibility. Jaxon prayed that he wouldn't move any further. Unfortunately, Francisco reacted just as the security guard had hoped. He leapt from behind the laboratory table toward the exit door.

"Watch out, Clay!" Jaxon yelled from above.

It was too late. The guard had already squeezed the trigger, launching bursts of plasma right at Francisco. The first two blasts shot wide, but the third impaled Francisco at center mass. Francisco's body jerked back from the blast, sprawling across the floor. He didn't move.

Jaxon screamed. "No!"

Startled by Jaxon's voice, the guard raised his rifle up and was about to fire. Jaxon, however, was prepared for the assault. He squeezed his own trigger, firing directly into the top of the guard's head. He dropped to the ground in a bloody mess.

Jaxon holstered his pistol and climbed over the rail and dropped himself to the ground below. First, he toed the guard, ensuring his lifeless state. Satisfied, he ran to Francisco's body, sliding down to where he lay.

"Clay!" Jaxon said, jostling his arm and shoulder, being mindful of his ghastly chest wound.

After a moment of shaking, Francisco blinked his eyes open halfway. Gurgling rose from deep in his chest. "J-Jaxon," he said, fighting to speak.

"Dammit, Clay! You should have stayed put."

"W-was s-sscared," Francisco said before a bout of coughing overcame him.

Jaxon looked over Francisco's body, realizing that the blast no doubt broke the majority of his ribs and possibly lacerated his lungs. It was only a matter of time before he bled out.

"It's okay now. I took care of the guard," Jaxon said. "What do you say we get out of here?"

"G-Guzman ... gone?" Francisco asked, fighting for breath for each word.

"No, he's just ... taking a siesta. I left him breathless," Jaxon said, an attempt to make a joke to cheer Francisco up in his final moments.

Francisco's eyes drifted shut as he smiled and forced a

guttural laugh. "Y-you do have a way with w-words," he said.

"Did you find what you were looking for, Clay?"

Francisco lay motionless for several seconds before lifting his left hand, which clutched a flash drive on a lanyard and several baggies of opalescent pills. Francisco smiled widely.

"Good job, champ. I'm sure the director will be pleased."

Francisco dropped his hand to the ground, releasing his grip at the same time. He rolled his head toward Jaxon then forced his eyes open. "D-did I do good, b-boss?" he asked, borrowing Oliver's moniker for Jaxon.

"You did great, Clay. I'm honored to have you on my team. What do you say we get out of here now?" Jaxon asked again. "Hopefully, Camille found us a ship to get us out of this hell hole."

Francisco's eyes drifted closed again, but he remained facing Jaxon. "N-no, just leave me. We both know … it's too late and … I'll just slow you d-down," Francisco said as blood began to seep from the corners of his mouth.

"Listen, buddy. You know I can't do that. You're going, and we're leaving right now," Jaxon said as he began to gather Francisco and his scavenged belongings.

"Wait," Francisco pleaded. "Y-you have to prom … promise me something."

"Anything, Clay," Jaxon said, lowering him back to the ground.

"S-save the girls," Francisco said. "Save them for me." Francisco coughed, bringing a mouthful of blood up from his lungs.

Jaxon looked down at Francisco, unsure what he was talking about. *Something must have happened on Delta Station, but what?* "You got it, Clay. Consider it done." He only hoped that he didn't just promise something that he couldn't deliver.

Francisco opened his eyes and smiled up at Jaxon. Then, his head rolled to the side and his eyes glazed over as his last breath passed his lips.

"Dammit, Clay," Jaxon muttered. He dropped his hands

over Clay's eyes, closing them gently. "You weren't supposed to die. Nobody was supposed to die."

Jaxon stood and rushed to the side of the dead guard and secured his plasma rifle. He returned to Francisco and hoisted him up and over his shoulder before heading for the exit.

As Jaxon opened the lower level door, a new alarm and warning began to blare.

"Warning: Station implosion imminent. Hull breach irreversible. Locate escape path immediately."

"All right, dammit. I'm on my way!" Jaxon said as he stepped into the familiar corridor that led through the central thoroughfare and toward the station's docking bay.

59

Jaxon rushed into the berth, and found it mostly deserted. Rightfully so, he mused. The space station *was* about to explode. Thankfully, there was one ship remaining, and it looked strangely familiar. It just happened to be the ship that brought him on board. Praying that his companions had secured it for their own departure, Jaxon charged ahead and right up the boarding ramp.

Once in the main hold, Jaxon lowered Francisco onto the flight couch and covered him with a shipping blanket before heading for the cockpit.

Stepping in, both Oliver and Camille stared at him expectantly.

"Cutting it a little close, aren't you? Francisco on board as well?" Camille asked.

Jaxon nodded. "Yeah, get us out of here."

"What about Guzman, boss?" Oliver asked.

Jaxon took Francisco's station behind Camille and looked ahead. "He's about to get his just dessert."

Oliver fired the engines and drove the throttle ahead to full.

As the ship approached, the bay doors flashed a warning before slowly parting open. He knew their ship was compact, but Oliver was accelerating much faster than he was comfortable with.

"So ... Miles. Everything good?" Jaxon asked, not questioning his piloting skills outright.

Oliver remained silent as the ship jetted ahead. The closer they got, the more apparent it was that the outside edges of the ship were going to collide with the opening doors. Then, suddenly, Oliver adjusted the pitch of the ship sideways, and it shot out into space, just meters to spare all around.

"Jesus, Miles," Camille exclaimed. "What are you trying to do? Give us all a heart attack?"

Jaxon leaned back and smiled. He had the sudden recollection of his own escape from Taloo Station and was absolutely confident that Oliver was the right man to pilot.

Suddenly, proximity detectors began to blare, and Camille quickly brought up the sensor array on the main view screen.

"My God, they have us surrounded," Camille said. "Hold on. Those appear to be our own ships! Those signatures are GSA standard frequencies."

"Looks like they got my message," Jaxon and Camille said in unison.

"Your message?" They both asked, again, at the same time.

"I ... sent a message to the director right before landing on Delta Station," Jaxon said.

"And I sent a message to the assistant director right after you were captured," Camille said. "Assistant Director Evans practically demanded a multipoint check on all personnel."

"Strange. Director Howe asked me to keep him updated at every point along the way as well. He asked me to contact him directly and in private."

"Huh, same here."

"I don't give a shit what's brought them out here, I'm just thankful that they're here," Oliver said as he throttled back on the accelerator.

Then, the lead ship in front of them fired a warning shot across their bow.

"What the hell?" Camille asked. "Don't they know it's us?"

Jaxon already had his control panel queued up for the ship's stealth device. He activated it, reducing the ship's shields to minimum.

"Well, the ship's insignia and classifications are that of the Guzman family, so as far as they know, we're not even on this ship," Jaxon explained. "Miles, why don't you divert our course down and away from the surrounding ships? Stay as close to the space station as you can."

"You sure, boss? That station might explode at any moment."

"Well, if we're lucky," Jaxon said confidently.

The surrounding GSA ships remained in their positions but ceased firing. Oliver steered the ship to the back side of the space station and hovered just meters away from the exterior wall.

Within minutes, the space station began to self-destruct, the explosion beginning at the top and working its way down the center shaft. Jaxon sat at his controls with his hands at the ready. As the explosions neared their location, Jaxon quickly deactivated the stealth device and put all of the energy into the defensive shields just as the station exploded right next to them.

The blast jettisoned their ship outward, along with massive chunks of debris. As soon as they were clear of any collisions, Jaxon reactivated the stealth device, minimizing the shields once again.

Both Camille and Oliver turned in their chairs and stared at Jaxon, dumbfounded.

"What? It's a little maneuver I recently used—"

"Why not just radio them and tell them who we are? Why all the cloak and dagger again?" Camille asked.

"Because our mission isn't done quite yet. We have one more stop to make before we head home," Jaxon said.

He proceeded to tell them about Francisco and his final request. Neither Oliver or Camille cried outright, but they were both shook up at hearing of his demise. Camille explained the entire ordeal that Francisco witnessed. They all agreed that the next stop was unavoidable.

J axon, Oliver, and Camille walked through the hand-carved wooden doors of The Pleasure Gauntlet. As they entered, Madame Elina looked up. She first saw Jaxon and smiled. Then, upon seeing Camille and Oliver, her happiness turned to worry.

"Ah, Marty. It's been so long. Where have you been?" Madame Elina asked, stepping around her podium and walking directly up to Jaxon.

Jaxon made no action to divert from the approaching Madame but glanced nervously toward Camille, who was giving him a questionable look.

Jaxon accepted a brief hug from the Madame then pushed her away. "My priorities in life ... have changed. Quite some time ago," Jaxon said. "We're actually here on another matter."

Madame Elina looked at Jaxon cautiously before returning to her podium. "If it has anything to do with these two, I have no idea what you're talking about," she said.

"It's about your girls, Madame. I know that Pablo Guzman is behind your operation, and I'm here to inform you that there's a lot of changes coming your way," Jaxon said dutifully.

Startled by the mention of Guzman, Madame Elina straightened her posture. "I have no idea what you're talking about. Who's this Pablo ... Guzman fellow anyway?"

Jaxon sighed. "Oh, Madame. Let's not waste each other's time. I know that he's behind your operation, and he's been trafficking girls throughout his entire network. I'm here to tell you it's over. Guzman's dead and I'm here to save the girls."

Madame Elina smiled nervously before she lunged toward the control panel on the side wall. Her fingers were millimeters away from the security call button when Camille stopped her.

Jaxon stood by, motionless. "Why must you make this difficult? We know they're here, so why don't you save us both a lot of heartache and just tell us where they are?"

Madame struggled with Camille but was incapable of escape. Camille gripped both of Madame's arms and twisted them behind her back, driving them up into her shoulder blades, perilously close to snapping.

"Ah! You don't have to be so rough," Madame Elina cried. "Suppose you're right and Guzman is my main benefactor. Why should I believe you that he's dead?"

"You can believe me or not, lady. I just want the girls, then we'll be on our way."

"Well, you're too late. There're no girls here. Just leave now and I ... promise that I won't tell Pablo about this incident."

"You want me to kill her, boss?" Camille asked.

What's with this boss thing? Jaxon wondered. Oliver certainly had started something.

"No, we might need her. Hold onto her while Oliver and I go look for them. If we're not back in ten minutes, you're more than welcome to take care of Madame Elina in any way you see fit."

"I swear!" Madame Elina said. "They're gone. The girls aren't here."

Jaxon and Oliver stepped past the women and into the cordoned off pathways of pleasure. "Which way were you guys when Francisco … left the room?" Jaxon asked.

"This way, boss," Oliver said, leading the way to Gigi's room.

Down the hall and to the right, Oliver stopped in front of the third door. "We were in here," Oliver said, motioning toward the door.

"And did Clay say anything else? Which way he went when he left the room?"

"Sorry, boss," Oliver said.

"Looks like we're going to have to do this the hard way. We're going to have to start knocking on doors—"

Before the words were out of Jaxon's mouth, Oliver walked up to the next door in the hallway and burst in.

"Sure, let's just throw discreetness right out the door," Jaxon said, catching up to Oliver.

Walking into the room, they found an aging man tied to the bedposts with a velvet rope. He only wore a pair of silk boxers. The prostitute in the room was wearing a satin-stitched horse head with leather straps around her neck. She completed the ensemble with a horse tail protruding out from between her butt cheeks.

Normally, Jaxon didn't react so adversely to the perversion of others. But he felt a little flush in the face at the sight. "Sorry, wrong room," he said before pulling a reluctant Oliver back out into the hallway.

"From now on, let's just crack the door open and peek in. If they're having sex, we move on. The room that Francisco described earlier was at the end of the hallway somewhere, isn't that right?" Jaxon asked.

"Yeah, something like that."

They continued down the corridor, popping their heads through doors randomly, witnessing various states of sexual promiscuity along the way.

Finally, at the end of the hallway, they came to a door that was different than the rest. "This has got to be it," Jaxon said, opening the door and walking in.

The room was pitch black, and both he and Oliver fumbled for a light switch. Finally, Jaxon found it and flipped it on. There were more than two dozen cages lining the side walls, stacked two high. Unfortunately, they were all empty.

"Sonofabitch!" Jaxon exclaimed. "She was telling the truth."

Before returning to the front, Jaxon and Oliver exhausted their search in the room, looking for a possible secondary exit. Coming up blank, they began to retrace their steps to the lobby.

As they walked down the corridor in silence, Oliver began to slow his pace. "I got an idea, boss."

Jaxon stopped and turned to face his companion. "Go ahead."

"I think we should stop and talk to Gigi. I think she was into me enough that I might be able to get some information out of her. Maybe, just maybe, she knows something about those girls."

Jaxon considered Oliver's suggestion before nodding his head. "It's worth a shot, Miles."

They retraced their steps a few doors before Oliver knocked and walked in.

Gigi was kneeling at the foot of the bed, stark naked and wearing a strap on dildo. Her pleasure companion was not a male, as expected, but a female, which was a rarity in itself. Both Oliver and Jaxon flushed red at the embarrassment of the situation.

"Ryan, what are you doing here?" Gigi said as she climbed off of her feminine patron.

"Sorry to just burst in like this, Gigi, but it's important," Oliver said, averting his eyes away from the naked girls.

Jaxon pulled out the last of his paper credits and handed them to Gigi's client. "Hey, sorry about this. Here's enough to buy you two more sessions later, but we need to talk to Gigi now."

Awkwardly, the woman dressed and bolted from the room.

"What's all this about?" Gigi asked.

"We're looking for some girls," Jaxon said.

"Well, you just found two and scared one away," Gigi said angrily.

"No, I mean we're looking for the young girls that were in the cages down the hall. We're here to save them," Oliver said. "When my friend and I were in here recently, he left the room and found them. Now we're here to set them free."

"Good luck with that," she said. "Madame Elina will never let that happen."

"That's not going to be a problem," Jaxon said. "We have somebody on that situation. Now if you please, can you help us?"

"I'm not sure what I can do."

"For starters, you can tell us where they take the girls. We found the room and the cages were all empty," Jaxon said.

"That's because they've already been taken upstairs for conditioning."

Jaxon felt a pit build in his stomach. He didn't like this sound of that. *Were they too late?*

"What do you mean?" Oliver asked.

"It's something they started about a year ago. Any new girls coming in go through a conditioning process where they erase memories of their past. They still know *who* they are, but they don't know who they *were*. It makes them more agreeable to our profession. If the girls don't know any better, they're less resistant to the demands of the clients. Hence, makes much more money for Madame Elina."

"And Pablo Guzman, no doubt," Jaxon said.

"You know about Pablo?" she asked.

"You mean, knew? Guzman's dead. I'm sure word will get around eventually, but until then, I want to know where these girls are. I want to set them free before it's too late."

"It might already be too late," Gigi said. "They took them up to the treatment lab late last night."

"Can you tell us where it's at?" Oliver asked.

"I'll do one better. Give me a minute to get dressed and I'll take you there personally. If what you say is true, I'm done here."

Five minutes later, Jaxon led Oliver and Gigi back toward the foyer. As they rounded the corner into the final corridor, they came to an open door. Cautiously, Jaxon slowed his pace as they approached, not remembering if it was open on their way in. As they stopped in front of the door, the three of them stood, staring into the room in disbelief. It was Camille and the Madame in a questionable situation.

"What's ... going on in there?" Jaxon asked with a grimace.

Camille craned her neck and peered out the door at the three of them gawking. "Oh, hi honey. Just taking care of Madame Elina."

Madame Elina was naked and strapped spread-eagle to some exotic sexual platform device, exposing what God had given her for all to see. To finish her off, she had a ball gag in her mouth.

"When you guys didn't come back, I didn't have the heart to kill her, so I ... tied her up."

Jaxon, Oliver, and Gigi all cringed as they stared in awe.

"What?" Camille asked innocently. "We couldn't very well

have her triggering some kind of alarm, now could we?"

"Tie her up, I get. But like that?" Jaxon said.

"Hey, don't question. She obviously has no consideration for any of the girls she has working for her. Might as well let her have a little bit of her own medicine, don't you think?"

"You're a cruel, cruel woman. And for that, I love you," Jaxon said.

"And I love you, honey," Camille said, leaning in and kissing him on the neck.

"I kinda hate to break up this lovefest, but we have some girls to save," Oliver said.

Camille slapped Madame Elina's bare ass. "Okay, let's go. Who's your friend? Miles, is this your doing?"

"Camille, Gigi. Gigi, Camille. She's going to take us up to where the girls are being held," Oliver said.

"Okay, that's fine and all, but I'll have to catch up with you. I have some other things to take care of first, right boss?" Camille said.

Jaxon nodded.

Gigi gave directions for Camille to find them as soon as she completed her part of the mission and then she disappeared. Gigi led Jaxon and Oliver through a series of dark corridors before coming to a discreet flight of stairs leading up to a single door on a narrow platform.

62

At the top of the stairs, Gigi stepped to the side of the landing and allowed Jaxon and Oliver to enter first. They opened the door and silently stepped through, taking in the horrific surroundings. There were several dozen hospital beds scattered throughout the room, most of them with girls strapped to the bed frames. The girls ranged in age from preteen to what appeared to be middle age. At the center of the room, there were two men in lab coats administering something to one of the girls. Their backs were toward them so their element of surprise was intact.

Jaxon held a finger up to his lips and looked at Gigi.

She nodded.

Silently, Jaxon and Oliver approached the technicians. As they got closer, it became clear that they were adhering electrode patches to the girl's forehead and temples. The wires led to an archaic machine on a trolley that had a very large rotator dial and what appeared to be an amp or voltage meter.

Just as they reached the men, one of them stood and approached the trolley, ready to twist the dial.

"Don't even think about it," Jaxon said as he placed the barrel of his pistol to the side of the doctor's head. The other doctor sprang from his chair and lunged toward the side wall, where a panic alarm button waited. Oliver chased after him, tackling the doctor to the ground.

"Who are you?" the first doctor asked.

Jaxon sighed. Then he raised the butt of his gun high above the doctor's head and dropped it down with great force, knocking the doctor unconscious. Oliver, watching from the far side of the room, mimicked Jaxon's actions.

"Gigi, start untying all the girls," Jaxon said as he began to remove the wires from the girl nearest him.

Oliver started to help but then turned his efforts to tying up the doctors in case they woke up before their escape.

"Miles, when you're finished with them, find the girls some clothes. They can't very well go out into the station naked," Jaxon said.

"There should be some in the operating room next door," Gigi said. "I don't know if there's enough to go around, but anytime I've been in here for ... a procedure, I've seen them in a side cabinet."

"Procedure?" Jaxon asked.

"Don't ask. Let's just say Madame Elina doesn't want a bunch of babies running around the space station."

The ever-present pit in Jaxon's stomach grew even more. The atrocities of what was happening on the space stations, all at the hands of Pablo Guzman, made him sick. He couldn't believe how much of his own life was wasted with regret for taking El Tonto's life and maiming Pablo. Now, seeing what kind of psycho he was, he felt a certain satisfaction about how Pablo's life ended.

As the three of them continued untying and redressing the girls, some of them coherent, some not, Camille walked in and froze.

"My God. It's all true," she said in disbelief.

"Yes, but with your help, we can get out of here even

sooner. Let's get them all ready to go so we can move. They're weak, but they all appear able to walk."

Camille rushed in and helped dress the remaining half dozen girls as Gigi and Oliver began gathering up the girls that were ready and leading them toward the door. They waited in line, patiently, as Jaxon and Camille corralled the remaining few girls.

"Okay. Is everyone set?" Jaxon asked.

"On your mark, boss," Camille and Oliver said in near unison.

"I wish everybody would stop calling me boss," Jaxon exclaimed.

"Whatever you say, boss," they said again.

Jaxon shook his head and opened the door. He pulled his gun out and checked to see if they had company. They were alone.

Oliver and Gigi took the lead, guiding the girls down the stairs, two by two. Camille and Jaxon brought up the rear, making sure all the girls exited safely. Halfway down the stairway, the station's security alarm began to blare.

"Looks like they found Madame Elina and triggered the alarm," Camille said.

"It was inevitable. I was hoping to at least make it through the pavilion before it happened, but that's what your plan was for. Go ahead and pull the trigger, Cam."

Camille waited to get to the bottom of the stairs before she brought up her commPad to activate the devices. Bright digital numerals displayed on her panel, and three, two, one counted down. Then, silence.

The silence only lasted a moment before a noticeable shimmy could be felt throughout the station's floor. The lights flickered and dimmed then went out completely. Emergency lights kicked on within seconds, and then, more alarms. Warnings began to blare about hull breaches and evacuation directions followed.

"Well, there goes the lower fifty floors of this shit hole,"

Camille said. "I placed the charges right where you said, in the elevator shaft just below level one."

Jaxon smiled. "That should keep them distracted for a while. Plenty of time to get off this sinking ship."

With catastrophic failures commencing throughout the space station, the security guards normally stationed at the space dock entrance were nowhere in sight. No doubt called to other parts of the ship to regain a semblance of control. Having one less obstacle to worry about made gaining access to their ship practically a walk in the park.

"I'm sorry, girls," Jaxon began, "but we really weren't prepared to have quite so many guests on our trip home. But I assure you, the ride will be quick, and you'll certainly have more space and freedom than you ever had with Madame Elina."

Jaxon scanned the cramped cargo bay, analyzing each of the girls' faces as he did so. Nearly a third of them had blank stares on their faces, having already been processed through the mental manipulation device. The remaining girls' emotions ranged from fear to jubilation for being freed from the confines of their metal cages. As he continued looking at each of the girls, Jaxon couldn't help but think about how Francisco would be overjoyed at their success of the rescue. Jaxon smiled warmly.

"Now, Camille here will help you each find a place to get comfortable. We're limited on bunkrooms, but as soon as I move out of my quarters, I'm certain that there will be enough space for four or five of you to have some privacy."

Camille, who was standing next to Jaxon, nudged him kindly. "Same with my bunk. I'll just follow along where the boss goes, freeing up more private space for you all." Camille slipped her arm around Jaxon and held him tight.

Oliver also offered his bunkroom to the girls, but both Jaxon and Camille agreed that although it was a nice gesture, he'd be able to share his bunk with at least Gigi for the ride home. Not surprisingly, the suggestion was agreeable to both of them.

Hours later, Jaxon and Camille had assembled a makeshift cot in the corner of the cockpit for their two-day trip back to earth.

Having settled most of the live cargo, Oliver walked into the cockpit.

"I think we're good, boss," he said, standing between to two rear stations. "Gigi is taking a nap and all the other girls are tucked away in the various bunkrooms we have. It's tight, but everyone's attitude is positive at this point."

"That's great, Miles. Why don't you take a load off and relax for a bit?" Jaxon said.

Oliver lowered himself into Francisco's seat and tilted the chair back, tossing his feet up onto the console. "I was thinking, boss. You want us to pass around ... a picture of Celeste to the girls? Maybe they've seen her."

Jaxon looked at Oliver fondly. "That won't be necessary, Miles. I already know where she is. Or at least I have a good idea about her location. When I was interrogating Guzman, he didn't come right out with her exact location, but he did say that Brutus has her personally. As soon as we get to earth, I'm dropping you two off, along with all our hitchhikers, then I'm going to rescue her."

"There's no way you're going alone," Camille said, kicking Jaxon's heel with her toe. "Wherever you go, I go. You got that, mister?"

"Same here, boss," Oliver said, holding his thumb up in the air.

"I appreciate the gesture, guys, but I can't ask you two to do this. Whether I'm right or wrong on who Brutus really is, I stand a good chance of being court-martialed because of my approach. I might very well spend the rest of my life in some GSA jail cell."

Neither Camille nor Oliver flinched.

"Just the same, boss, I'm there for the duration. Besides, what are our alternatives? I was already kicked out of the GSA once. What else do I have to lose?"

"Here, here," Camille said. "If you're right, you're going to need our help all the way."

Jaxon was taken aback by their loyalty. He had a sneaking suspicion that Camille wouldn't let him out of her sight for the rest of her natural life and expected it. As for Oliver, he was a tough man to read, and was constantly full of surprises.

"Okay, then. You're on. As far as the GSA knows, we're all MIA, so were not landing in San Francisco. We're actually going to land back where we took off, out in the New Mexico desert's spaceport."

"Do you think that's wise?" Camille asked. "The place isn't exactly a top-secret facility, but it's still highly populated by the GSA."

"Yeah, I know," Jaxon said. "But, if my plan works, we'll only need a few moments of surprise before anyone's the wiser. Once we land, we can hand our passengers off to the GSA and duck out in the process. Besides, our destination isn't terribly far from the port anyway."

Oliver and Camille both perked up at hearing Jaxon's conceived plan. "Do tell," Camille said.

Jaxon spent the next several hours explaining what he'd

discovered through Guzman's interrogation and his plan of attack. In the end, all three were in agreement that it was the only feasible approach. Their first step was to determine exactly who Brutus was. They each had their suspicions as to who.

The rest of the journey back to earth passed in relative normalcy. Something new for them for a change.

64

Jaxon sat in the driver's seat of the sport UTV that he and Oliver drove from the safe house to the spaceport a few weeks earlier. Having returned to that same vestige, he sat idle, under the cover of the forest canopy. From his position, he had eyes on the front door of the safe house.

Having been back on Earth for a little less than a week, he and his companions remained undetected by the GSA. Their covert existence allowed them to fully plan their imminent operation. It also allowed them to secure multiple tools of the trade along the way.

Jaxon reached up as if to scratch the back of his ear and gently tapped at his skin. "Hummingbird, what's your status?" he asked. Hummingbird was the codename he'd given to Camille. He thought assigning codenames at that stage was foolish, but with Camille's limited experience in covert field operations, she felt … not necessarily special, but secure by the implementation of them.

Within a few seconds, she replied. "All is quiet from my end, Saber. Over."

"Ladies Man?" Jaxon asked, referring to Oliver's self-declared codename.

"I was just about to call you, boss, er, I mean Saber. A black, GSA-licensed SUV just turned off the main road and is heading your way." After a few moments of silence, Oliver spoke again. "Over."

"Here that, Hummingbird? The game is on," Jaxon said, feeling his anxiety build.

"Roger that, Saber. Would you refresh our minds on what your signal will be? Over."

"It's Clay Francisco, obviously. Over," Jaxon said with a grin.

Within moments, the SUV came barreling up the dirt road and stopped in front of the rustic cabin. Jaxon continued to watch, anxiously waiting to see if the director followed their precise written instructions. *Come alone.*

The director exited the vehicle and cautiously looked around at his surroundings. Having once been a covert operative himself, Jaxon recognized the honed skill set. After a few moments of hesitation, the director climbed the front steps and walked into the cabin.

"The falcon has landed," Jaxon said. "The sparrow is already in the nest, and our party is complete. Ladies man, please come up and join us. I will signal when it's time for your arrival. Over."

"Roger that, boss," Oliver said, forgoing the codename nonsense.

Jaxon took in several deep breaths, exhaling slowly with each. He knew that the moment he walked through the door, all bets were off for a potential life in seclusion. But none of that mattered when it came to saving Celeste.

Jaxon checked himself once again and made sure that he had both his primary weapon as well as a snub nose at his ankle … just in case. Satisfied, he gunned the UTV and careened out of the brush and onto the dirt road. Seconds later, he parked next to the director's vehicle. Not wasting a moment's time, Jaxon sprinted up the steps and blasted through the front door, startling both Director Howe and Assistant Director Evans.

The heads of the GSA were seated at a small kitchen table, looking both confused and surprised.

"Jesus, Jaxon. We thought you were dead," Howe said, pushing himself to his feet.

Jaxon watched both of their facial expressions as he walked further into the cabin. "Well, I've been told that I'm a tough man to kill, and I'd like to keep it that way."

"When did you ... get back?" Evans asked, standing to join Director Howe.

"Oh, I've been back for a ... while. I've just been kind of laying low and taking care of some personal matters."

"Such as the location of your daughter?" Director Howe asked.

"That, and trying to determine the identity of the mole."

Jaxon watched, and neither Howe nor Evans flinched.

"Are you positive there's actually a mole?" Howe asked. "It's only been speculation—"

"I'm all but positive, director. And from what I've learned over the past few weeks, I've just about narrowed down his identity."

"Well, that's absolutely sensational news," Evans said.

Jaxon perked up at hearing the assistant director's choice of words. "Yes, it is, Perry. I've also learned that his codename for Pablo Guzman is Brutus. Is that equally sensational? Assistant director?" Jaxon asked, resting his hand casually on the butt of his gun.

"Whatever do you mean?" asked Evans. "I've ... not heard that name before," he stuttered as he crossed his arms defensively.

"What's going on here?" Director Howe asked.

"If I'm right, director, Assistant Director Evans here is Brutus."

Evans gasped. "That's absurd. Whatever would give you

that idea?" he asked, letting his hand slide to the inside of his coat.

"Well, you see, Guzman and I had a fairly in-depth conversation shortly before his tragic demise. He told me everything," Jaxon lied, "including the fact that you have my daughter. And from my understanding, she's here, somewhere, right now."

"That's preposterous," Evans said. "You're going to take the word of a known international criminal? Good Lord, the man had his hand in every crime-oriented business in the galaxy. From the obvious, drug manufacturing and distribution, to—"

"Human trafficking? Prostitution? Racketeering?" Jaxon added.

"Precisely. Not a very upstanding citizen, I'd say," Evans said, resting his hand on the butt of his own gun, tucked inside his jacket.

"The thing is, Perry, all the GSA knew about was the drug business. I just added the human trafficking statement after I discovered his activities in the outer ring. Until now, that was only known to him and his entourage. People like you, Brutus," Jaxon said, stepping closer to Evans.

"Let's just slow down," Director Howe said. "Those are sizable accusations, Jaxon. I've known the assistant director for many years, and I'm sure he has explanation for—"

Before the director could finish, Evans withdrew his gun and thrust it into the director's rib cage. "What? You want me to prove my innocence? You want me to assure you that I'm not Brutus? Well, let me tell you," Evans said, pulling back the hammer on his pistol. "I'm done explaining things. I'm done. I've been in your shadow for far too long, and things are going to change."

Howe winced at the pain caused by Evans' pistol gouging his side, but remained silent.

"Where is she, Perry?" Jaxon demanded. His hand was now fully gripping his own holstered pistol.

"You're in no position to demand anything, Jaxon. As I see it, I have all the control. Now, why don't remove your pistol from its holster, slowly, and drop it to the floor?"

Jaxon stared intently into Evans' eyes. He knew that his honed skill set was much stronger and more accurate than Evans' was, and he was almost positive that he could draw on him, aim, and fire long before Evans could get a shot out himself. But it was the director's life that would hang in the balance if he was wrong. Finally, Jaxon nodded slowly and followed Evans' direction. He slipped the gun from his holster and dropped it to the floor.

"Now kick it away," Evans demanded.

Jaxon did so, nudging it across the floor.

"Tell me, what gave me away? I know that Pablo would never disclose my identity."

Jaxon slipped his hands into his pockets, casually, and leaned against the wall. "You're only half right, Perry. Pablo didn't tell me who you really were, but he did leak out some hints about your inflections. Isn't that absolutely sensational?" Jaxon asked, adding more inflection to the word.

"That's all you were basing this on?" Evans asked. "My pretentious word choices?"

"That, and a number of other things that I've added up over time. It seems that you've been giving me just enough information to string me along. Then I learned that you'd given Camille specific direction to maintain contact throughout the mission, and that drove everything home. I'd already agreed to report to the director personally and any further communication beyond that would not have been sanctioned by the GSA.

"You traitor!" Howe said. "I've given you every opportunity for advancement, and this is how you repay me?"

"Oh shut up, you windbag. I should be in your position, and you should be—"

"But you have to earn this position. You've never given me reason for promotion. You've always been a follower and never a leader. This position—"

"Shut up!" Evans demanded, shoving the director to the ground.

Jaxon had to move cautiously if he wanted to keep everyone alive. He also knew that he couldn't just outright kill Evans until Celeste was safe. As far as he knew, he could have Celeste at a completely different location and their weeks of tracking his movements could have all been a ruse.

"So, what's your play, Perry?" Jaxon asked. "You don't think that by simply eliminating Howe and myself that you'll just be able to step into the director's position, do you?"

"That's exactly what I think, Jaxon. There are a very small number of people who know this place even exists, and as soon as I kill you both, I've eliminated the majority of those involved."

"Aren't you forgetting about Miles Oliver, Camille Parker, and Clay Francisco?" Jaxon asked, queuing his team into action.

Evans swung his pistol back and forth between the director and Jaxon. "Let's just start with you two first and then I'll track down everyone else and eliminate them with equal vengeance." Evans continued pointing his pistol back and forth between the two men, as if playing eeny, meeny, miny, moe.

Suddenly, the front door burst open at the precise moment that Evans had his gun pointed at the director. The commotion startled Evans enough that he squeezed the trigger, driving a bullet into the director's stomach. Howe screamed from the pain and dropped to the floor.

Just as swiftly, Evans pointed his pistol toward Oliver, who had dropped to the ground himself in a defensive posture and fired two shots in quick succession. Both shots went wide.

"Wait!" Jaxon said, pleading for Oliver not to return fire. "He still hasn't told us where Celeste is."

"That's right," Evans said, pointing his gun right at Jaxon's head. "Celeste is the key, and unless your partner over there drops his gun, you'll never know what has become of her."

"Drop it," Jaxon said. "Drop it now."

Oliver reluctantly lowered his semiautomatic rifle to the ground. He shoved it to the side.

"Good boy," Evans said, pulling the hammer back on his pistol. He pointed it at Oliver, and just when he was about to pull the trigger, a shot was fired from the rear entrance of the cabin.

Camille's shot hit Evans in the shoulder, causing him to drop his gun. Jaxon sprung forward and plowed into Evans, taking him to the floor and pinning his arms behind his back.

"Quick, take a look at Howe. He's been shot!" Jaxon exclaimed.

Camille rushed to the director's side. He clutched at his stomach. "How bad is it?" she asked.

The director squeezed his eyes closed as he lifted up his blood-soaked shirt, exposing a bullet hole on the left side of his abdomen. Camille gently touched the side of the director's waist and slid her arm around to his back. She pulled her hand out, and it was covered in blood.

"It looks like it was a through and through. If we get you some help fast, I think you'll be okay."

"There's ... a medical ... room in the basement," Howe said, fighting to get his words out.

"Without proper training, we wouldn't know what we're doing," Camille said, pulling the director's shirt back down over the wound.

"I might be able to help," Oliver said, kneeling down next to them. "I had a little training as an EMT before coming on to the GSA. I generally get weak at the knees at the sight of blood, and knew right away that it wasn't my desired career choice, so I changed. But, in an emergency like this, I think I can manage."

By then, Jaxon had made his way to the group. "Well, you're just full of surprises, aren't you, Miles?"

"That's right, boss. I feel it's best not to reveal too much of one's own being prematurely. Don't you agree?"

"You got that right, boss," Jaxon said with a wink.

As Camille and Oliver helped the director up, Jaxon returned to Evans for more information.

"Are you ready to talk yet?" Jaxon asked, standing above Evans, who was lying on his stomach.

"If you're going to help him, why don't you help me as well? Then I'll tell you where she is."

"Sorry, Brutus. You first," Jaxon said as he rested his foot on Evans' back.

Evans moaned in agony. "Okay. She's down on sublevel six."

"You mean she's here?" Jaxon asked, incredulous.

"Yes, she's been here the whole time. Nobody goes down that far and—"

"You fucking bastard!" Jaxon said, driving his foot harder into Evans' back.

"Stop! You're killing me."

"You should've thought about that before you killed Lily and took my daughter."

Jaxon removed his foot and headed for the basement door. Evans called after him.

"Aren't you going to take me down? I'm bleeding here."

"I tell you what, Brutus. If she's down there and is okay, we'll patch you up. But until then, you can lie there and bleed for all I care."

Jaxon turned and walked through the basement door.

65

After stopping by the medical wing on the first sublevel, Oliver had already stopped the director's bleeding. Confident that he was in good hands, Jaxon continued down the stairwell to sublevel six. Unsure if Evans had been completely truthful about Celeste's location or if he was walking into a trap, Jaxon had his gun out just to be safe.

As he approached the stairwell door leading out into sublevel six, Jaxon leaned his ear against the door and listened intently for any sounds.

Silence.

Jaxon gripped the door handle and twisted. A slight tug and the door swung open. Cautiously, Jaxon popped his head through the doorway and quickly scanned the environment. It was a dimly lit corridor that plunged a dozen feet away from the stairwell before it veered to the left. There was nobody else in sight.

A crackle in Jaxon's ear startled him.

"Where'd you go, Jaxon?" Camille asked.

"Down five levels. Approach with caution. Radio silence."

"Got it," Camille said. "I'll cover your rear."

Jaxon proceeded down the dungeon-like passageway, slowing his pace as he approached a corner. He paused to listen.

Silence.

Instinctively, Jaxon pulled the hammer back on his gun and rounded the corner.

There were two security guards on either side of a single door at the end of the corridor. Neither of them noticed Jaxon approach. At first. As he neared, the closer guard caught sight of him out of the corner of his eye and reached for his gun. It was too late, though, as Jaxon fired, dropping the guard to the ground.

The sudden clamor caused the second guard to move much more quickly. He already had his hand on his pistol grip and was bringing it up when Jaxon's second bullet pierced the guard between the eyes. He dropped next to his partner.

"Jesus, Jaxon. Was that you? I could hear the gunfire in the stairwell," Camille said in Jaxon's ear.

Jaxon remained silent. He moved forward and rested his hand on the door handle. With a deep breath, he twisted the handle and walked through.

The room was similar to his temporary bunk several levels up. A toilet and sink hung from the wall to the side. There was a Bureau across from the door, sitting next to a single wide cot.

Sitting on the bed was Celeste. She sat there, staring back. She appeared to have been reading a book and had a startled look on her face from all the commotion.

Tears of joy almost overcame Jaxon as he finally saw her face. He checked himself and quickly extinguished the waterworks.

"Celeste? Are you okay?"

Celeste dropped the book and raised her legs up in front of her chest, wrapping her arms around them. "Who are you?" she asked, staring intently at the gun in Jaxon's hand.

Jaxon quickly holstered his pistol and raised his hands up

in the air. "It's okay. I'm here to rescue you. I'm not going to harm you; I'm not going to let anyone harm you."

Celeste rocked back and forth as she stared at Jaxon. Her eyes welled up, and she began to cry.

Jaxon rushed to her bed and kneeled down beside her. "Did he hurt you? Are you okay?"

"I'm … fine. They hurt me a little, but I'm just scared. Is my mom, Lily, okay?" she asked, wiping her tears away.

"I'm sorry, Celeste, but Lily didn't make it. I'm sure that she fought to give you a chance to get away."

Celeste began to cry even harder.

Seeing the pain and anguish on her face tore deep into Jaxon's soul. It became increasingly more difficult to keep his own emotions in check.

"Hush, hush," Jaxon said, trying to soothe her pain. "It's going to be okay. I'm here now, and I won't let anything hurt you ever again."

Celeste stared at Jaxon quizzically. "Who are you?"

Jaxon heard footfalls echo in from the corridor, and he instinctively reached for his weapon. Seeing Camille approach, he dropped his hand away and focused on Celeste.

"I'm Jaxon. Did Lily ever tell you about me?"

Celeste sniffled and wiped more tears away. "N-no," she said, continuing to stare at Jaxon curiously.

"I'm … I'm your father, Celeste," he said.

Shocked awareness came over Celeste's face, but she remained seated on the bed. Jaxon instantly regretted telling her the truth so quickly. He hoped that he hadn't just made a big mistake.

"Celeste? Are you—"

Before he could finish speaking, Celeste sprang from bed and threw herself at him, wrapping her arms around his neck and squeezing. Jaxon felt her tears fall down his neck. He held her for a long time, unable to hold his own tears back.

Their silent reunion, precious for them both.

Jaxon and Celeste walked out of the stairwell into sublevel one. Camille had already retreated to give the two of them some privacy to reconnect and was standing next to Oliver just outside the medical room.

As he approached, Jaxon spoke. "Hey everyone, I'd like you to meet someone special. This is Celeste, my daughter."

Camille reached out and took Celeste's hand warmly. "It's a pleasure to meet you, sweetheart. I'm so happy that you're okay. You're all that Jaxon's talked about for the last three weeks."

Celeste smiled shyly. "Nice to meet you," she said.

"Hi. I'm Miles. Your dad here is one lucky guy to have found you once again," Oliver said, shaking her hand.

Celeste smiled and nodded.

"How's the director?" Jaxon asked.

"I patched him up as best I could. But thankfully, being the head of the GSA has its privileges; they had a chopper ten minutes out. The medics just got here and are in there with him now," Oliver said. "He said that he wants to talk to you right away."

Jaxon nodded and looked at Celeste, contemplating whether he should leave her just yet.

"Go ahead," Camille said. "I'll watch after her. We can have some girl talk while you're gone."

"Oh, great," Jaxon said as he hugged Celeste before walking into the medical room.

Two medics were attending to the director lying on the operating table. One of them looked at Jaxon as he approached. "You shouldn't be in here," he said.

"No, it's okay," Howe said. "I need to talk to him. Come closer, Jaxon."

Jaxon did and stood near the head of the table.

"So, quite a mess, wouldn't you say?" Howe said through gritted teeth. "But I would've appreciated a little more heads up before you made your move."

"I couldn't have been sure, director. Not until that instant. We were fairly certain it was Evans, but it could have been you all along throwing everyone off your scent as the mole. I had to do this on my terms."

The director moaned slightly as one of the technicians sutured the bullet hole. "Regardless, that's not exactly how we do things at the GSA. You, above everyone else, should've known that."

"I understand, sir," Jaxon said, opting to take the reprimands from the director without question.

"I understand that you found Celeste?" Howe said.

"Yes, sir. She's been here the entire time. Evans had her in sublevel six from the start."

"And she's okay?" He asked.

"She's scared, but no physical injuries," Jaxon said, thankful. "With any luck, she won't suffer any lasting effects from the traumatic situation."

Howe nodded, half focusing on the conversation and on the stitching being performed on his abdomen.

"Director, are you on any kind of pain blockers right now?

You look like you're in agony."

"Nope. I'm ... forgoing any form of narcotics. These gentlemen know that it's imperative that I remain cognizant throughout this whole procedure. They've assured me that they will not cause me any undue pain," Howe said. "Isn't that right, gentlemen?"

The two medical technicians nodded but maintained focus on Howe's injuries.

"I suppose congratulations are in order," he said, looking back up at Jaxon. "Guzman's operation has been neutralized?"

"Yes, sir. Guzman will not be a problem for anyone ever again."

"And what about Francisco's directive? Was he able to secure any documentation or procedures of the drug's production?" Howe asked.

Jaxon didn't blink. "Unfortunately, no. By the time my team penetrated the labs, they had already sabotaged all of their computers and records. All that was left was a useless pile of burning circuitry."

Director Howe frowned. "That's quite unfortunate. Having physical proof of his operation would have smoothed things over with the oversight committee ... in addition to serving as defense for your future."

Jaxon's eyes narrowed and met the director's. "Future? What are you saying?"

"You have to understand, Jaxon. The GSA functions on a mandated set of rules and regulations. Without them, there would be corruption. I can't say for certain right now, but after each of you have been debriefed, the company will analyze your individual situations as to what sort of repercussions will come out."

Jaxon began to feel anger build deep inside. "Repercussions? We were sent on this mission to stop Guzman's operation. We followed those orders to a T, in addition to saving the lives of dozens of innocent women before they were thrust into the life of prostitution. Jesus Christ, director. You should be pinning medals on each and every one of us."

"Relax, Jaxon. It won't be as dire as it sounds. But without the evidence that Francisco was to obtain, I have no control over the outcome. There's a very good chance that none of you will ever see each other again. And for some of you, you might not even recall what happened over the last month," Howe said as he stared into Jaxon's eyes.

Jaxon felt his face flush with anger. He stood there, silently, as he drove his fingers into the palms of his hands.

"On the other hand," Howe said, glancing at his now bandaged abdomen, "if some kind of an arrangement can be reached, with each of you individually, I'm certain we'll all have a bright future."

Great, Jaxon thought. *First, he threatens me with the possibility of having my memories scrubbed, then he finishes up with some kind of bribe, most likely to come back to the company. What a character.*

Jaxon placated a smile before walking out of the medical room, without another word.

67

The comforting aroma of freshly brewed tea lingered in the air as the soothing sounds of flamenco guitar echoed throughout the Celestial Teahouse. The hour was early, and very few people were out circulating through the Pavilions of Taloo Station. Celeste was at the front of the store, pulling chairs off of tables and sliding them underneath as she prepared to open for the day. Despite being right next to the front windows, she failed to notice the first customer walk up to the store.

Ding dong.

The door chime melody drew Celeste's attention.

"Hi there. Is it too early to order a cup of tea?" Camille asked as she approached the counter.

Celeste smiled. "Of course not, ma'am. What would you like today?"

"Oh, I hear that Angorion Spiced tea is really something special. Mind if I try a cup of that?" Camille asked.

"So, your usual then?" Celeste said with a grin.

Camille shrugged. "Creature of habit. How are you today,

Celeste?"

"I'm good. I'm done with classes this semester and my professor tells me that my grades are good enough to get me into college this fall. Now, I just have to figure out how we're going to pay for it too."

"That's fantastic, Celeste. Why didn't say anything sooner?"

Celeste shrugged, still fighting the demons of shyness. "I guess I get so wrapped up in my own personal space that I forget you guys are around."

"That's understandable. You're a teenage girl. Cherish this time, Celeste. It's a wonderful time."

Celeste bobbed the tea infuser into a cup of steaming hot water and slid it across the counter to Camille. "Here you go. Don't tell Jaxon, but this one's on the house."

Camille winked at Celeste. "It's our secret. Speaking of, is the boss around?"

"Yeah, he's back in the stockroom. We just got a shipment of some new kind of tea or something. He's been back there all morning, and he's been giddy as a child."

Celeste pulled open the curtain separating the front of the store from the stockroom and called out, "Hey, boss. You have a visitor."

Jaxon stepped out from the back room, flakes of tea scattered all over his face and shoulders. He looked up and saw Camille and smiled. "Fancy seeing you here," he said as he walked up and kissed her.

Camille returned the embrace, before playfully pushing him away, so as to not cause any undue discomfort for Celeste.

She noticed and smiled. "It's okay, Camille. It's nice to see that Dad has someone that he loves."

"He loves me, does he?" Camille asked with a smirk.

"Of course I do, baby. Haven't I told you that every day since we've been here?" Jaxon asked. "By the way, how'd it go this morning?"

Camille stepped back from the counter, her feet close

together, and her back arched upright. She held her head high and said, "You are now looking at the new regional director for the GSA on Taloo Station. Overt classification."

"Ah, that's wonderful, Camille," Jaxon said.

"Thanks. They initially offered me a covert position, but I had to turn them down. I told them that I was tired of all that top-secret spy lingo. Just not my style."

"Wow, that's really fantastic," Jaxon said. "And quite a relief, too."

"What's a relief?" Camille asked as she sipped at her tea.

"I mean that you're the head of the overt sector. God, I'd have hated to report to you if you'd been appointed as the regional *covert* supervisor." Jaxon winked.

"You better watch yourself, Mister. I'll still have some pretty strong pull inside the GSA. One false move from you, buddy, and—"

Jaxon kissed her on the lips, interrupting her obviously rehearsed spiel.

"Oh, God. Get a room," Celeste said before she disappeared into the back room. Jaxon and Camille laughed.

"For what it's worth, being in this position will allow me to see a little bit more of what's coming down the pike for you. I'm still surprised that you accepted Director Howe's offer in the first place."

"Ah, it's okay. He promised me it's only going to be on an *as-needed basis*, and I get to keep all my memories. And, for that matter, so do you and Miles. Speaking of, I don't think you properly thanked me for such a selfless gesture on my part."

"Oh? What was last night? Didn't I thank you enough?" Camille asked as she remained in his bear hug grasp.

"That was a thank you? I thought you were just being kind to me."

"Oh, stop. If gratitude is what you want, when I get home tonight, I will thank you all night long."

Jaxon raised his eyebrows with excitement. "You've got a deal."

ABOUT THE AUTHOR

When not practicing architecture, Paul works on his writing. He lives in Littleton, Colorado, with his wife and daughter.

To learn more about him and his books, visit www.Paul-Kohler.net

www.ingramcontent.com/pod-product-compliance
Lightning Source LLC
Chambersburg PA
CBHW020333180626
46812CB00001B/178